WHISKEY SHIVERS

THE VOODOO BASTARDS MC
BOOK 2

A.J. DOWNEY

BOOK TWO

Published 2022 by Second Circle Press

Text Copyright © 2022 A.J. Downey

ISBN: 978-1-950222-39-1

Editing & book design by Maggie Kern @ Ms.K Edits
Cover art Dar Albert at Wicked Smart Designs

DEDICATION

To all the educators who keep on keepin' on despite feeling like you're trying to ice skate up hill. I see you, you badass motherfuckers. Keep doing what you're doing and fight the good fight for the wages you deserve.

PROLOGUE

*H*ex...

"Hey, no running!" Her voice, while trying to sound authoritative, didn't quite reach the mark. I looked up the hallway to the beautiful brunette standing outside the doorway to her classroom. Despite her attempt at a stern warning, she couldn't stop her smile. She never seemed to stop smiling and I had to say, it did things to me.

Corliss Legare was a beauty. One that dressed a little too plain for my tastes; but then again, she was a high school language arts teacher, and had to follow the dress code just like the rest of us. Still, she was beautiful without the benefit of makeup or revealing clothes. She tended to stick to the same tried-and-true outfits day in and day out, and that was alright with me. Her long brown hair was typically up in a ponytail, and today she had some escaping tendrils she reached up to tuck behind her ear.

Her captivating blue eyes met mine and she gave me a wink. I felt my lips tug in an answering smile.

"Hey! Slow down, there." I stepped in front of the two rowdy boys and they laughingly and begrudgingly slowed their asses down, walking past me, paying me no never mind.

Not a big deal. The desired effect had been achieved. Corliss's smile grew even wider and she tipped her chin in a nod in my direction. I gave a nod back.

One of the things I liked about her was she treated me with respect. There wasn't a lot of that to be found for the school custodians, but Corliss Legare didn't care. She treated everyone with kindness and respect, and I liked that about her. Everyone did. She was a light in the halls and the hearts of faculty and students alike at Lakeside High.

I went back to pushing my mop, giving my head a bit of a shake at the kids making their way through the halls, parting around the adults like water, flowing over the linoleum I mopped a spill of soda off of in a babble and a rush of excited chatter.

I risked a glance at Cor's shapely ass as she strode back into her classroom. Her jeans hugged it oh so perfectly. I shot a look around me to make sure no one had caught me looking and thought to myself just how much I wished I could watch it stride through the doors of my club. The things I would do to that woman if she'd let me.

What could I say?

I was definitely hot for this particular teacher.

CHAPTER ONE

*C*orliss…

"Hi." I leaned down to kiss my fiancé Mark. He absently looked up from his computer screen, giving a grunt of annoyance and jerking back at first before his mind seemed to calibrate into the here and now. He quickly pecked me on the lips.

"Working from home today?" I asked.

He made a non-committal noise and asked me, "What's for dinner?"

I fought not to roll my eyes and kept my sigh of defeat to an inward one.

He was letting his job take over *everything,* and I was starting to feel like I didn't matter. That I was only here in a support role to make his life easier. That I was more of an assistant than a girlfriend, or wife… which was discouraging to say the least.

I mean, I had moved all the way out here with him so that he could take this job. Uprooted my entire life from Houston and left all my friends to move to a city I didn't know, away from the only area that I had ever known, for him. Lately, it was like he couldn't even give me the time of day.

"I don't know," I said. "Have a taste for anything?"

He was wholly focused on his computer screen and frowning. "Just whatever, babe. It's fine."

I tipped my head back and felt my shoulders drop in utter defeat. I stood there for several moments, willing him to pay me just *any* mind. When it didn't happen, I let the sigh building escape me and went into the kitchen to figure it out on my own.

I'd done *a lot* of figuring it out on my own. My whole life, really.

I'd been born to drug-addicted parents and had been in and out of the Texas child welfare system, bouncing back and forth until my mother had finally OD'd when I was twelve. My dad wasn't anywhere to be found, and my grandparents were physically incapable of taking me. They had pretty much both died within a couple of years of my mom. My grandmother on her side had had a stroke years before and my grandpa was her sole caregiver until he'd died of a cardiac event. My grandmother eventually died in some home somewhere – at least that's what I had to assume. I never heard and couldn't find her. There was just no information.

I'd ended up aging out of the system, had taken the full amount of government aid offered to me, and had gone for teaching – working my ass off and taking a shit ton of student loans to put myself through college. I knew I'd never be able to pay them all off, but I had to do something with myself. My heart was into maybe being that saving grace to another kid with a rough background like mine. Like one of my English teachers had been for me.

I'd met Mark in college. Some of our classes overlapped even though his degree was completely in Internet Technologies and Business or whatever. I couldn't follow all his computer jargon and coding. I was all about English and language arts. I'd been a reader my whole life, disappearing into books to avoid the crazy that my life was by no choice of my own.

Mark had made being with him easy, and when he'd asked me to move with him, and marry him, I'd jumped at the opportunity – especially knowing that I could maybe make a difference when it came to the school I'd been hired at.

Let me tell you – teaching a bunch of inner-city ninth graders from a poorer ward or neighborhood? It wasn't easy. It was mentally and emotionally exhausting on a good day, and entering into my second year of teaching as I was now? I was still worried about failing. You know? I mean, all but three of my students passed last year, and none of them were held back a grade, so that was something? Right?

You would think, but I was less worried about failing as a teacher in the getting them all to pass regard, as I was failing them individually by giving a single one of my students the feeling like they couldn't come to me about anything or for anything. Especially the ones with a maladjusted home life.

I started playing some Billie Holiday on my phone and went to the fridge, opening it up with a heavy sigh and letting my eyes rove its contents.

Mark cursed under his breath from the other room and I waited for it. Sure enough…

"Can you turn it down? I can't concentrate."

It was barely playing, but this was becoming typical.

"Sure," I said. I switched the music off and set to work, fixing dinner in silence.

There was a reason I'd been holding off on actually *planning* the wedding. I guess I wasn't quite to the point of throwing in the towel, but I certainly didn't think that at the rate we were going, things were going to last. And damn if that didn't hurt.

CHAPTER TWO

*H*ex...

"You're here late," I said. I didn't even bother to hide the surprise in my voice as Corliss Legare looked up from her laptop screen at her desk, putting her readers up on top of her head. I raised an eyebrow at that and said, "A little on the young side for needing those, aren't you?"

She smiled and raised her arms over her head, giving a long stretch like a cat.

"There's no accounting for crappy genetics. My fiancé is running late at the office. My car is in the shop. He's supposed to give me a ride home, but I expect I'll be taking a rideshare or something." She made a face.

All I really took from that was that she was off the market, so I downshifted from my intent to flirt some to just plain being her friend. There was just something in those blue eyes of hers that radiated a fractured sort of ache. That said, she could use one right now.

"Oh, well, I've got about an hour left. I could swing back by if you need and see if you're still here? If you are, I live over down in the ninth. If it's your direction, too, I could give you a lift."

She looked thoughtful as I picked up the trashcan by her desk and emptied it into my big rolling can.

"No pressure, not trying to be forward or anything. Just trying to be helpful," I added when she mulled it over just a little too long.

She smiled, looked up, and said, "Thank you." Then, nodding, she said, "If I'm still here, I would gratefully take you up on that."

"No problem," I said.

She turned back to her laptop and I went about my business in her room, collecting the trash and wiping a few things down. I didn't run the canister vac I was packing around on my back. I didn't want to disturb her any more than necessary – plus, the floor of her classroom wasn't that bad. It could wait until tomorrow.

I fully admitted my disappointment when I came around an hour later and her classroom was both locked up and dark.

Looks like her ride had shown up. I didn't blame her for not finding and telling me. The school was a large one and had multiple floors. I could have been anywhere. If I'd been down in the boiler room or the custodian's pen, she likely wouldn't have been able to find me at all. This old building could be a maze and none of the teachers knew it like the custodians and maintenance guys did.

I got out, locked up, and waved goodbye to ol' Curtis, the custodian in charge. I guess you could call the lanky black man my boss, but he didn't like it. Nah, he liked to see the custodial staff as equals. Said there wasn't no need for a man in charge, even if he was the one who had to sign off on shit. He was a good man. I could respect him.

I drove my truck home. I didn't ride to the school very often and when I did – never with my colors on. I liked my job. I dug fixing and cleaning things. It reminded me of my old man growing up. He was a school custodian too, and everybody at that school adored him. He'd been into some shit like me outside of school – nothing as heavy as the Voodoo Bastards, though. No, my dad had just been an old-school Appalachian moonshiner. Still, it'd been damn useful the things he'd taught me both on the right and the wrong side of the law.

His motto in all things had been "*work smarter, not harder*" and he had a penchant for some good 'ol redneck ingenuity. He'd also had a pretty unhealthy dislike for authority, which had gotten him into trouble more than a time or two. It was certainly something he'd passed on down to me – his only child.

By comparison, I didn't have the best relationship with my momma. Hell, she'd been the reason I'd moved all the way out here. My daddy always said she was a good woman – a woman he'd certainly loved dearly right up until the day he'd died; but *goddamn,* did that woman try to smother me. Always with the damned unattainable expectations and shit howdy, it was like she hadn't known my fuckin' daddy at all. Constantly with the refrain of how disappointed my daddy would be with me for not doing this, that, or the other.

It was one of the reasons I didn't come around too often to the old homestead out in Tennessee. I just couldn't bring myself to deal with her nitpicking. It'd like to drive me insane.

My phone went off the second I'd planted my butt in my seat of my truck, and I checked the screen.

It was Louie, our newest member, going on a year or more now.

Louie: You coming by the clubhouse tonight? I got that part you were looking for!

I grinned.

Me: Well shit, howdy! Good on you, boy! Yeah, I'm leaving the ol' day job now. I'll be by in the next couple of hours.

Louie: Sweet, I'll see you then.

I started the truck and sighed, turning the dial and putting it in reverse, backing carefully out of my spot and heading on down the road in the direction of home. At a stoplight, I pulled up on the passenger side of this expensive-looking Beemer and just happened to look down.

Leaning in the window, a finger along her cheek, her middle finger curled and pressed to her lips, which were tight with disapproval, was little Miss Legare. I guess I'd just missed her. By the vacant and dull look in her blue eyes, she was tuning whoever was in the driver's seat out. I couldn't see him from this angle, but I could see plain as day – she wasn't happy. It sent my heart to pinging off my ribcage in a sensation that was unfamiliar to me.

I didn't know if I quite liked it, but it certainly was something. Something very real.

It stuck with me the whole drive home and even through me stripping off my coveralls and the clothes I had on underneath them. I put them straight into the wash and straightened, feeling mighty fine now that I had the constricting clothing off. I hated clothes. Had never been a fan. I tended to walk around my place as naked as a jay bird every chance that I got.

I went to the fridge and cracked open a cold beer. I was *still* thinking about Corliss Legare and the look in her blue eyes as she stared vacantly out the window. She'd been completely unaware I was there, which made me think about La Croix and his little Alina. I think I was beginning to understand the old boy's distant obsession with the redheaded woman up in the apartment window. An obsession he still had today, over a year and some change later, after making her his. Everything about their relationship was unconventional as fuck, but goddamn if they didn't somehow work. Thick as thieves, those two, and sometimes, just sometimes, I found myself green with fuckin' envy looking at 'em.

I went in to take a shower, getting in and living for the tankless water heater that I'd put in. Never-ending hot water on demand – fuck yeah.

I took another drink off my beer and set it in the nook I had in the tiled shower wall that I kept aside for it. I'd tiled it myself. Hell, I did all the work on this place between my day job and all the club goings-on and happenings.

The hot water pulsed against my back at the base of my neck, between the top of my shoulder blades, and I just would not be distracted. The look on her face as she stared out that window unnerved me, damn near haunted me. She was all smiles and sunshine, laughter and light, and it bugged me that she could be such a chameleon and hide whatever she had going on at home.

I found myself feeling voyeuristic, balling my hand into a fist against the ceramic subway tiling of my shower wall, as I leaned under the spray and let it try to pry the new tension taking hold out of my back.

I wondered if the prick driving had ever laid a hand on her.

I didn't like the thought.

I finished my beer and stepped out of the shower, lookin' like a boiled crawdad. My stomach growled and I found myself wondering what to do for dinner. I also knew I had to get my ass over to the club. I was excited to get the part for my project out in the garage from Louie.

I was rebuilding a classic 1963 Harley-Davidson FL Duo-Glide. Literally, from the frame on back up. A long while back, we'd dragged this damn thing up out of the swamp while magnet fishing. I'd done the right thing, getting it checked out with the local PD. It'd gone into the water probably sometime in the eighties. The original owner was dead, and the local boys didn't want the paperwork of hauling it off and were more than happy to let me take it off their hands.

As much as I'd hated cozying up to the pigs over it, I would have hated even more restoring the fuckin' thing, getting a *go faster* award on it, and getting a set of silver bracelets for all my trouble and a record I did not want for stealing the damned thing. Hell, I amazed myself that I was still out here truckin' along and keeping my job at the high school – no one any the wiser that I was some kind of rough-around-the-edges criminal, out here livin' by his own set of laws.

Did I have an arrest record? Yeah, but that didn't count for shit without a conviction, and I did *not* have me one of those.

I suppose it was an eventuality, maybe even an inevitability, when you lived this life – at least for most… but I refused. I knew there was a better way. A smarter way. Just like my daddy'd told me.

I got dressed in more comfortable clothes, shrugging into my jacket, and cut for the short ride over to the club.

It felt good to have the wind in my hair, and yes – riding without a helmet was illegal in Louisiana, but fuck it. The ride was short and the only time the cops came rolling through this neighborhood was when the gangbanging was fired up, which it hadn't been after we'd moved in. We didn't have the time or patience for that kind of back-and-forth. Not on our turf.

"Ridin' risky, ain't ya?" Axeman asked when I got off my bike.

"What are you, my fuckin' mother?" I asked him. He gave me this cheesy shit-eating grin that made me snort as he took a drag off the doobie that he'd rolled up for himself.

He held it out, and I wrinkled my nose and gave my head a shake.

"Nah, I'm already hungry. That'd probably edge my ass into hangry with the munchies coming along with it."

"Crawfish boil goin' on out back," he said. "Cypress brought in a haul."

"My man," I muttered. "Good deal. I was just tryin' to figure out what the hell to do for dinner."

"Well, should be puttin' it on sooner rather than later," Axe said, looking at his watch.

"Nice," I muttered and went on through into the club.

"Hex." La Croix nodded from one of the leather couches in our living room setup.

Alina was lounging against him, a book in her hands. She looked up over the top of it and said, "Uh-oh, I know that look."

I raised an eyebrow and slid onto one of the bar stools. "You do, do yah?" I asked.

Chainsaw turned around from selecting a bottle off the shelf back there and gave me an inquiring chin lift. I threw him some chin back in the affirmative and wordlessly he pulled the bottle of top shelf whiskey that I liked down and went for some glasses.

"I do too, brother." La Croix's voice was low, dark, and stormy. I held up a hand and waved him off.

"You boys need a minute?" Alina asked, uneasiness clouding her clear eyes, and I shook my head.

"It ain't club business, darlin'. You're good right where you're at."

She visibly relaxed.

"What's goin' on then?" La Croix asked.

I sighed and accepted the rocks glass from Chainsaw and tossed the double that was in it back.

I savored the light amber liquid, rolling the fire and smoky goodness over my tongue, and swallowing, eased out a breath.

"Just think, I might have an inkling now what it was like for you," I said, eyeing Alina. "You know, before y'all got together."

She shaded a pretty pink, but her green eyes never wavered from mine. She was fearless now, held a confidence that looked good on her with La Croix at her back. La Croix's dark gaze was affixed to the copper of the top of his lady's head.

He nodded slowly, those creepy fucking tattooed eyeballs of his flickering up to mine and fixing there. Something passed between us then. A new understanding. Something primal, beyond brotherhood and bike. A curious thing. His lips quirked slightly on one side, a smug little smile tugging at his lips. An answering smile spread my own until I was grinning, teeth and all, and lookin' like a fuckin' loon.

"Yeah, laugh it up," I told him and his smirk grew to a smile – the closest thing to a full-on belly laugh that this motherfucker ever got. Which, come to think of it, was probably a good thing. If La Croix was laughin'? The devil him-fucking-self was walkin' the earth. It was that terrifying of a sight to behold.

CHAPTER THREE

*C*orliss…

    I sighed softly with frustration and checked my watch. My car had needed to remain in the shop another day and Mark was supposed to pick me up… and he was late… again.

I looked up as my classroom door opened and the school's custodian, the attractive one, rolled his bin through.

"Here again?" he asked and smiled, and it was something.

I smiled back, hoping that it was just friendly and he didn't take it as flirty. I just didn't need *that* drama. I gave him a breezy, "Yep! For sure. I should be able to get my car back today if my fiancé, Mark, would just get here on time for once." I rolled my eyes, unable to contain my frustration.

"You try an' call him?" he asked, and I shook my head.

"I'll give him a few more minutes," I said.

"Offer stands from yesterday," he said, as he emptied my trashcans around the room into his bigger bin.

"I appreciate that. If it's much longer, do you think I could trouble you for a ride to the mechanic's shop?" I quailed inside just asking. I mean, how cringey, having to ask your coworker to get to the shop, to get your car, when your *fiancé* had already said… but Mark was proving to be unreliable as hell lately and I just didn't know what his problem was.

"No problem. What's the name of the place?" he asked.

"Roald & Son's Auto Repair," I said, coloring lightly. He gave a slow smile.

"Cheap, but they do good work." He gave a nod. "I know where it's at."

"Then thank you, Mr. Johnson," I said.

He stopped and said, "My friends call me Hex."

"Hex?" I asked, and he gave me a bit of a serious look.

"Not sure why I told you that. I mean, I ain't told anyone at the school that before. Mike works just fine."

"Hex." I turned the unusual name over in my mouth and had to ask, "How'd you get a name like that? I like it."

He stopped his cleaning again and straightened, turning.

"I'll answer your question if you answer one of mine first."

I cocked my head and took off my reading glasses.

The very temperature, or barometric pressure in the room, shifted to something more serious, his gaze from across the room holding a weight that hadn't been there a moment before. But it was the weight of curiosity – nothing uncomfortable. Not yet… although I felt as though it was a tipping point. That we were suddenly on the very precipice of something here. I didn't know what it was, but there was a tenuous thread of, I don't know, *hope?*

He unfastened his canister vacuum from in front of his chest and shrugged out of it, setting it on the floor next to his rolling bin. I perked up when he came toward me, pulling up a chair across from my desk and settling into it, leaning forward, his muscular forearms atop his knees, the sleeves of his school district issued pine-green coveralls rolled back over them. There was something very blue-collar but still *very* alluring about that. Almost as hot or hotter than when a man rolled his shirt sleeves back in a white-collar position.

My thoughts drifted to Mark. I rolled my lips and flirted with danger out of my annoyance and hurt when it came to the man I was supposed to be set to marry.

"Ask your question," I said, leaning back in my seat and almost surrendering in the moment to whatever may come out of Mike 'Hex' Johnson's mouth next.

What came wasn't what I had expected, not at all.

"Are you happy?" he asked me.

I blinked in surprise and my gaze flicked to his intense brown eyes that were light enough they weren't quite black but were darker still to give that effect that they were molten and deep.

My breath stilled in my lungs, and my voice sort of issued forth without my thinking about it, blurting out, "Beg your pardon?"

He gave me a crooked grin and huffed out a slight laugh, leaning back in his seat.

"It's not a complicated question, Miss Legare," he said. His voice was warm and slightly teasing, dragging an answering smile to my own lips as I shook my head to clear it from whatever spell he was trying to put on me.

"I mean, in what context?" I asked to buy time. His expression changed, like clouds scudding over the sun, dimming things, turning him cold almost.

"Here at school?" I asked, and quickly followed up with, "Of course I'm happy. I love my job."

He cocked his head and I felt a bit put on the spot. He said, "I confess, I pulled up alongside y'all at the stoplight up the road yesterday. You didn't look happy then and I just got the impression I should check on you, is all."

"Oh," I said, and the silence that word escaped into was so profound I felt as though my utterance should have echoed. He watched me, waiting me out, and I felt my shoulders drop as though the proverbial jig, as they would say, was up.

"I… I wasn't happy," I confessed. "Mark and I were having a bit of an argument." I cleared my throat as his chin lifted almost imperceptibly and I smiled wanly. "He can sometimes get a little wrapped up in work and things, that's all. Things are fine now."

"Is that why he's late today, too?" Hex asked gently.

I said, "I don't know. Probably. I can't get through to him on his cell phone. He turns it off for meetings and sometimes forgets to turn it back on." I blushed and was low-key angry at myself and damn sure resentful of Mark for having to make the excuse. I mean, he was a grown-ass adult. With how addicted the lot of us were to our phones nowadays, I didn't understand what was so hard about remembering I was waiting and turning the damn thing back on.

"Tell you what." Hex planted his hands on his knees and stood up. "I'll just let ol' Curtis know I'm takin' you on down to the shop to get your car and I'll be back in fifteen. We'll go now. I'm sure you'd be a lot more comfortable grading papers at home and it'd sure take a load off of you, getting your car sooner rather than later."

"Oh, I can't ask you to do that," I said and laughed a little.

"It's no problem. I want to, so I will," he said and jerked his head toward my classroom door. "C'mon."

I looked at the clock and then at my dormant phone on the edge of my desk and scraped my bottom lip between my teeth.

"Can you give me a few minutes to gather up my things?"

He was right. Mark wasn't answering his phone. I had no idea when he would be here, and I really did want to get my car before the shop closed, otherwise I would just be doing this all over again tomorrow… potentially with an added overnight storage fee, considering my car was completed. They had it clearly posted that any vehicles that had their work completed were subject to a daily storage fee until picked up. I was *barely* going to scrape getting it out and I didn't have the extra to just let it sit.

"Sure thing," he said. "I'll just go find Curtis and let him know. Back in a few."

"Okay," I said.

I gathered up my things. I just knew this would start a fight with Mark later, but damnit… he wasn't exactly making any of this easy. And if he couldn't turn on his phone? Well, to hell with him.

Hex stopped outside my room and rapped his knuckles twice against the doorframe. I looked up from where I was shoving the last of my students' papers into my bag with my laptop and smiled gratefully.

"Thank you for doing this," I said. "I really appreciate it."

"It's no trouble. Let's get you back on your rails," he said with a smile and a jerk of his head. I felt my smile grow as I slipped past him out into the hall and he locked up my classroom behind us.

"Thanks for letting me borrow Mr. Johnson for a ride," I said to Curtis, the lead custodian for the school.

The older black man, who had to be in his early seventies, waved me off and said kindly, "Oh, that's no trouble, Miss Legare, no trouble at all. Mikey here is a good worker and he'll be back to finish the job. Ain't got no worries about that."

I smiled and Mike looked pleased and said, "Appreciate it, my guy." He clapped Curtis on the shoulder lightly as we passed.

I slowed when the lights flashed on the big Dodge RAM pickup in the employee parking lot.

"Oh, wow," I said. I couldn't keep how impressed I was out of my voice. "This looks really new!"

"It's actually two years old," he said. "I just like to keep my shhhh-htuff nice."

I laughed a little as I opened the passenger side door. It was immaculate inside the truck, but that wasn't why I was laughing.

"Don't worry about keeping it clean around me," I told him. "I aged out of the foster care system. I've heard it all and then some."

We both shut our doors at the same time as we settled into our seats. He gave a low whistle as he buckled up.

"That must have been tough," he remarked.

I nodded. "It wasn't easy, but here I am," I said brightly and with a bit of a false sense of bravado. I mean, there were definitely days where I didn't feel like I belonged here, and by "here," I didn't mean in New Orleans, or even at Lakeside High. What I meant was I didn't feel like I should be this educated or proficient in my work. I didn't feel like with how I grew up or how I'd pulled through all the opposition stacked in front of me that I should have made it. I felt like I should be at some Dollar General somewhere, pregnant with my third or fourth kid, on my second or third father of that child, watching the clock so I could get out and have a drink or my next hit of whatever. I felt like I should be my mother.

What's more, and I don't know why, but I felt comfortable enough around Hex that I said as much.

He raised an eyebrow and glanced in my direction as we rolled up to a stoplight. He said, "Sounds like you had it rougher than most growing up. Says something about you that you *are* here and not there."

I smiled to myself and looked out the window, leaning back into the plush leather seat of his truck and letting my eyes drift up to the wide, fall, blue sky stretching out endlessly above us.

"Yeah, I guess so," I said, and I was charmed to be sure. It'd been a while since I'd met anyone so easy to talk to.

"So, where'd you move here from?" he asked.

"Sorry? How'd you know I'm not from here?" I asked.

"Accent's different, but hey – I'm not from around here, either. I moved out here from the good ol' Volunteer state. The great state of Tennessee."

"Ah, I was about to say, your accent isn't from here, either. The answer is Huston, but my momma was originally from these parts. Her parents were, anyway. They up and moved to Huston after she was born."

"They couldn't take care of you?" he asked, and I shook my head.

"No, my grandma had a stroke and my grandpa wasn't in the best of health, either. The state decided foster care was best."

"Well, I'm glad it worked out the way it did and you're here," he said. "Lakeside High was in sore need of a teacher like you. You're one of the best, if I do say so myself."

I laughed and said, "I guess that's because I live, sleep, eat, and breathe work. It hasn't been the easiest for me to make friends since moving here. Mark never really wants to go out unless it's a work function, and he's been taking me to less and less of those. I don't get out much."

"That's a damn shame," he said, turning down the street to Roald & Son's Auto Shop.

"I just don't like going out by myself," I said with a shrug. "I guess it's as much my fault as anything else."

"You should get out more, go on down to a café, sit and read a while, something – I don't know. One of my buddy's girls, she goes out and sits and paints watercolors. Got into mixing her own paints and stuff from natural things and opened her own shop. You got any hobbies?"

"Nothing I've picked up in a while, but I have a few," I said.

"Well, there you go. Maybe you wanna pick some of it up again."

I smiled and said, "I just might." He pulled into the lot.

"Well alright, then," he said, turning the dial on his dash to put the truck into "park."

"Thanks for the ride," I said, and he rested his wrists on the top of the steering wheel, loosely lacing his fingers as he let his hands hang.

"I'll see you bright and early, Miss Legare," he said, and I smiled, looking back over my shoulder before I slipped down onto the ground.

"Please, call me Cor, or Corliss. Feels weird having my friends call me Miss anything."

His grin grew into a smile, and he gave me a nod. "See you tomorrow, Cor."

"See you tomorrow, Hex," I said. I shut the door behind me, feeling… good. I felt good. Like I'd genuinely made a new friend.

My phone rang as I was settling up at the counter for my car.

"Hey, I'm here," Mark said absently after I picked up.

"I couldn't get a hold of you," I said. "I had no idea when you would be, so I'm already at the shop. One of the custodians gave me a ride."

"Goddammit, Liss," Mark huffed out, irritated, and I felt my spine go rigid.

"Well, maybe if you'd answer your fucking phone and weren't late to everything all the damn time, we could have avoided this situation. I'm trying to pay for my car and get out of here. I guess I'll see you at home and we can continue this conversation there," I snipped out. Before Mark could say anything, I ended the call on my end and turned off my phone.

I smiled politely up at the man behind the cash wrap and asked pleasantly, "Now where were we?"

He gave me a dubious look and, with a bit of a laugh, said, "I'd hate to be him right now, boy. I just need you to sign here." He pointed with the pen at the line and handed it over, and I scribbled my signature.

"'K, great," I said. "Thank you for getting this done so quickly."

"Yes, ma'am. I'm just sorry we didn't get it done yesterday."

I shook my head. "It's alright, things happen." We finished our transaction and they brought my car around – washed and vacuumed.

"Aw, thank you!" I said, beaming. "You didn't have to do that."

"All part of the customer service experience over here at Roald & Sons, ma'am. Y'all have a better day now, y'hear?"

I smiled and accepted my keys. "I will, thank you."

I still beat Mark home by minutes. Boy, did we have a go at each other that ended up in both of us going to bed angry and giving each other the silent treatment.

Jackass.

CHAPTER FOUR

*H*ex...

"Hey, Mike, how's it going?"

"Another day, another dollar," I answered Mrs. Donal, the school principal. "What can I do you for, ma'am?" I asked, genially tipping my non-existent hat.

"Second-floor girl's restroom. I don't know what these kids are doing and I'm sorry, but all but one of those stalls is out of order. Every one of those toilets are clogged with something."

"Ahhh, kids," I said with a wink. "I'll get right on it. Let me grab my toolkit."

"Thanks, Mike!" she called after me as I backed out of the office and left her to resume her conversation with the school's main secretary.

It'd been a few weeks since I'd given Cor a ride out to the shop to get her car, and we'd struck up a good friendship since then. I took any excuse I could to go on up to the school's second floor and to pass her door. We'd even sort of struck up a once-a-week standing lunch date in her classroom. Just an unspoken thing that'd started up casually and had organically evolved over the last two weeks into lunch every Thursday.

It was tipping into the downhill slide that was late October and I was curious, since Halloween was supposed to be on a Monday this year, what Cor had planned for dressing up. Myself, I'd got a pair of those familiar blue-gray coveralls and a good ol' fashioned William Shatner mask that everybody recognized these days as Michael Myers. Had to get Mrs. Donal's permission. She'd nixed the obviously fake big butcher's knife with the squeeze blood handle and collapsible blade but I'd sure tried talking her into letting me do away with her at the school assembly that'd been planned for that day all in good fun.

She agreed to let me chase her off the stage at least.

Even the grownups had to have fun sometimes.

We had a grand ol' Halloween bash planned at the clubhouse on that Saturday night and I was sorely tempted to invite Cor for a first-time get-together outside of school… yeah, even though she had some guy, was living with him and engaged and all that.

I had a good feeling that wasn't gonna last. She never talked about him, and anytime the conversation turned toward him? She'd conveniently change the subject.

I took my hand-carried toolbox with me and went up the stairs. I had to pass her classroom to get to the bathroom that was having problems and was surprised to hear a bunch of loud and rambunctiousness coming outta the room almost as soon as I set foot on the second floor. It was after school hours. Most if all o' the kids were supposed to be long gone – unless she had detention duty this week. I know it rotated through the teachers so it was a distinct possibility.

I slipped just inside the classroom door and barked out, "Hey!" The classroom of five or six settled right the fuck down.

"Where's Miss Legare?" I demanded calmly.

"Bathroom," one of the girls said.

"She's been gone a while," another kid said. He was a class clown type – funny as hell but didn't know when to quit. Still, he was a good kid.

"Thomas followed her out a few seconds after she left," one of the other girls said and I felt the first stirrings of dread tick down my spine. I didn't know who Thomas was, so that meant maybe he was one of the quiet ones. The quiet ones gave me the heebs. Why? Because *I* had been one of the quiet ones and I was into all kinds of shit.

"Y'all sit here and be quiet," I said. "She'll be back in a minute."

I ducked back out, shut the door behind me, and went for the bathroom down the hall.

The second red flag when it came to this situation came in the form of Cor's brightly colored and sparkly tumbler from a popular coffee chain lying on its side, water spilling out in the middle of the hallway's linoleum.

"Shit, Fable…" I muttered, absentmindedly calling her by the pet name I'd given her over lunch last week. She'd told me about how myths and fables had gotten her through, given her a place to escape, when her mom was deep in her shit and bringing creeps home to hook up with for a fix. How she'd literally locked herself inside her bedroom closet when the creeps couldn't get their rocks off with her mom and had come looking for her.

It'd been a tale as old as time, a familiar one, but one that'd still pissed me off no matter how much she'd assured me that by some grace of some higher power she'd never been touched. The conversation had turned then to religion, and how she didn't believe in God. How she was a pagan, more spiritual, than anything.

How it made more sense to her.

It hadn't been the first time I'd had the thought that she and Alina would be a pair, and what'd gotten the wheels in my head to turning that she maybe should come around the club someday. If I could trust her to keep that secret for me.

There was a sinking pit in my stomach when I pushed open the door to the girl's bathroom up here. A pit that yawned open, the bottom falling out.

Every man's got a monster that resides in him. One that when you push the right buttons? Well, his other side comes roaring to the surface. Some men were so broken, that like La Croix, and maybe Axeman, their others were more their full selves than their selves anymore.

I happened to be one of those men who jived with that other. Who

23

managed a level of control that was unmatched. I'd never had my MC life and school life collide so hard as it did when I saw what that kid was doing to Cor.

The blood on the tile, channeling through the grout, the way his ass cheeks flexed with every thrust. The way her hand, pale and limp, swished back and forth through the puddle leaking out of her, the crimson thick and wet.

First thing I did was drop my tools with a crash. The kid was some kind of blessed that I didn't think to grab a wrench or a hammer or something when I started to wail on him. I grabbed him by the back of his fuckin' hoodie and ripped him off her prone bloody and beaten body, and I bodily *threw* his ass sideways into the wall.

He hit with a grunt, some of the old pink tiles cracking and shattering behind him. He slid to the floor, and I hauled back and buried my steel-toe booted foot in his guts. I kicked him. And when I say I kicked him, I mean I beat that motherfucker until he stopped moving, kicked the ever-loving shit out of him, beat his fucking ass like he was a grown-ass man. Guts, chest, head, it made no never mind. I wanted him dead but was only stopped up short by screaming coming from the fuckin' doorway.

I rounded on the girl from Cor's classroom and bellowed, "Get down to that office and call 9-1-1, *now!*"

I went to Corliss's broken body and moved swiftly, dragging my radio off the floor where it'd flown from my pocket. I rambled into it, calling for help, my eyes trying to make sense of things.

She had a puncture by her neck, another down on her ribs. Her pants and panties were gone, her shoes too. The only thing she was wearing from the waist down were her fucking socks and I had nothing to cover her with.

I put my hands over the wound that seemed to be bleeding the worst, pressing down. Her breathing didn't sound so good, and I recognized the sound. I'd been around a fair few to make it, friend and foe alike.

"Hang on for me, babe," I muttered and I pressed.

"Oh, damn!" I looked up and said, "Gimme your jacket!" Tyrone pulled off his black hoodie and for having so much melanin, the kid looked ashen. He covered her up and I said, "Good, good, you read my mind. Now go stand at the door. Make sure nobody but an adult comes in here."

"What about him?" he demanded.

"You wanna get a lick in on your way out go ahead. I ain't see shit," I said.

"Fuck, man," he muttered and to his credit, he kicked the unconscious fucker in the kidney area on his way out.

It felt like fucking forever before help arrived and when it did, it was old Curtis.

"Aw, hell!" he cried and went to check on the kid I beat the fuckin' brakes off of. I let him. If the kid died, it'd be my fuckin' ass. I didn't think I'd gone that far, but shit – I'd lost control. I knew that.

A moment later, the principle showed her ass up, on a phone, barking into it.

"Oh, God!" she cried, a hand over her mouth at the scene in front of her.

Shit went fast after that. Like all the time had stretched and then snapped, events rocketing forward at the speed of sound to the point I couldn't be sure what was what.

I seemed to come back to myself at the double doors in the front of the school, on the first floor, a hand on my shoulder holding me back as they loaded Cor into the back of the wee-woo wagon.

"She's in good hands. You got to her. They'll take care of her."

I swallowed hard and turned to look at the pig with his hand on me. I shook it off and said, "You want anything or can I go?"

"I need to take your statement, find out what happened here, then you can go," he said.

I nodded, and swallowed hard, reining in my adrenaline, my rage, and hiding the shaking in my hands.

You're a good citizen, I told myself. *Act like it, you fucking fool.*

"Sorry," I said, after getting it together. "She's my friend…"

The cop nodded solemnly, pity in his eyes.

"I understand. Not many people encounter this level of awful in their lives."

I swallowed hard and asked, "What about him?" All the while I chanted rhythmically in my head, *don't be sus, don't be sus, don't be sus… do what the normies would do, do what the normies would do, do what the normies would do…*

The cop, to his credit, was a good man. He looked over at where the kid was handcuffed to a gurney and being wheeled out – headed for the back of an ambo of his own.

"What about him?" he asked dryly, voice deadpan in that 'I don't give a fuck' tone.

I gave him a look, a grim set to my mouth and gave him a nod of respect that he deserved.

"Ask your questions," I said and swallowed hard.

"Let's go back inside." He put a hand on me and I stiffened, but I let him lead me back inside.

No telling if I would need the club's attorney or not, but you better believe, I was gonna contact him.

CHAPTER FIVE

orliss...
    Everything was fuzzy. Everything was a blur, a rush, a barely there blush of light and sound. Movement and frenzy, pain, and a haze of wild energy that I couldn't quite grasp what was here nor there... and then nothing again.

I was in and out, aware I was in a hospital. Breathing was hard and I didn't want to wake. Still, people and voices persisted, touching me when I didn't want to be touched, yelling questions over and over until I tried to bat them away like the annoying pests that they were.

Then there was a gentle touch to my hair, a rough hand smoothing it away from my face, soft lips to my forehead, then next to my ear. A pleasing voice, at once familiar and unfamiliar, and then there was nothing more again.

I was lost to the underworld of warmth and dark, drifting along the River Styx made of pain killers and drugs, and I worried vaguely about that.

Addiction ran in my family.

I didn't want to be my mother.

I would rather be in pain... but my mouth was filled with hard plastic and unpleasantness and there was nothing I could say...

CHAPTER SIX

*H*ex...

I kissed her forehead and brushed her hair back from her face, wincing that it was crunchy with her dried blood in places.

"Hey, uh, you got anything I can clean her hair up with? Like some baby wipes or something?" I asked softly.

The nurse that was in here punching buttons on her IV machine looked my way.

"Yeah, if you can just hang on and give me a minute, I'll see if I can't find something for you."

"Thanks," I murmured.

I'd lied my ass off to get in here, claimed I was her brother. Didn't have to wait long to do it, either. Her piece of shit fiancé had been up and hadn't lasted five minutes before taking off. The nurses didn't like him. Told me he'd basically said to call him when she woke up and had bounced.

I didn't bounce. I stayed right here and gripped her hand lightly in mine, sitting by her bed vigilant. What for? I couldn't tell you, but I was here.

"Here you go, honey." The nurse passed me a packet of these hospital-grade wet wipe things that were the size of a paper towel when you unfolded them. I'd seen 'em used on another patient while I'd lurked in the hallway outside the ICU's doors.

"Thanks," I murmured.

"You're not her brother, are you?" she asked as I got one of the cloths out.

"As far as you know, I am," I said tersely and the nurse smiled at me.

"Oh, quit it. I like you. You're much better for her than that other one."

"Thanks," I muttered and I wiped at her hair, swallowing hard at the rust-colored tinge it left behind.

"Just... if he comes back... we don't need any drama, okay?" she asked and I nodded without looking at her.

"You'll get none from me. I can control myself," I said.

"Are you the one that put her assailant in the ICU over at—"

"Yes," I said. "But that was different."

She nodded.

"Glad to hear it."

"If there's anything that she needs..." I said after hesitating and the nurse smiled.

"Eventually, she'll need clothes and the like to get out of here."

"How long do you think that will be?" I asked over the shush and beeps of equipment.

"That depends on her," she said.

"Thanks," I murmured as she went for the door. She turned back and nodded, her short blonde pixie cut starting to gray, the wrinkles fanning out from her eyes in crows' feet as she smiled.

I wanted her to leave so I could pick up her chart and see what was what. I didn't think the nurse would tell me if I asked. She knew I wasn't family. Probably thought I was too dumb to understand the medical jargon and shit. I was alright with that. I waited and picked up the binder thing off the rolling table and started looking through it.

Collapsed lung from a stab wound that was written in a bunch of fancy ass medical terminology that meant her side, sort of toward the back, under her arm. I had to guess her arms were up to ward him off

29

when that one fell. It wouldn't have stopped her from screaming but the blow to her head that was listed would. The major scary stab wound was up top, in front where he'd stabbed down at her shoulder with the pair of scissors that'd been found on the bathroom floor. That one had nicked her subclavian artery, or the one that ran up under or around her collarbone – which had snapped under the blow that'd been dealt by that weasley little fuck.

Still, back to the whole artery thing. That'd been the bastard that'd kept her in surgery for so long. Repairing that had been a bitch, probably. I don't know. I was used to putting people full of holes; not the business of patching them up.

All in all, she'd bled, *a lot*. They'd had to put it back in by even more, and she'd almost died on the operating table not once, but a couple of times.

It was a miracle she was still here if you believed in that sort of thing.

I didn't. There was no god as far as I was concerned. Not one that'd let her miss all the things she'd been up against only to take her down with this now… *fuck*.

I put the chart aside and resumed doing my best to clean her up, talking to her softly, making every promise I could that this would be the last fucked-up thing to happen to her if I could help it. That no one would touch her without asking first ever again, or I'd break every fucking bone in their damn hand – no, their *whole fuckin' body*.

I didn't know if she could hear me, but I'd like to think for the sake of my own sanity that she could.

"Yo, MAN, YOU GOOD?" Saint called when I walked into the club that night.

"Why?" I asked. "What you hear?" I scowled. I hadn't called anyone or said anything to La Croix or none of them.

"Shit, man… it's all over the news – your high school, *custodian* –

that's fuckin' you. You wanna tell us what the fuck is going on?" La Croix looked pissed and I couldn't say I blamed him.

"Who all is missing?" I asked tiredly.

"None of us," Bennie answered.

"We're all here," Axe echoed, sliding a whiskey down the bar. I picked it up and downed it, nodding.

"Church," I said, and everyone wordlessly ditched their phones on the bar and filed toward the back while Axe gathered them up and dumped them into the mylar signal blocking bag we kept them in, zipping it closed.

Smart man, he dragged the bottle of my favorite off the shelf and thrust his chin at me to silently tell me to keep my glass.

I nodded tiredly and we filed back into the chapel.

"So, what the fuck is going on?" La Croix demanded sternly.

I told them. Everything. About how I'd gone up to fix the fuckin' toilets, about how I'd found her bleeding out on the bathroom floor, that kid... the kid raping her.

Stone silence rippled around the table.

"I'm honestly surprised this shit made the news," I said. "Shit like this happens every fuckin' day in our schools and it never hits the media..." I ran a hand over my face. "I mean, maybe not quite this bad, but *fuck*... the news? Already?" I worried about Corliss. I scooted my glass over to Axe who had the bottle poised and ready to pour.

"That's *why* it's on the fuckin' news, though, bro," Bennie said, shifting uncomfortably in his seat.

"The kid ain't a kid," Axe said as soon as I finished swallowing.

"What?" I demanded.

"He's some twenty-three-year-old dude *posing* as a kid," Collier declared.

"That's why it's all up on the news," Bennie practically repeated himself. "Nobody knows what to do with any of this."

"What the fuck?" I demanded softly, incredulously.

"They say you put him in ICU," Saint said.

I caught his eye and gave a curt nod. "Goddamn right I did," I said, and there were nods of respect going around the table.

La Croix grunted at the head of it and I caught his creepy inked-out eyes. Something passed between us. A… a tiredness almost.

"We ain't getting any younger," I said. "I've especially been feeling it. Slowing down some, you know? Like this ache in my soul for something… quieter. A longing for something good. I've lived fast. I have no intention of dying young – ain't none of us do. We've fought long and hard to mark out this turf as our own and by God, we've won it and defended it against all comers."

"You drunk already?" Saint asked with a wink. A smattering of uncomfortable laughing went around the table.

"No," I said and rubbed the back of my neck, pulling on the back of my head to ease some of the tension that'd been riding my shoulders all afternoon and evening.

"We put Ruth and them down with the intended goal of living another life," La Croix said.

I nodded.

"We saw something better – we all did," I said.

"Quit beating around the fucking bush," Chainsaw grumbled.

"There's no getting to this motherfucker now," Saint said and sighed. "He's safe as can be in that hospital."

I nodded.

"He hurt someone close to Hex. That means exactly what you think it means – all of you. You ain't dumb," La Croix declared.

"Shit, Saint's right," I declared. "Ain't nothing we can do about his ass right now but yeah. I won't let that shit stand. Cor… Cor's a good person. Sweet. Been through a lot and still managed to dodge, well, *that,* right up until today."

"How's she doing?" Louie asked, and he looked genuinely concerned. But our boy Louie? He was still on the young side and he always was a soft touch.

"Not good. He stabbed her a couple of times with a pair of classroom scissors, the old-school kind with the metal handles. Collapsed a lung, nicked an artery. She's in intensive care until further notice. I had to lie to get in there with her. Pretty sure in addition to the blood loss, they're worried about infection. She was in surgery a long time. They almost lost her twice."

"What can we do?" Cypress asked.

"Right now, we can agree or disagree we're gonna do something about it. For now, that's all we can do. When the time comes and a plan gets made, we'll figure out the rest, I reckon," I said.

"You know we're with you, bro," Axeman said, and I gave a nod.

Murmurs of assent went around the table.

"For now, you focus on your girl," La Croix declared.

"She's got a tough road ahead when it comes to healing up, believe me," Louie declared and he didn't look happy. All I could do with that was nod. He'd been stabbed himself last year pretty good. Came within a hair's breadth of getting hooked on Oxy. It was tough for him, the pain. He was scared as fuck – had confided in me a few times he was afraid he'd go down that rabbit hole and he ain't never see the light of day again. But that was what we were for. To keep him straight and from going down that road if he didn't wanna.

I worried about it for Cor. She had a similar family history from what she'd told me. She was tough, though. Just like Louie'd been tough.

We were quiet around the table for a while and I finally scoffed, making a noise of disbelief.

"Now how the fuck does a twenty-three-year-old man pass himself off as a fourteen-year-old kid?" I wondered aloud.

"Ain't that the fuckin' question?" Collier asked, leaning back in his own seat.

"And the citizens want to call *us* the crazy ones," Cypress said, staring off into space.

"A-fucking-men," Chainsaw said with a bit of a chuff.

I shook my head. The whiskey was working like a charm now, my mind and body quieting down, and suddenly all I fucking wanted was a hot shower and some sleep.

"I think I'm gonna go home and go to bed," I said. I got a couple of slightly worried looks.

The guys knew I was into Cor, by a fair bit – but they also knew she was spoken for, that things were new, and I wasn't as serious as all that for the time being.

I think within a matter of seconds that'd changed this afternoon and that, next to the helpless rage I felt, is what pushed me over the edge into a fuckin' freefall, arms pinwheeling with absolutely nothing left to ground me. At least not until she woke up. Not until I knew she would be okay and just how much more damage had been done.

Her body would heal. I worried more about her heart and her mind.

CHAPTER SEVEN

*C*orliss…

I woke in the intensive care unit and I had absolutely no recollection of what'd happened to me. None. The last thing I remembered was the bell ringing for the end of a period. I knew it was one that was after lunch, but beyond that I couldn't say… and that in and of itself was terrifying.

The police came to talk to me, and I felt genuinely bad that I couldn't help them but at the same time… the powers that be had seen fit to bless me that even though I was hurt, and badly at that, the reason why was a complete mystery to me.

"I'm going to head back to the office," Mark said. He barely pecked me on the forehead, dragging his hand from mine almost as soon as the police detectives had left.

"So soon?" I asked, disappointed.

"Well, yeah. There's nothing really that I can do here and you know I hate hospitals, babe."

I swallowed hard and hated the bitter taste his words left on my tongue.

Yeah, no, we were so over when I was out of here. This was fucking bullshit. I didn't know how I was going to do it, how I would figure it out… but no. This was *stupid*. However, I could also appreciate that if and when I could leave the hospital, I was going to need help for a little bit. Like it or not, Mark was the only person that I knew that could. It was just a question of if he would, which I highly doubted at this point, and I was scared for a whole different reason.

You've done everything on your own to date… why would this be any different?

The voice was a familiar one to me, rock hard and steely with determination. The one that constantly urged me to be smarter than the problem and I would. I would have to.

I slept after that. The drugs sucking at the edges of my consciousness until I was out, drifting in an almost state of in-between worlds. Sometimes I would hear things, like the nurse come in to check my vitals. Sometimes it was something unpleasant, just on the edge of dreaming that would jolt me awake. Mostly it was the sensation like I was falling although I was perfectly still.

I hated heights. I always had. The sensation of being high and falling, falling, falling, wasn't a good one – not for me.

The next time I jolted awake, a rough hand was in mine and another one smoothed my hair back from my face. The sensation was so achingly familiar, though I didn't readily know why.

"Hey, you. Hi…" the voice was rich and melodic, familiar with a southern accent but not Texas, and not Louisiana. I opened my eyes and I felt tears spring to them as Hex looked down at me with warmth in his rich brown eyes, a tremulous smile painting his lips even as worry creased his brow and bracketed those lips with deep lines of concern.

"Hi," I murmured back, and he pressed his lips to my forehead and retook his seat, gathering my hand gently between his, careful not to bump all of the IV apparatus stuck to the back of it.

"How did you get in here?" I murmured softly.

"Lied and told 'em I was your brother," he said.

I stifled a laugh but it was too late. Enough of it got through, sending pain, racking through my chest and body.

"Don't make me laugh," I scolded and his smile grew.

"Think of it this way," he said. "The pain lets you know you're alive."

It was a bit of a sobering thought.

"I don't even know what happened," I told him. "I don't remember anything after fourth period. I'm so confused. One minute, the bell is ringing and the next thing I know, I'm waking up in the hospital."

"Police come by yet?" he asked.

"Yes," I told him. "They said…" I swallowed hard. "They said I was attacked by a student. That… that I was…" I didn't want to say it out loud.

"Shh, it's okay. You ain't gotta tell me. I was the one who found you."

I tore my gaze from my blanket-covered lap to his face. His look was half-shuttered, like he was trying to hide all the bad things from me. I didn't know how I felt about that to be honest. I wasn't a child but at the same time…

"I want to know, but I don't think I'm ready to know right now," I told him.

He nodded slowly. "And that's just fine," he said. "I'm not going anywhere."

He gave my hand a light squeeze and I tightened my grip on him. I didn't want him to take it away yet.

"They might move me to a regular room tonight or tomorrow," I said softly. "Still, they said it's going to be awhile before I can go home."

"What's that look for?" he asked gently when again I couldn't look at him.

"I guess it says something that you're here but Mark…" I pursed my lips to fight back tears because damnit… it hurt. It hurt a lot.

"Yeah, I hear that," he said. "You need anything?"

"Are you leaving already?" I asked.

"Nope," he said simply. "I'm here as long as you need me."

I smiled but it was probably more of a grimace as the tears switched from hurt to gratitude at the drop of a hat.

"Then you might be here a while." I tried to joke and his smile grew, a soft wheezing gentle laugh escaping him despite his best efforts to remain serious.

"An' that's alright with me. I ain't got nothing but time, Fable. I ain't got nothing but time."

I sniffed and nodded, stopping when it pulled on my neck and shoulder. I realized my right arm was in a sling and had been this whole time. *God and Goddess, these drugs,* I thought with dread. They screwed everything up.

"How are my students taking it?" I asked, and Hex swiped his thumb across the backs of my fingers.

"The whole school is just wrecked. They're scared for you," he said.

"You have your phone?" I asked.

"Yeah, why?"

"Help me look a little less scary, and a little less like death has had its hand on my shoulder," I ordered.

"Yes, ma'am," he said. He got up and helped sit me up some, shoving pillows behind me to hold me up.

The nurse came in and asked me, "What are you doing?"

"Having my fr-brother record a message to my students, letting them know I'm okay," I said.

"Oh. Well, hang on. Don't try to do too much. Give me just a moment and I'll bring in some professional help. We don't want you hurting yourself."

We waited. We got propped up, and Hex took the quiet time to fix my hair into something less ghastly.

I didn't look great – pale with dark circles under my eyes, a shadow under the hollows of my cheekbones from too much trauma and drugs. It drove me a little crazy that I looked so awful when I couldn't remember why – no matter how much I told myself that I was blessed for that universe-given mercy.

Who in their right mind would *want* to remember something like that?

Certainly not I, and I hoped I never would. But by the same token, I was absolutely certain that I would *never* forget Hex and the kindness he showed me here today.

I swallowed hard and made him take a few takes until I was satisfied with the message I intended to convey correctly. I mean, I was a freaking language arts teacher. I had better get it right.

CHAPTER EIGHT

*H*ex...

"Oh, Mike... what can I do for you?"

I stepped more fully into Mrs. Donal's office and asked, "Got a minute?"

"Of course," she declared. Before I could even get the door shut all the way, she asked, "You aren't ready to come back so soon, are you?"

I smiled and went around the pair of chairs in front of her desk, taking a seat across from her in one of the two uncomfortable wooden chairs with no padding she had set out.

"Truth be told, I'm going a little crazy around the house. I understand why you wanted me to have some cool-down period, but I was ready to come back to work Monday after... well, after..." I played it cool, acting like I was more bothered about the whole thing than I could honestly say that I was. I lived in a secret world steeped in fuckin' violence. Nothing honestly surprised me anymore. The only thing that especially bothered me about this whole thing was how badly it'd affect Cor... but me? I could compartmentalize that shit just fine.

Still, the rest of the world expected me to be some kind of traumatized, so traumatized I would be. Seemed to me like it was somehow becoming chic to be some kind of fucked up; and to be honest, while I'd never begrudge a person their feelings on any given subject, there were a lot of people out there that didn't know the first fuckin' thing about what being traumatized really meant.

I mean, you didn't see or hear me whinin' or cryin' about seein' my daddy shot in front of me. Dyin' in my fourteen-year-old arms over a dispute over his latest batch of shine.

Tell you what though, where the law'd failed my pops? I hadn't. And those motherfuckers ain't seen my eighteen-year-old self comin'. Their bones still rested up in some remote holler of the Smokies and I slept just fuckin' fine about it. Still, I missed my pops every damn fuckin' day.

"You know it's okay to not be okay, don't you, Mike?" Mrs. Donal asked quietly, and I smiled at her.

"Oh, I know it. I just find it helps to keep busy. I'm just tryin' *not* to tear into another room of my house that don't need it. Been tinkerin' out in the garage some, but this place gives me purpose. Y'know?"

"Well, if you're ready, far be it from me to stop you coming back, now," she said.

"Actually, that's only partially why I'm here," I told her.

"Oh?" She settled back in her seat. Mrs. Donal was a grand old lady, her short, iron-gray hair perfectly coifed and she always wore an impeccable and professional skirt suits that reminded me of the same sort of thing the principles in my school wore when *I* was a kid. Like there was some sort of dress code or some shit, unspoken throughout the land. I don't know… still, she looked on at me with some interest from behind her rimless glasses as I pulled my phone from my back pocket and I cued up one of the two videos that'd I'd recorded for Corliss.

My voice emanated from the small screen, *"Okay, it's rolling – you can say what you want."*

Mrs. Donal's smile was both sad and amused as she listened to my Fable say how much she missed everyone and how very sorry she couldn't be with them. She also lit up when Cor mentioned she would record a second video for the students to tell them how much she loved and missed them all and how she would work hard to return very soon but that it would be awhile. The first video was the truth, the second was a kinder and gentler thing to let the school know that she was alright and would see everyone as soon as she could.

"That was very sweet of her," she said, handing the phone back to me. "Very kind of you to have been to see her, Mike... although I know an ICU when I see one." She winked at me.

"Yeah, well, I had to see for myself, you know?"

Mrs. Donal gave me a look over the rim of her glasses and said gently and so very kindly, "You know she's engaged, right?"

I smiled. "I do." Then the lie slipped out nice and easy, "Nice guy."

She smiled and seemed to relax some, and I said, "We're just friends. Got some things in common and she's easy to talk to. I'm... I'm glad no one holds it against me, me comin' unglued on that feller. I mean, I didn't know he wasn't a real student when I did and... I just couldn't fathom anybody hurting Miss Legare like that."

"It's alright, Mike. I can't imagine seeing something like that myself. I'm glad you were there to save her life."

I nodded and said, "You want I should email these to you?"

"Yes, please."

We went through all that stupid shit and I effectively dismissed myself. Good deed done for the day, I took myself back to the hospital.

CHAPTER NINE

*C*orliss...

"The hospital says I could come home in a few days, so I need some clothes. I'm sorry to bother you but…"

"Yeah, no, babe, it's no bother! I've got most of my afternoon clear. I'll bring them right now."

"You're sure?" I asked.

"Yeah, yeah! I'm sure. I'm glad you're feeling better. I bet you're ready to come home."

"Honestly, I just want to shower in my own shower," I said.

"I bet. Do you want anything specific?"

I gripped the phone just a little bit tighter and thought to myself just how *weird* it was that Mark was all of a sudden being nice. Attentive even… I'd had more than a few suspicions already. He hadn't visited me at all while I'd been in ICU except for the one time, and he'd only been once or twice since I'd been discharged from ICU into a regular room, each time for a maximum of ten to fifteen minutes. Like he couldn't *wait* to get out of here. That led me to be suspicious it was because he had someone else that he was more interested in being with out there. I didn't have any other evidence, mind you, but I just knew in my gut, it was more than just not liking hospitals.

After almost two weeks in here, I was so ready to go home, but I was also extremely nervous about it. I mean, there was no way I was in any shape to take care of myself, not with the broken clavicle and my arm in a sling. Doctors warned me it could take up to *ten weeks* for the bone to heal and I would be in the sling a minimum of eight of them.

I didn't know how I was going to do it, and I *really* didn't know how I was going to get through it without pain meds. I was already trying to wean myself off them. I didn't request them, and I went as long as possible between doses – much to the consternation of my nurses.

It hurt. A lot. My hands perpetually shook and it was impossible to get comfortable.

"Um, I can't use my arm so nothing that has to be pulled over my head. So, a button down of some kind – as loose fitting as you can find it. Other than that, just jeans, socks, and underwear."

"You got it," he said. "I'll get it taken care of and bring it up in just a bit.

"Alright," I said. "Thank you."

"No problem, like I said." He hesitated and then added belatedly, "Love you."

The two words at the end almost felt like a bucket of cold water. I mean, the way he said them… it was almost, for a fraction of a second, like having the old Mark back. The one I'd fallen in love with and the one who had loved me enough to ask me to marry him before the new job and the big move and the chaos of all those big changes.

"I love you too," I said softly, and I meant it. I did love that Mark. Even though I didn't really know who he was anymore, I would always love who he was in some small part. You know? Still, I didn't know if there was any saving us, not when I so clearly had so much to think about.

"Be there soon," he promised.

I chuckled at the sudden enthusiasm in his voice and said, "Okay."

"K, bye." He hung up first and I hung up the receiver to the phone in my hospital room. My cell phone was in my purse which was locked up in my filing cabinet in my classroom, along with my house keys. I would need those too.

They would be getting here eventually. I'd asked Hex for them and he'd said he would bring them after work.

I looked at the big bouquet of flowers over by the sink and picked up one of the books off the stack that Hex had brought me unasked and unprompted.

Things I'd never read, but things he'd thought I would like because we'd talked about some of my favorite things over lunch once and he'd remembered… he'd *bothered* to remember.

Talk about conflicted, I thought to myself.

I rested my good hand atop the book I'd been reading. It was, indeed, to my tastes and I was enjoying it when I could concentrate on it. It was a modern retelling of the Hades and Persephone myth. I did love my Greek mythology. Fractured fairytales were a guilty pleasure of mine and of the small pile of four books that Hex had brought me along with the flowers? I'd only read one of them before and it happened to be one of my favorites.

I thought about him. He seemed to occupy my thoughts quite a bit lately. It certainly didn't hurt that not a day had gone by here at the hospital that he hadn't come to see me. In the beginning, I would wake to him sitting by my bedside, either asleep himself in the chair or watching my television with whatever he could find that wasn't boring on the screen.

Sometimes, when I didn't wake, I would still know that he'd been here. Things would be left for me – a treat of fresh beignets or a note. The first time had been the book I was reading, with a note written on the cover page saying that if I needed anything to not hesitate and to call him, along with his phone number.

It'd been late when I'd seen it, so I hadn't called, but I'd called to say "thank you" the next morning. He hadn't answered the phone, so I'd left a message. He'd called me at lunch and had said he was back to work already and that everyone had missed me. He'd said there was an afternoon assembly planned to play my message to the students and that had made me smile.

Honestly, I couldn't quite be sure the order of any and all the things had happened in since I'd come to the hospital. Not with the steady haze of pain medication and with just how much I slept. I swear by everything, the long and unregulated sleep schedule, while necessary for healing, had really thrown off my sense of time.

Now, frustratingly, the tables had turned and I spent more time awake than asleep and it felt like I could only wait. It was these long stretches of agonizing consciousness that were the worst. Being in the hospital was *boring*. Even more so when your arm didn't work and you couldn't even have your fiancé bring you a craft to work on or anything. Not that I'd honestly thought that he would. His good mood and prompt attention on the phone just now had honestly shocked me.

Still, my hospital stay had become nothing but pain and boredom until Hex arrived to keep me company and then the time just *flew* by. It was maddening, and it worried me that I didn't even *miss* Mark all that much and spent most of my time thinking about Hex.

I took a deep breath and ended up sucking it in sharp at the end, as the motion sent a jolt of pain through my neck and shoulder. Having a broken collarbone *sucked*. It was going to be hard figuring out how to do everything on my own.

And that was the whole crux of it, wasn't it? I was about to find myself wholly reliant on Mark. Mark who was barely there since this had happened and honestly hadn't really been there at all in the weeks leading up to my attack.

I worried about that. I didn't have any place else to go and no one else who I could rely on. I was scared.

Truthfully, all I wanted was a hot *shower* when I got home. In my own shower. You know? I longed for it. I wanted my own soaps and shampoos and to be genuinely *clean*. They didn't much worry about any of that here in the hospital and I still had several days to go. The sponge baths with wet wipes just weren't doing it for me, and I would honestly give *anything* for my hair to be clean.

It was all I could think about, to the point of obsession. Then there were the whispering doubts in the back of my mind of *would Mark help me? Or would I just be treated as inconvenient, as I had been before all this happened?*

I didn't know anyone else, really... except Hex, and I was more than slightly cursing my introverted ways at having not made any real friends in the last year or more since moving here.

I'd somehow let Mark be my end-all of be-alls and looking back, all I could do was ask myself how I could let something like that happen? Not that Mark had really done anything to discourage it... quite the opposite in fact. He'd told me multiple times when I'd expressed an interest in going out and meeting new people that I didn't need to do that, that I had everything I'd needed right there at home with him.

At the time, my heart had melted, but with his growing distant, now I was just angry with myself for not seeing it for what it was – a control tactic.

Like I said, I'd had entirely too much time here alone, on my own, to think...

When Mark did arrive, it was with flowers and one of my travel bags from home. He stepped into the room and peeked out from behind the carnations and smiled. I forced a smile to my own lips and said, "Pretty, thank you..." of the flowers, even though I couldn't stand carnations. They reminded me of my mother's funeral. I know that at some point I had told Mark that and it hurt my heart that he couldn't be bothered to remember. I mean, maybe I was being too harsh, but *honestly.*

"Oh, these are nice," he said of the flowers that Hex had brought me. "They from the school?"

"Yeah," I said. I mean, it wasn't *exactly* a lie, even though it certainly felt like an untruth. I don't know what bothered me more – well, that was another lie. I knew it bothered me more not that I'd just lied by omission to my fiancé but that it didn't bother me one bit to do it.

I pressed more of my smile out to the surface and knew it for the brittle farce that it was when he came over to lean down to kiss me.

"You look a bit better," he said, and I tried to nod but stopped short.

"They said my incisions are healed nicely, but the collarbone is going to take a while," I said. "I'll need help with showering and the like for a while and I won't be able to go back to work right away."

"Yeah, no. I don't think you should go back to that school at all," he said and I rubbed my lips together.

"I-I haven't decided on that," I said. "I need more time with that one."

He sat on the edge of the hospital bed by my knee and asked incredulously, "What, you aren't seriously considering going back, are you? I mean, will they even take you?"

I frowned at that. "What? Why wouldn't they?" I asked.

He stared at me, surprised, like a deer caught in the headlights and I stared back, waiting him out.

"Well... I mean... uh..."

"Well, you mean, uh, *what*, precisely?"

"Nothing, babe."

If I could have crossed my arms, I would have.

"No, really... what did you mean?" I pried. Was I picking a fight? Maybe. But I was so screaming frustrated mad with him, with his apathy, and how he paid me no attention. With how he'd barely been here throughout this whole thing and with how he was seriously testing my last nerve with making it sound like my school was going to treat me like this was somehow my fault.

"I mean, you had sex with a student," he said lamely, and I felt myself reel back as though I'd just been slapped.

"You don't honestly believe that, do you?" I demanded.

He was silent, his eyes locked to mine, bouncing slightly in their sockets, entirely too wide as he searched my face. The silence just continued to stretch on and on between us.

I fought not to cry, but not because I was hurt. No, oh no, I was *angry.* I was absolutely out of my mind *furious.*

"No, not at all," he said and I could *see* him recalibrating in real time. I watched his thought process scrambling to find a way to backpedal gracefully out of this.

"Then why even bring it up like that, Mark? Seriously. Why? I didn't *choose* to get attacked in a high school bathroom. I didn't go in there to get stabbed and – and – and *raped*! He wasn't even a *student!* He's some sicko, pretending to be fourteen, who hasn't been fourteen for a very long time! Are you for fucking real right now?"

"Look, it came out wrong," he said and he looked at his watch. I knew what was coming next – it was the same thing he always did.

"Yeah, yeah, *work*," I bit out and my tone was acid.

He sighed and his face collapsed into lines like a parent trying to get a hold of their anger. I could almost watch him count in his head.

Just what exactly did he have to be upset about? Good Lord!

"Am I interrupting?" I looked sharply at the door to my room and Hex standing there, my briefcase over his shoulder, my purse in his other hand.

"Who are you?" Mark asked.

"Mr. Johnson is one of the school custodians," I said coolly in Mark's direction. I met Hex's eyes and tried to convey a silent apology. His timing was awful, but that wasn't his fault.

I broke eye contact and looked away as Mark said, "Oh, what can I do for you Mr. Johnson? My fiancé and I were just talking."

Hex's eyes flicked to me. I felt like my face was burning up with equal parts anger and embarrassment now. I mean, *had he overheard anything Mark had said to me just now?*

"Ah, nothing," Hex said genially. "I just came to bring Miss Legare the things she asked for out of her classroom." He held up my things and set them aside on the nearby chair in my room, saying, "Took me a bit to break into your filing cabinet. Sorry I had to. We couldn't find your faculty keys. They might have been taken into evidence or something."

"Thank you," I said. "I'm sorry it was such an inconvenience—"

"No, hey, not at all." I looked up at the sharpness in Hex's tone. My eyes met his and despite Mark's presence in the room, Hex said clearly, "You are never an inconvenience to me." Then as Mark stood, he attempted to lessen what he said, sort of, by saying, "That's what friends are for." *Or was he..?*

It was hard to tell.

"Right, well… I, uh." Mark cleared his throat. "Why don't you just call me when they're ready to release you. We'll sort the rest out when we get you home." I jumped slightly when he squeezed the top of my thigh and caught Hex's body language subtly change out of the corner of my eye.

"Leaving already?" Hex asked, his tone made out of winter.

I bit the inside of my cheek to keep myself from full-on choosing violence with Mark. I so wanted to snarl something about him and his bullshit *job*. I was *this close* to just full-on snapping but I couldn't… not without having any place to go. Not without having some sort of plan in place.

Mark made his excuses and left me sitting in that damn hospital bed, his stupid, *stupid* words lingering in my heart and mind, ravaging the shit out of them both.

I had turned my head to stare at the sky outside my window and sniffed.

"You alright, Fable."

An angry tear snuck free and trickled down my cheek. I sniffed again, wiping it away with my good hand.

"No, I'm angry," I said. "But not at you."

I turned back to a kindly look from Hex, a small hint of something like pride in the way he smiled at me.

"How are you even with that chode?" he asked and I wheezed a laugh.

"I don't even know who he is anymore," I confessed quietly. Hex took my hand between his, massaging it, working his thumbs across the back of it.

"Yeah, well, I heard everything he said in case you were wondering."

I closed my eyes and sighed out, defeated.

"Don't judge me for staying," I said. "I don't know anyone else out here and I don't have anywhere else to go. I have to figure some things out, but you better believe I'm so done. I don't think there's any coming back from that. I-I-I can't."

"Shhh, easy there, darlin', you don't owe me a thing. Certainly, no explanations or anything like that. Your life is your own and I get it – believe me."

I sniffed again, my nose running along with my high emotions.

"Hang on there," he said, and he got up from where he'd replaced Mark at my bedside... but that wasn't right. Honestly, if anything, the place at my side felt like it belonged to Hex – not Mark. It honestly felt like *Mark* was the usurper, which was problematic all on its own. I mean, Mark was the one I was supposed to be engaged to.

I looked at the container on my bedside table that I think was typically reserved for dentures but had my jewelry I'd come into the hospital wearing in it. I'd had to argue with them to let me keep it, and I kept meaning to have Mark take it home but...

"You want some help with that?" Hex asked, taking up the container that was somewhere between a very 1950s blue and green. That's to say, a color that'd been popular in the fifties. It was frustrating just how much my brain was scrambled and I didn't know if it was all the pain medicine or the blow I'd taken to my head or what.

"Yes, please," I murmured. "Keep it safe for me?" I asked as he opened it and saw what was inside. "The nurses keep trying to lock it in some hospital safe but I don't want that. I keep meaning to have Mark take it home but I always forget. He's here so infrequently—"

"Yeah, I noticed that too," Hex muttered under his breath, but to his credit, he didn't say more. He just put the container in the pocket of his leather jacket.

I reached out with my good hand and ran my finger over the zipper at the outside of the cuff of one sleeve of his coat and said, "A little warm for this out there, don't you think?"

He chuckled and said, "I ride. I'll take a little warm over road rash any day."

"Somehow that doesn't surprise me," I said with a bit of a smile. "That you ride, I mean. You seem like you're the type."

He chuckled and asked, "I do, do I?"

"Mm-hm." I rested back against the bed and sighed, the tiredness rushing back in.

"You want me to lower this for you?" he asked softly.

"No, I'm okay like this. You only just got here – don't you leave, too."

His eyes met mine, so very serious when he said, "Wouldn't dream of it, beautiful. I'm here as long as you want me to be."

I closed my eyes and thought to myself, *forever is a very long time to commit to...* but I didn't say it out loud. Instead, I simply put my hand over his where it rested by my hip and gave it a squeeze.

"Besides," he said. "It's sort of become our thing, watching *Jeopardy* in the evenings. I wouldn't want to miss out."

I smiled wanly and said, "Yeah, but it's not the same anymore without Alex." The longtime host of the program had died of pancreatic cancer and had been such an indelible mark that it really *wasn't* the same.

"True that," Hex agreed, and there was a quality in his deep brown eyes when I opened mine that sent the blood rushing through my veins and quickened my heartbeat. He stared at me carefully, and a little too intently.

I looked away, blushing, and made mention, "*Jeopardy* doesn't come on for a few hours."

He smiled at me and said, "So what do you feel like talking about? Or do you just want to rest?"

"Mm, how about a little of both?" I asked. He chuckled, and I said truthfully, "I have no idea what to talk about really."

"How's the book?" he prompted and I smiled.

That was a good and safe subject.

"It's really good," I said.

"Oh yeah? What they got going on?"

I didn't think he was interested at first, at least not really, but he listened and asked questions. When I made mention he should read it, he just looked at me with a twinkle in his eye and said, "Why do I need to go and do that when I got you to tell me the story?"

I laughed then and it ended in a pained moan.

"Sorry," he said and looked sheepish.

"Never be sorry for making me laugh," I told him. "After all, laughter is supposed to be the best medicine, isn't it?"

"In that case," he said. "We'll have you healed up and out of here in no time."

"You're sweet," I told him.

"Yeah, well… you bring it out of me."

Somehow, I highly doubted that. I think that was honestly just the way he was.

CHAPTER TEN

*H*ex...

I dropped onto the other end of the couch from La Croix, who was lounging back with a beer on his knee. He was grease stained and had put in a hard day's work at the ol' salvage yard by the looks of him.

"Where's your girl at?" I asked.

He silently jerked his head in the direction of the apartments across the street.

I gave a nod, but I fully admit being lost in a lot of thought. They kept circling around a certain brunette with the prettiest blue eyes.

"What's eating you?" he asked and held out the beer in his hand. I took it. It was cold and full. I don't think he'd even gotten to take a drink.

He pulled one up from the six-pack hidden down behind his leg where he had one boot planted against the concrete floor. He twisted off the top and took a pull off his beer and I drank up, too.

"Her useless prick of a man was at the hospital today when I got there," I said.

La Croix grunted.

I sighed and told him the full meal deal. After a few moments of silence I said, "Let me ask you somethin'. If a man spoke to Alina like that boy did Cor, what would you do?"

"Knock every fuckin' one of his teeth out of his fuckin' head," he answered promptly. "But you know that, so why you even askin'?"

I lowered the bottle from my mouth and swallowed the mouthful of rich lager I had in it, and said, "Sometimes you can be too close to somethin' and it's worth gettin' an outside opinion," I answered.

He looked thoughtful then nodded sagely.

"Priorities," he said, and I smiled at him then and nodded.

"You're learnin'," I said with a wink, and he cracked a smile back.

It was something my dad had instilled in me and was somethin' I was forever sayin' to La Croix. It was one of the biggest reasons ol' Ruthless had to go. Ruthless had lost sight of his priorities where this club was concerned, and I couldn't afford to lose sight of the priorities where my Fable was concerned.

"What're your priorities?" La Croix asked me.

"First and foremost, will always be this club," I answered.

He nodded his big bald tattooed head and said to me, "This club is straight. You ain't got no worries about us or what's goin' on."

I met his creepy blacked-out and intense gaze and I had to nod. "Ah, yeah," I agreed.

"So, what's next?"

"Cor," I answered softly. "Gettin' her healthy, makin' sure she's good."

He raised his chin and looked at me imperiously, and I crooked a smile that was nothin' short of chagrinned.

"You ain't gotta say it," I said and he stilled.

"Now you're gettin' it." He echoed the sentiment of what I'd said just a moment before.

"It's like a fever," I said. "An obsession. Like she's the light and I ain't nothin' but a fuckin' moth to the flame."

He was nodding slowly and took a pull off his beer. After swallowing, he said, "More intense than anything that's come before."

"Yeah, but I gotta say – between you an' me? I at least *know* Cor. Talked to her, I mean. Wasn't obsession at first sight like with you."

He didn't smile, his expression as serious as I'd ever seen it as he simply raised one shoulder in a one-off shrug and said, "When you know, you know."

I laughed outright then and said, "You gon' start sounding like the kids these days."

He shook his head and took another drink off his beer. Lowering it and swallowing, he stared at the bottle in his big mitt and said, "When you find the right one, you feel just like you did when you was sixteen. A world of possibility opens back up in front of you as long as she's by your side."

"That's about as poetic and profound as I've ever heard you, my friend."

He nodded and was his usual quiet self.

"Your list doesn't end with club and woman," he said.

"No, it does not," I agreed.

"Which one?" he asked and I knew what he was asking.

The boyfriend or the brute.

"That's up to her," I said.

He nodded. "Just like my Alina with me. She points, I slay."

I nodded slowly. "Only seems right. My Fable is the aggrieved party in all this."

"If she's a soft touch?"

"Then I'll handle it myself, my way, quietly," I said, and that put a smile on La Croix's face.

"We will," he said. "I have a feeling one or the both of 'em will need some special handling."

I took another drink of my beer.

"That remains yet to be seen," I answered him truthfully.

"In any case," he said, clearing his throat. "It'll be handled."

"Yes. Yes, it will," I agreed. We toasted on it, clicking the necks of our bottles, and taking a drink a piece before settling into comfortable silence.

When we took up talkin' again, it was about my classic bike and the restoration I was doin' on it. It was a good way to end my night despite the restlessness I had goin' on in my soul. I wanted to be by her side, but she'd chased me out gently at the end of the half-hour-long show. I hadn't argued, no matter how much I'd wanted to. I could see the emotional and mental exhaustion in her face and the way she looked so small in that hospital bed. She looked fragile, like the thinnest glass, and I wasn't about to be the thing to make her shatter.

She reminded me of when you dripped a drop of molten glass into a tank of cold water. It simultaneously made one of the strongest fuckin' things but at the same time, something so fundamentally flawed that you nicked it, or hit it just right? The thing would explode back into a powder like substance much like the sand it'd been created from in the first place.

Like that drop of molten glass, she was beautiful in her resilience, but she wasn't immune to the pressures. She could withstand a lot, but if something struck her just right... I didn't want to see that happen, although I was certain she would rise again, stronger than before. Even more resilient. But I would love to see that happen without the benefit of her having to break completely. I would love to see her forged in this fire. into something equally as beautiful as that glass but infinitely harder and more flexible like steel.

By all accounts thus far, my Fable was the stuff of legends anyhow. She'd certainly gone way above and beyond surviving a bunch of shit circumstances. By all accounts, she'd *thrived,* and I aimed to make sure this wouldn't be any different.

Still, I had to tread carefully. Part of what appealed to me about the woman was her strength and the fact that for the first time, I felt like I'd encountered the perfect dream. A true match for me in not only determination but brains and tenacity.

She seemed the other half of my coin, the light to my dark, soft to my hard, and I wanted to see how we could grow entangled if circumstances would let us.

I went home that night and when I pulled out my phone, I noticed some new messages I'd missed.

Unknown Number: Now you have my number, too. The nurses charged my phone for me so I could text you; although, texting one-handed is hard and is taking me forever. Thank you for bringing my

things to the hospital for me. I'm going to read some more of my book and get some more sleep. Goodnight.

I saved the number as *Fable* in my phone and sighed. I'd missed her message by an hour or more. The other one was just a cat setting off my front door camera several times – which was annoying but alright. At least it let me know my cameras were still working.

I took a hot shower and took myself to bed, sending a quick couple words back to her.

Me: Goodnight, Fable.

Still, I couldn't help it. I lay awake a long time, staring at the ceiling and dreaming up random acts of violence to befall her soon-to-be ex who couldn't appreciate what he had right in front of him.

Fucking idiot.

CHAPTER ELEVEN

orliss…

"I'm sure he'll be here any minute," I said when the nurse came back into my room. I was dressed, my hair pulled up into a ponytail by the lovely woman charged with taking care of me today, to disguise how greasy and oily it was until I could get home and take a shower.

I'd spoken to Mark only yesterday to tell him they were letting me go today and when he could come and get me… but he'd acted distracted and now? Well, he was encroaching on more than an hour late and I could feel my face burn with embarrassment.

I was in a wheelchair, all of my bags neatly packed and sitting on the bed. The books and things that Hex had brought me stowed carefully in the bag that Mark had brought my clothes in. My briefcase and my purse leaned against it.

I sniffed and tried not to let the threatening tears spill. I was gutted. I wasn't angry this time. I was just *hurt*.

When she came back to check on me after another half an hour, I asked for the specific book that'd Hex had written his number in and for the phone. Mine was in my purse and I didn't want to waste any more of the poor woman's time, digging around for it.

It took some fumbling one-handed to get the cover of the book propped open and to handle the phone at the same time, but I managed.

He picked up on the first ring. "Hello?"

"Hi, um… it's me," I said. I *hated* doing this to him after he'd already done so much already.

"What's wrong?" he asked immediately.

"Um, they're ready to let me go here and Mark knew what time to pick me up. It's been a couple of hours and, well, I'm still here…"

I couldn't even ask him for a ride home. He just said, "I'll be right there," and I heard him call out to someone in the background and the line simply went dead.

I closed my eyes and listened to the silence over the line and just breathed.

I think my panicked mind was working a little overtime by this point. I mean, I had abandonment issues, I knew I did, and Mark… well, he knew too, and yet he kept *doing this to me*. I mean, it wasn't the first time. Still, what was making me angry now was that I felt like such a doormat in that I couldn't stop worrying about him and making excuses in the echoing back chambers of my mind. Things like *what if he was in an accident on the way here? What if he was downstairs in the emergency room right now. and I was up here mad at him for something that wasn't his fault?*

I tried his phone one more time. carefully pushing the numbers on the handset with my thumb.

"This is Mark Chetta. Please leave your name and number and what this is regarding after the tone."

I sighed and hung up, knowing if I left any kind of message, saying what I *wanted* to say, it would just cause a fight later.

I took several deep cleansing breaths and wrestled the handset back up onto the bedside table. I pulled myself forward with my feet against the floor to slide my book back into the open top of the bag in front of me.

I swear it wasn't ten more minutes of me sitting and fretting before heavy boot tread fell behind me and I twisted as much and as carefully as I could to see Hex, once again, coming to the rescue.

"Hey," he said and the hand he put lightly to my back at the base of my neck was both heavy and warm, yet gentle and light, with its touch. A shiver went down my spine and I swallowed hard.

"So, uh, you don't just ride, you're a biker?" I asked.

He frowned slightly and then looked down at himself and swore softly. "Uh, yeah, about that…" he said, coming around and dropping onto the bed to be a little more even with me when he met my eyes.

"I keep it on the down=low because the school and all of that, but I'm actually the VP of this particular club. I know it's got a bad reputation but La Croix – that's the president – and myself, we've been workin' hard the last year or two to clean it up."

I could read the sincerity in his eyes and tried to make light of things by swallowing hard, nodding carefully, and saying truthfully despite how my voice shook, "Actually, I think it's kind of hot."

He snorted a laugh and bowed his head, bouncing it in a nod before finally looking up at me and asking, "No call – no showed on you again, huh?"

I bit my lips together and turned my head very carefully to look past him and out the window behind him. I sniffed.

"Oh, hey, don't do that, Fable," he said consolingly. "I'll get you home, no worries. We can decide what you wanna do from there."

I nodded slowly and said, "Thanks."

"Let me get your things together and have a quick chat with your nurse. Okay?"

"Okay," I murmured, and I felt my tense posture ease. All I could think to myself was how I should have honestly called Hex in the first place. That by God, it was *nice* when he stepped in to handle things. That it took such a weight and a pressure off me.

He disappeared out into the hall, and I worked my feet against the floor and turned the wheel on my chair with my one hand so I could see out my room's door. He leaned over the nurse's station and I felt my mouth just absolutely water over the fit of his jeans over his ass. Broken in and comfortable looking, the denim faded around the square of his wallet.

I followed the chains of his wallet up where they disappeared under his leather jacket covered by the rough-looking leather vest with its dirty but colorful patches. At the skull leaning out from the big gold fleur-de-lis with its rictus grin and purple top hat, it's one green eye bulging from behind its monocle.

I hadn't heard much about the Voodoo Bastards but what I'd heard wasn't exactly *good*. It shocked me that he was one of them.

It confused me, too. I mean, could they really be that bad if their vice president was a high school custodian? I mean, you had to pass background checks, drug tests, and all the things to even think about working at a school, which, *clearly*, he had if he was working there now but...

He turned to look at me and gave me a smile as one of the nurses approached him and said something. His attention whipped back to her but that half-smile of reassurance he had just cast at me left me sort of numb and reeling.

I mean, the temptation was *right there,* and I couldn't help but think how things could be so different. How it was so easy to talk and to laugh with Hex and how he'd so selflessly been here for me when my own fiancé, the man who was supposed to love me until the end of time, couldn't even be bothered to show up.

I looked down at the tan line on my empty ring finger, my hand kept tucked in close to my ribcage in its sling, my posture corrected by a series of figure eight straps and craziness to allow my collarbone to heal, and it was a profound moment.

I thought of Mark and everything felt desolate, cold, and ashen. Whatever love I'd held for him was gone, slowly burned out of me with his inattention and abandonment.

When I looked back up at Hex's broad shoulders tapering down to a narrow waist, all I could think about was how warm he made me feel and I wanted that. But it broke my heart too, knowing that it could and probably would end in the same way.

How many times had I been treated like a shiny new kitten with a set of new and eager foster parents, only to be passed off to the next set weeks or months later? How often had I switched schools and how many nights had I slept on an office couch in some child protective services building because there hadn't been any available places to put me?

How often had I been shifted out of a loving environment for once because I was a good kid and easier to place than the next kid who needed this home more than I did?

…and now here I was, a fully capable adult, a contribution to society; and still, *still* it was like no one saw me. Like no one cared… not even the person who was supposed to care for me the most. I was both so very sad and so very angry and just full of resentment over that fact.

I sat red-faced in that damn wheelchair and waited patiently once again for others to figure out what to do with me because the people who were supposed to care and be responsible for me couldn't be bothered to show up. Dammit, I hated it. I loathed it. I felt just like that unwanted child, that invisible teen, and my heart hurt so badly and still, *still*, a part of me worried about Mark, and I hated that, too.

Hex racked a stack of what was presumably discharge paperwork against the wraparound the nurse's station and gave a nod to the nurse standing there who blushed a pretty pink. I sighed inwardly, thinking to myself, *girl, same.*

He returned to me and tucked the papers into the top of the bag and said, "Someone's going to wheel you out front where I can pick you up easier. Then I'll take you to your place. We're going to stop at the in-hospital pharmacy first and get your scripts—"

"No pain meds," I said with a grimace. "I want to try and get off those."

"Yes, pain meds," he said. "I won't fuckin' argue with you about it. You don't have to take 'em but if you wind up needing them, it's better you have them than you don't, I reckon."

I glowered at him and he smiled and huffed a laugh. "You're adorable when you do that," he said, peeling off the prescriptions from the top of the paperwork and setting them apart from everything, before zipping things closed.

"We are not friends for five whole minutes," I grumbled under my breath, and he laughed.

"That just means you'll be over it by the time you need to get your pretty little ass in my truck," he said.

I scowled at him, my mood pretty bad, but still trying to lift under the starry twinkle in his liquid-brown eyes.

"Let's get you out of here, beautiful. You definitely deserve your freedom." He gently set my purse in my lap and I put my good hand over it to keep it from sliding. The rest of things he shouldered and a volunteer appeared a few moments later to wheel me where we needed to go.

I made sure to say goodbye to the staff that was here who'd taken such good care of me on my way out. A thing that Hex didn't begrudge me at all. He simply stood aside and waited patiently, not saying a word.

Had it been Mark, I was sure at this point, that he would have rushed me.

The pharmacy downstairs was a bit of a wait, and I apologized to the poor volunteer, an older woman in her late sixties, perhaps early seventies, who just chuckled lightly and waved me off.

Hex gathered the white paper bag with everything in it and paid before I could even get my purse open, by tapping his phone against the screen at the payment kiosk thingy.

"Okay, I'm going to go on ahead and get my truck. You ladies take your time, and I'll see you out there, alright?"

"Alright, we'll be there!" My volunteer chuckled and wheeled us in the direction of the hospital lobby as we watched him forge on ahead of us.

"You're very fortunate," she remarked mildly.

"Oh, we're just friends," I murmured, as much to not let me get my hopes up and wind up hurting my own feelings as anything.

"Oh, I don't know about that," she said. "That boy dotes on you. I think it's more than that, yeah? In any case, the only thing nicer than watching him coming, is watching him go."

I spluttered and couldn't help but laugh, which jarred my shoulder and sent a lance of pain through my neck and chest from the broken bone.

"Oh! I'm so sorry," she cried.

"No, it's okay," I said. "It was just unexpected. To be honest, I needed that laugh."

She chuckled and said, "He reminds me of my late husband. My Harold was like that."

"Aw, I'm sorry," I said.

"Oh, no… it's been several years now and it's alright. That's part of why I come here, though, to be useful and keep busy. Much better than pining away at home alone."

I said, "I understand."

"Still, when a man treats you like that, you'll want to hang on to them," she said with a wink, putting the brakes on my chair and standing next to me under the overhang along the pickup-and-drop-off zone outside the hospital's main entrance doors.

"I'll keep that in mind," I murmured and simply breathed in the muggy fall air of late October New Orleans, with its green smell of the Mississippi River and surrounding swamp. Sweet, living, with its slight edge of decay underneath.

"Are we close to the river?" I asked.

"Not terribly so," she answered. "Just the wind blowing in the right direction, I think."

We made small talk about the weather and the smell when the rhythmic sound of a big, well-oiled, diesel engine brought me looking up to the intimidating gray work truck in front of me.

"Oh, dear," the woman tsked as Hex came around the front.

"It's not as bad as it looks," he promised, opening the door. The runner board whirred down and clicked into place. I took a deep breath as she straightened from putting the wheelchair's foot things up out of my way.

"Easy, darlin'," Hex said, taking my purse and opening the back door of the truck to put it atop my other bags. He shut it and came around to my right side, reaching down to brace me. I put my hand in his warm, rough one, and leveraged myself up out of the seat, groaning a little bit.

Two weeks essentially in bed the vast majority of the time certainly hadn't done me any favors.

"Go on and get up there. I'm here to catch you," he said. He stood at my back as I pulled myself up onto the runner board first by the "oh-shit" handle, pausing there for the pain to diminish before hoisting myself carefully the rest of the way into the truck.

It wasn't that bad, but it wasn't good either.

"Thank you," I called down to the volunteer who smiled up kindly and gave me a wink that made me blush as Hex shut me safely into his truck.

I turned my head to watch him get in. He pulled the seatbelt across me and clicked it into place for me.

He'd taken off his colorful vest and it hung from the back of his headrest of his seat.

"It doesn't really bother me. You didn't have to take it off," I murmured, and he smiled at me, this little smile like he thought I was cute.

Hanging his hand off the top of his steering wheel by his wrist, he said, "It's not that. It's a rule, you don't wear your cut in a cage. It's a disrespect to the colors. We don't do disrespect. Same principle as not letting this great nation's flag touch the ground kind of a thing."

"Oh," I said.

"You wanna tell me your address? I'll put it into the GPS here and we'll get going."

I told him my address and he put it into the big screen in the middle of everything, and took a deep breath letting it out slow.

"Alright, now, let's go," he said, twisting the dial into "drive." Checking things out, he pulled smoothly into the drive to take us on our way.

Anxiety crawled along my skin and I honestly felt like my stomach had turned to lead. I guess we would find out why Mark wasn't answering his phone on a Saturday.

CHAPTER TWELVE

*H*ex...

She was quiet but practically crackled with nervous energy on the drive. I tried breaking the silence and her discomfort by asking, "Now that you're out of there, what's the first thing you want to do when you get home?"

She didn't even hesitate. "I want a *shower*. A real one. My hair feels gross and I don't feel like I've been genuinely *clean* for forever. I just want a shower in my own shower, with my own shampoo, and my own conditioner, and my own soaps and face wash and smell-good comfort things."

I nodded, smiling to myself. I'd never heard someone sound so wistful or longing over a damn shower before. It was cute. What was not cute was that her fiancé hadn't picked her up, her level of agitation, and that she practically vibrated with emotion – none of them good – in the seat beside me. She was stressed, which in turn was damaging my calm and was making me want to damage her useless fucking boyfriend.

Following the turn-by-turn directions on my screen and keeping a watchful eye on the flow of traffic, I tried to keep the light banter up but I wasn't being very good at distracting her. People drove like assholes in and around the city and I was just as defensive driving my damn truck as I was on my bike, but probably even more now than any other time with the precious fucking cargo I had in my passenger's seat.

I didn't want to hurt her any more than she was likely already hurting, and I really wasn't enjoying the idea of leaving her in this place alone to take care of herself. I damn sure didn't picture him doing *anything* useful for her if he couldn't even be bothered to spend more than ten minutes at a time in her presence while she was laid up in the fucking hospital.

I smoothly pulled up to the curb in front of the address she'd given me and it was a nice little house. Probably a one bedroom by the looks of it out here.

"Stay put, let me come get you," I said, and I pushed the button to turn off my truck and exited to come around and help her out. I grabbed my cut without thinking and shrugged into it as I came around the front of the truck where I could keep an eye on her. To her credit, she did good, and simply undid her belt and popped the door when I got to her side, waiting for me to be in a position to catch her if she needed it.

She got down on her own under my watchful eye, and I relaxed a little once she was settled onto terra firma and looked steady.

I got into the back seat and got her purse.

She looked good, some kind of Texas with her Wranglers on and her pair of boots. Up top, she wore a fitted white cami tank top under an open turquoise, black, and white plaid country snap-button blouse that made her eyes practically glow. She looked like she'd just stepped off a Texas dude ranch and looked comfortable enough, which is honestly all I cared about. It wouldn't have been what I would have picked for her first set of street clothes after an ordeal like hers, not with the complexity involved with the form fittingness of it.

I had to imagine there was some weaponized incompetence there. I know she would have asked for something loose and easy to get her arm through.

I definitely wouldn't have chosen layers.

I got into her purse at her behest to extract her keys and helped her key her way into her front door.

"Thanks," she murmured, and I stared down at her from the few inches that separated us.

"I'm not letting you go in there by yourself, babe," I said softly. "I'm not leaving here until I'm sure that you're safe and good to be here, and that he's going to do right by you and take care of you."

She stared up at me, her color going something white as snow.

"Hex, I'll be good no matter what," she said gently, and I could see a certain amount of stubbornness start to surface; a defiance in her eyes.

"I know you're tough," I said gently with a smile. "Still ain't leaving you here by yourself to face whatever's goin' on inside that door."

She swallowed hard and nodded, and I gave the knob a twist to let us inside.

CHAPTER THIRTEEN

*C*orliss...

The front door opened to our dimly lit living room, Mark's desk space in the dining room, and the kitchen beyond that which was all empty... but that's because we could hear them in the bedroom.

I bowed my head in embarrassment and humiliation with a heavy dose of defeat.

Hex was staring at me, his face unreadable as he waited me out to see what I would do.

I took a deep breath and walked loudly, my cowboy boot heels clacking against the hardwood floors dully as I went to the back of the house and to the bedroom, pushing open the door flush to the wall.

Mark was cursing and trying to pull up the sheet to cover himself but the blonde was working against him, tugging on the same sheet to cover herself too.

"Stop, just stop!" I barked, loudly, but just so damned tiredly. "Just what the fuck, Mark?"

"Don't you what the fuck me!" he cried incredulously, "What the fuck, *you*? You're not supposed to be here!"

I felt Hex at my back, the energy, the vibration coming off him the same as anytime you stood outdoors, pending a violent electrical storm. The air around him practically humming, the heat coming off him scorching my back and fueling my fire as I exploded.

"You were supposed to pick me up from the hospital today, you piece of shit!" I screamed at him. "You left me sitting there for fucking *hours,* waiting on your lying, cheating apathetic ass to come get me! I finally had to call Hex! All the while you're in our house, in our bed, fucking—" I spluttered. "I don't even know who the fuck you are! Who are you?" I demanded.

"Doesn't matter," Hex grated. He gently moved me aside and grabbed Mark by the back of his neck and fetched him up against the wall by the door. He planted a fist next to his head and slapped a hand against his chest, pinning a bunch of money to it.

"This is what's going to happen," Hex declared, and Mark spluttered. Hex put his fist through the sheetrock next to Mark's face.

"You're done talking!" Hex bellowed in his face. "Now, you're listening!"

Mark, to his credit, shut the hell up. The skeeze in our bed had managed to cover up with the comforter I'd bought and I wanted to puke.

"You take this money. You get in your expensive fucking car and you take this cheap-ass whore and yourself to the nearest hotel for the rest of today and tonight. By the time you come back, we're going to be gone and you're *never* going to contact Cor again. Do I make myself clear?"

"Who the—"

"*Do I make myself clear?*" Hex bellowed, and both myself and the whore in my bed jumped while Mark shrank like the pussy he was.

"Okay, alright," Mark said with his hands up in surrender.

"No, don't look at her. You look at me," Hex demanded when Mark tried to turn his head in my direction. I swallowed hard and stared at him. I would *not* give him the benefit of me looking away. Not this time. Not after all the times I'd overlooked every other little thing he'd done – or not done, as the case may be.

"Fable," Hex said quietly. "Step out into the hall."

I did. Most of the time I would be incensed at being told what to do, but right now, with everything crashing down on me, I was merely *grateful* that Hex was in control so I didn't have to be.

"You and the whore have three minutes to get fucking dressed and get the fuck out or shit's going to get violent," Hex declared.

"You can't threaten me in my own house," Mark rallied and tried to stand up a little straighter. Hex shut him down with a look.

"I just fucking did. What are you going to do about it?" he demanded.

The blonde had her phone and I went over and ripped it out of her hand and threw it on the floor, crushing it under my boot heel.

"You're lucky I don't slap the shit out of you, trying to call the cops on me in my own house!" I snarled. "Get your clothes, get your shit, and *get out!*"

"Fable, *hallway*," Hex ordered and his tone was less gentle with me than it'd been the moment before. I swallowed hard and did what he said.

I stepped into the hallway, thought better of it, and went into the bathroom, dropping onto the closed lid of the toilet after slamming the door shut.

No, slamming the door didn't make me feel better. I thought it might, but it didn't.

I shook with the vibrant energy that the adrenaline had sent coursing through my veins but at the same time? I felt like I was emotionally suspended in animation, things roiling and churning my gut but like I was having a physiological response. My thoughts and feelings were just... stuck. Very stuck. Very... I was angry but I wasn't. I was upset, but strangely calm, as though I resided in an echo chamber of my own shitty emotions but *all* I was getting was the echo – none of the initial shouting, though they'd been muffled somehow. I realized that I had to hold on to it. I had to stay calm and get through this. That I was just in that phase of the tsunami pulling back all the things from shore. That everything was rolling out like a video switched into reverse and that when everything *did* come roaring back in, it was going to be *devastating*.

Too much, my mind whispered. *Too much, too much, too much.*

The cadence of it was soothing even though the implication of the actual words was anything but.

"Fable?" A knock came at the door and I looked up from where I'd hunched and rocked myself on the toilet, the white knuckles of my good hand pressed against my lips, my jaw aching from how I clenched it.

I went to the door and opened it.

"Help is on the way to load you up and clear you out," Hex said gently, and I lowered my hand from my mouth, shaking.

"I don't have anywhere to go," I said, my voice sounding hollow.

"You just let me handle that," he said soothingly and reached out to cup my face with his hand, smoothing back some wisps of hair that'd escaped my ponytail.

"What have you got to pack up your things?" he asked.

I sighed, closing my eyes and going back to what I'd always known.

"Trash bags are under the kitchen sink," I said dully.

"Okay," he said. "Start with in here. Put everything you want to take in the sink."

"Okay," I said, and he disappeared from the doorway, leaving the portal open. I felt like all the air had been sucked out of the room with him.

CHAPTER FOURTEEN

H ex...

Fucking trash bags. I thought, but I wouldn't leave her here. Could I have made him pack up his shit and get the fuck out, giving her the time to figure shit out? Probably. I didn't like that idea, though. One look at the place told me all I needed to know.

This place was mostly his. The things on the walls and the furniture screamed *this fucking douchebag.*

The bedroom was the only thing that had her touch on it, and maybe the kitchen. She didn't even have a desk, just his, which was *clearly* his and not to her taste at all. A modern looking monstrosity of metal with a glass top. Unfeeling, with no character to it.

Where did she grade her papers and do her work? I wondered.

Didn't matter. I would make space for her. I would be everything this self-centered prick refused to fucking be.

I found the roll of bags under the sink and brought them out, heading back for the bathroom, shaking the white kitchen bag open. She handed me things one-handed off the shelf in the shower and off from around the bathroom sink and I stood patiently, taking the object from her and dropping it into the bag one-handed while she sort of only half paid attention to what she was doing. Like, she pulled her stuff, but at the same time? Her eyes were wounded, vacant, and staring… but of all things, they weren't surprised.

She was wooden with anger and her face was etched with lines of hurt that she hadn't even held in the hospital – but she was strong as hell and I could see she just fucking *refused* to fall apart.

As we were finishing up with her bathroom stuff, I heard the roar of the bikes outside.

I'd sent a simple SOS and dropped a pin to the club's group text and boy; I could hear hell comin' with 'em.

Saint and Cypress were the first through the front door.

"Where's the fire at?" Saint demanded, and I tossed him the bag of toiletries I had in my hand.

"Out to my truck. We're moving her out of here and to my place," I said tersely, and Saint and Cy exchanged a look.

"Make a line," Cy called out the door and that's what we did. Fable and I filled a bag and sent it down the fuckin' line where it was put in the back of my truck. There wasn't a whole lot – just clothes and books; a few knickknacks and things she wrapped in clothes and worried about. I sent orders down the line on what was fragile and to put it in the back seat.

Pictures came off walls, some she smashed in the middle of the living room, leaving the wreckage on the coffee table and floor.

I didn't say a fucking word.

"The blanket there and that's it," she said.

"Our turn," Bennie said and nudged Louie.

"Light bulbs and batteries?" Louie asked with a savage grin.

"Every left sock," Axe declared.

Bennie frowned at him. "How do you tell a left sock from a right?"

"Some are marked," Axe said with a shrug.

"Alright, alright, do your thing boys. I'm taking Cor home. No property damages. This fuck is apt to get petty and she don't need it."

I steered her out the front door and found La Croix leaned up against the side of my truck. He gave me a nod and took a drag on his joint. He held it out to Fable who shook her head miserably and mumbled, "No thank you."

La Croix simply shrugged and looked at me. I gave a light shake of my head, and he threw me some chin in understanding.

"Later," I said, and he nodded.

I got Cor tucked into my rig and shut the door.

"See you at your place to unload it. Let these fools have their field day."

I had to grin at that and nodded. La Croix let out an earsplitting whistle and waved his hand like a magic wand to round the rest of the boys out here up to fall in.

Bennie stuck his head out the front door and I called out, "My place when you're done." He gave a nod and raised his hand in farewell. I went around and got into the truck.

Fable's wide and shocked blue eyes met mine.

"Let's get you home and bring this stuff in. We'll have plenty of time to figure it all out after we're done."

She nodded and I heaved a sigh, pressing the button to start my truck and giving the shifter dial a twist.

The ride to my place was made in a sort of shell-shocked silence.

"THANKS BOYS," I muttered as they filed out of my place. My living room was piled with a crazy amount of shit, lookin' like a cheap plastic snowdrift from all the white kitchen bags stuffed with her things.

"She gonna be good?" Louie asked, and I nodded. The kid was a good kid, had heart, and was just the right fit for what La Croix and I were looking to achieve with the club. Were we ever gonna be on the right side of the law? No. Not fuckin' hardly. Did we want to achieve a modicum of peace within this life? Yeah. Yeah, we did. We didn't think we would ever tone down to the degree of the Kraken; but we'd like something like it, in our own way.

I looked back into my living room where Corliss stood, looking battle weary amid the crazy and the wreckage of yet another new fucking beginning. She looked strained and about ready to snap. I gave Louie a pat on the back and sent him out the portal of my front door. I shut it with a sigh behind him, threw the deadbolt, and twisted the lock in the knob out of sheer habit.

Was I afraid of anything coming through my door? Hell no. Anyone showed up here uninvited, they'd have a bad fuckin' day. That didn't mean I was in the habit of makin' things easy on a motherfucker, nor did I make a habit of invitin' any kind of trouble in.

In fact, Corliss Legare was the first woman I'd ever brought to my home. On the odd occasion I'd felt the need for a regular hookup or anything else, I kept that shit to her place or the club.

"How you doing, baby?" I asked her gently, and she startled and turned, dragging those beautiful blue eyes up to mine.

She looked absolutely shattered when she said, "I just wanted a fucking shower in my own bathroom." She broke into a sob.

"Aw, hey, I got you. C'mere," I said, and I knew she was done. She'd held up like a champ but it was all too much for her and I felt some kind of way over knowing that she felt safe enough now, with me, to be so vulnerable as to fall the fuck apart. I towed her gently into my arms, and I held her like the fragile little thing that she was and just let her cry it out.

I didn't try to shush her or tell her to stop, which was my first inclination. Hell, I think it was anybody's inclination when somebody cried from a broken heart or just plain too heavy of a load to bear. No one liked to watch another person hurt. Not if you had a soul. Still, I think people needed to sometimes take a step back from their own discomfort and let a person feel any type of way that they needed to feel.

I could do that for her, for right now, and hopefully it'd get her through the storm a little quicker.

She leaned into me and I stood fast. When she'd quieted down some, she pulled away with a final sniff and wiped under her eyes, dashing at the wetness of her tears, trying to hide them and make them disappear.

"I'm sorry," she said with a decisive sniff, as though she'd made up her mind and that she was acting silly or something.

"Don't," I said, and the warning the word held had her looking up at me startled. "Don't you dare apologize to me after what you've been through."

She swallowed hard.

"You just tell me what you want to happen and I'll make it happen," I said, fixing her with my gaze.

She swallowed hard and looked frozen in her tracks, like a scared little rabbit. The only thing to tell me she wasn't going to keel right over and faint was the way her eyes glittered as they bounced slightly back and forth as she stared into mine.

"I want a lot of things," she said finally. "I-I-I want him to hurt too. I want him to feel the loss just like me. I know he never will and I hate that, but seriously, most of all, I just want a shower and to be clean, and to not be scared of what I'm going to do next and—"

"You don't ever have to be scared again. You're good here. Come on back here with me." I led her down the hall of my shotgun house, through the living room and past the little bar I had at the back of it that I was still working on putting in.

There was a bedroom that opened up just off the living room, but I intended to make that an office. Past it was the master bedroom, in size and by virtue that it had a bathroom attached and was the room that was mine. It was finished, as was the bathroom in there. That's where I took her, snatching up her bag of lotions and girl potions from the floor where I'd set them aside specifically when I'd found them.

She let me walk her, my front lightly bumping her back on occasion, as I pointed her in the direction that I needed her to go.

She sucked in a light breath when we entered the bedroom which, as I said, was finished, and her eyes were immediately drawn to the ceiling.

"How did you do this?" she asked and I smiled on the inside, her words stroking my pride.

"Cut into the attic space. Decided I didn't need it and I wanted the higher ceilings so it wasn't no thing. I still got some up there," I said, pointing vaguely. "It's just at the back of the house. I was planning on doing something similar in the living room when I got to it and leaving the ceiling sort of as-is for a low-ceilinged loft space over the front bedroom which I was planning on turning into an office. No need for three bedrooms, and that top space would make a good spot for something – I didn't know what, but now I'm thinking maybe a reading nook or something for you."

"Me?" she squeaked.

I chuckled and said, "It ain't no never mind," trying to play it off. She made me forget myself and I didn't want to move too fast.

Too late, asshole, I thought to myself.

"Here, sit," I said and she did, lightly, on the edge of my bed, her eyes drawn to the lofty ceiling that'd I'd tacked up wood like the ol' cabins up in Appalachia where I'd come down from. A little taste, a little sparkle of home, like the lightning bugs in the trees.

"Take a load off, Fable. I'll be right out to get 'cha," I said with a wink.

She nodded and looked sort of torn and apprehensive... no, *lost.* She looked lost, and I hated that for her somethin' terrible, but I can't say as I didn't understand it. You know?

I took her bag of girl shit into the bathroom and started the shower up, letting it get warm and reading the labels on everything to find a place for 'em. The shower shit went into the shower, the other shit? Well, I reckon I needed to build a set of shelves or something, but for now? For now, I put them up as nice as I could on the back of my damn toilet. I didn't know what else to do. If I put it all on the sink, there wouldn't be room to do nothin' else. It was like she collected this shit and had every sort of smell or whatever you could think of.

Not that I was complaining, mind you, I liked the way she smelled. Whatever she did, knocked it out of the park for me.

I went back out to the bedroom where she was sitting, looking a little forlorn, her sparkle considerably dulled.

I took a deep breath and kneeled in front of her, cupping one of her boot heels in one hand and gently supporting her leg above it, just below her knee with the other as I took it from her.

"Thank you," she murmured. "I don't know why he thought I would want my boots when I can't even bend over or use both my hands for anything."

"Because he was thoughtless, and only cares about himself," I answered, and she drew in a sharp breath and nodded carefully.

"You're right," she said.

"Wish I wasn't," I told her, taking up her other foot.

"Why?" she asked. "I mean, I know you didn't like him from like the word go," she said.

I took off her other boot, set it aside, put a forearm to my knee, and looked up at her.

"Because I care about how you feel. If you were with him, I could accept that, as long as you were happy. But he didn't make you happy, darlin', and I suspect he hasn't for a very long time."

She stared at me for a long, drawn-out moment and said, "That's probably one of the sweetest things anyone has ever said to me."

"Ain't that a fuckin' shame?" I asked softly, my voice pitched low, and I reached up to touch her face. She closed her eyes and tipped her cheek further into that touch, and I smiled. I was glad her eyes were closed. She was sweet as could be, and I wanted a chance but I wasn't willing to push her into anything. I also didn't want to be just a Band-Aid.

"Gonna take this nice and slow, okay, Fable?" I asked.

She sniffed and nodded, those blue eyes of hers opening back up, making me suck in a breath that I hoped she hadn't noticed. I wasn't in the habit of telling anyone in a position to hurt me just what they did to me. She was so beautiful, so sweet to me, so, just, *everything* that got me going, that I knew deep down, she posed a very real threat to me. I just didn't need *her* knowing that.

I hoped against hope that neither one of us damaged the other but rather made two halves of an incredible whole someday, but *priorities*.

...and my number one priority at the moment was to get her clean, get her into a shower she'd remember for a long time.

I started by working the straps holding her arm immobile free of their positions, paying close attention to how the contraption worked, but knowing step-by-step instructions resided in her discharge paper-work. The nurse had gone over everything with me in a cursory fashion but I tended to employ some good ol' redneck ingenuity where it was required and liked to figure things out on my own where I could.

"Okay," I murmured. "Let's get your good arm out first and give me some room to work with."

"Okay." She laughed a little nervously and had started to blush.

"Don't pay it no mind right now," I said, stopping her.

"Do what now?" she asked.

"The fact I'm a man and you're a woman, and I'm about to see you naked for the first time," I told her.

"Well, when you put it like that, that's honestly the *only* thing I can think about... but I like the way you said that just now," she said.

I felt myself frown a bit and asked, "What's that now?"

"That you're about to see me naked for the *first* time... implying there will be more."

I chuckled and she eased her good arm out of the sleeve of her blouse.

"You got me dead to rights, sweet thing," I said, and I admit to pouring on the charm just a little bit.

She turned her head and looked down her bad shoulder and said, "Honestly, I'm more nervous about you seeing the scars."

"Oh, baby, I can't promise I'll even notice 'em. I'm too busy lookin' at your pretty blue eyes."

At the cheesy line, her eyes predictably flicked to mine, her mouth dropping open slightly as she declared, "That was bad!"

I laughed and carefully eased the over blouse thing down off her bad arm. But true to my word, I kept my eyes fixed on hers as I asked, "Yeah?"

"Oh, God yeah. That was awful!"

I laughed outright and asked, "I got a few other bad ones, you want to hear 'em?"

She smiled and said, "No, I'm still trying to process that one."

"Fair enough, fair enough, Fable. Okay, how you got this damn thing on is beyond me." I gathered her tight cami tank top thing at the hem a bit.

"Well, bad arm went in first, then head, then we sort of dragged my good arm through and everything down so—"

"Take it in reverse?" I asked.

She dragged her good arm through the arm hole and down and took a deep breath.

"Don't worry about stretching things. Just sort of, I don't know…"

"I got you," I told her, and I gathered things slowly, concentrating like a motherfucker on getting this damn thing up over her head without jarring her collarbone on the side that was busted.

She breathed carefully, and I got things up over her head. I think we both let out a breath that neither one of us realized that we were holding.

"I feel like Indiana Jones and that bag of sand, trying not to set off that damn trap in the temple in the beginning of the one movie."

"Uh, yeah, except the only boulders here are in my over-the-shoulder boulder-holder which I'm not really great with it. I want this thing off so bad! I don't think I've ever wanted a bra off so bad in my life." She rolled her eyes and then grimaced.

"Well, you ain't gotta wear one around here, and we'll figure out a way you can go without on the odd trip out for the time being."

"Yeah, no." She laughed. "I don't think I could do it."

"Do what?" I asked.

"Go out without a bra."

"Why sure you can. Fuck what anyone has to say about it or what they think."

"I only wish I could be so brave," she said.

"Baby, you're braver than you give yourself credit for. I mean, just look at you. You're still here. Wouldn't give that dipshit boyfriend of yours the satisfaction of seeing you cry and you're fierce as hell."

"Am I?" she asked with a bit of wonder, and I smiled at her, reaching behind her, and unhooking her bra swiftly with a snap of my fingers.

She gasped, then threw back her head and laughed, holding her good arm across her chest to keep the garment from falling away.

"You know you are," I told her. "Trick is making damn sure you don't forget it."

"Good think you're here to remind me," she murmured and the look she was giving me... *fuck*.

"Damn straight I am," I said and looked down to her belt.

"Stand up for me," I ordered, pointedly ignoring the moment and how in a perfect fuckin' world or in a movie or some shit, I should have kissed her.

I didn't think either of us were quite ready for that. Not with how shook up the day had left either of us; her especially.

I peeled her jeans down her legs and her cotton panties, a match for her simple cotton bra, off her, down her legs which admittedly could stand a shave. Somehow, the thought of kneeling at her feet in the bottom of the tub, carefully drawing a razor up those legs of hers, turned me the fuck on and I immediately had to squash the desire with any and every method I had at my disposal.

I hate to say it, but picturing Mrs. Donal's wrinkled naked ass is what did the trick. She was a nice enough woman – but *no*.

I stood up swiftly, keeping things as respectful as I could by pointedly *not* looking as she found her bravery and left her bra behind on the bed.

"I'm going to get you in there and then I'll be in to join you and help you out, okay?" I asked. I knew my voice was a little rougher than it'd been a moment ago.

"Okay, if you think that would be easiest," she said.

I gave a bit of a laugh and said, "I can't promise something won't be hard, but what I can promise is to be as much of a gentleman as humanly possible, given I'm about to be naked in the shower with one of the most beautiful women I think I've ever laid eyes on."

The word vomit just sort of tumbled out of my mouth before I could stop any of it. I was pointedly looking everywhere but at her when I said it, as I led her into the small bathroom that I'd finished myself just in the last year.

She didn't laugh this time or call me cheesy. If anything, she'd gone just a little too quiet, and I had to look over my shoulder and check on her to make sure she was still behind me as I swept back the shower curtain and stuck my hand under the spray to make sure it was an acceptable temperature.

She was standing there mute, her eyes on me, her bad arm tucked into her side, her good arm hanging limp. I noted the fresh pink scarring on her shoulder and in the hollow of her collarbone, the ridge of a new pink scar just under her arm and barely peeking around her front from where he'd collapsed her lung.

Internally, I marveled at modern medicine and at how even with a lengthy emergency surgery they hadn't had to open her up from here to hell and gone, and how everything had been stitched neatly.

A few years down the line, you might not even notice the scars were there.

It was good work.

"Here," I said quietly. "Check that out and make sure it's not too ho. You can always warm up from cool but I'd hate to scald you."

She put her hand under the spray and nodded. "Thank you," she murmured.

I held out a hand and helped stabilize her as she stepped into the tub and stopped her just before she turned so that I could take down her ponytail.

I could see why she was so skeeved out and wanting a shower when her hair sort of tried to stick or remain in the shape it was in from the hair tie.

"Let that warm water work some magic and gimme just a minute," I said.

She said, "Okay." Her voice was a little smaller and a little breathy. I couldn't tell if it was because *now* her nerves were setting in or if it was from some form of excitement.

I was certainly hoping it was the latter. I know I was a little more excited than I needed to be at the moment, which is partially why I needed a minute. Not just to undress myself, but to get a fucking grip. If that meant quickly beating off in the next room then so be it.

CHAPTER FIFTEEN

*C*orliss…

I stood under the shower spray, turning it up incrementally until it was as hot as I could stand it – which was, I hoped, alright with Hex, who was taking a curiously long time to get in here. I hoped I hadn't said or done something wrong. That I hadn't overstepped, been too forward or made him uncomfortable… I don't know. It felt like my whole life had been tossed into the air. The whole puzzle that'd fit so nicely, its pieces snug, was suddenly dashed into pieces, all of them now strange and foreign and I didn't know how to make them fit.

Like in the dashing, the pieces scattering, the picture had changed on top just to add to the confusion of it all.

"Hey, babe, it's just me," he called out from the other side of the curtain and I jumped slightly. I was facing the water and I closed my eyes and listened over the shower spray as the rings whisked along the rod and the space suddenly seemed all the smaller than it had originally with his presence.

Not uncomfortably so. If anything, it had become cozier.

"Ooo, a woman who likes her water thermonuclear. I'd like to think I'd love you for that," he said.

"What?" I asked curiously.

"I love a good hot shower," he said, sticking his hand past me and under the spray.

Mystified, I turned and looked up at him, blinking in wonder and blurted, "I thought I'd find a unicorn before I'd find a man who liked my shower temperature. I mean, the unicorn seemed like the likelier scenario."

He looked down at me and broke into a wide grin, laughing too and gently putting a hand to my waist, sliding down and giving my hip a squeeze, before saying, "Turn around for me. Get that mane wet again."

I leaned back carefully and wet my hair under the spray, watching him watch me. It was as though the temperature increased pleasantly within the confines of the shower but it didn't have anything to do with the heat of the spray.

He took my bottle of shampoo and said, "Turn around for me," and I did. He worked the soap through my hair gently with his strong hands and I couldn't help but groan.

"It's not lathering up that great. May need to wash it twice," he said. "In fact, I'm going to." He spent some time massaging my scalp and where my skull met my neck, but it wasn't a deep enough or hard enough pressure. He was being so careful of me and I could appreciate that but still. A slightly frustrated sigh escaped my lips.

"What's that for?" he asked and I could hear the smile in his voice. I leaned back against him and told the truth.

"That feels good, but I wish you could do it like fifty percent harder."

He chuckled and went a little bit deeper with how he pressed his fingers and thumbs, but I would say only by like twenty-five percent. Still, for now, it was enough.

"Oh, God, that's divine," I said and sighed out in perfect pleasure.

"Happy to help," he said.

"You're going to spoil me," I murmured.

He chuckled, placing his lips next to my ear, his lips grazing the outer shell as he spoke, low and intense, "That's the whole point."

I shivered against his body, his voice as smooth as Tennessee whiskey, where I knew he was from. I don't think I'd ever swooned by a man's voice alone. He kept me up and kept me steady and pried the tension from my scalp and neck with his tender touch, rinsing my hair carefully, reapplying the soap, and washing the long strands a second time.

He worked conditioner through my locks and listened to me when I told him how to do it and left it in while he tended to the rest of me. I offered to do what I knew I could myself at every turn but he wouldn't hear of it, telling me to relax and enjoy myself for once.

It was *very* hard not to stare at him. He was a damn near perfect specimen of a man – so fit, with corded muscle and a to-die-for physique. I mean, he had abs and that delicious V that a man's hips made and women couldn't help but squeal over.

I don't think I'd ever been so close to a man that looked like him, or felt like him. The way he ran his soap-covered hands through my hair and over my skin like he was trying to memorize every inch of me by touch was something completely tantalizing and erotic. I found myself pressing my thighs together and hoping and praying the thrum of the hot water against my body would disguise how hard my heart beat against the inside of my ribcage, as though it held a humming bird trapped.

"You are so beautiful," he whispered against my ear and a whimpering, answering moan escaped my lips.

He chuckled darkly and pressed his lips gently over the pounding pulse in my throat in a chaste kiss, my back pressed along the front of his body. I felt his cock stir against my ass cheeks and my pussy gave an answering throb of desire.

"Turn around for me," he whispered and I complied as if I were his marionette, drawn by strings, that he so lovingly plucked and played.

By the time he was done with me, I was as clean and polished as I'd ever felt until I realized he wasn't done.

He turned me out of the water's spray and asked, "You trust me?"

"Of course, I do. Why?" I answered automatically, even though it caused fresh anxiety to fizz under my breastbone. He took up my razor and my can of gel stuff that turned to shaving cream when you agitated it against your skin.

"Oh," I murmured and he kneeled at my feet and lathered my leg up over the knee.

He carefully stroked the razor up my leg and I smiled and said "Push it down my leg. It's the best way to get the trapped hair out."

"What?" he asked.

I held down my hand and he handed me the razor. I stroked up but then immediately pushed it back down the track I had just made in the shaving cream and he looked a little startled, like the lightbulb had just gone off. He said, "Never thought of that. You ladies are hardcore."

I laughed a little and said, "I've never cut myself." I shrugged my good shoulder.

He took up my razor again and shaved my legs carefully, although he seemed a bit squeamish at first about the pull/push motion, but he got the hang of it fairly quickly.

He stood and turned me back into the shower spray to rinse off and said, "I can get under your good arm if you'd like but I'm not sure how far out you can bring out your bad one to get up under there."

I thought about it, and the thought of leaving it undone actually really bothered me, so I raised it very carefully, as far as I could, and he was swift about it.

"I don't think it's perfect, but it's better than nothing," he said as I lowered it carefully back down. The other side was a breeze and I honestly felt so much better.

"Thank you for thinking of that. I wasn't going to ask you," I said and he chuckled.

"You feel done or you want to hang out a little more while I take care of myself?" he asked.

"I can wait," I said and he double-checked.

"You're sure? I can get you out and dried off and come back in."

"I'd like to wait," I said blushing. "I wish I could return the favor so completely."

He winked at me and said, "I don't shave my legs, darlin'." I laughed and smacked him lightly on the chest with my good hand.

He laughed and we carefully traded spaces so he could take advantage of the spray.

He washed quickly and efficiently, a tactically precise shower, whereas mine had been a leisurely exploration of my body that'd left me totally hot and bothered. Still, watching the soap run down his chiseled body didn't help me in the slightest in that department.

He turned off the water and told me, "Hang tight. Don't try to get out yet," before whisking back the curtain. We'd been in long enough without the fan running in here that the mirror was water streaked and steam hung in the air. Also, it didn't feel cold.

"Shit, I always forget the damn fan," he said, switching it on. I expected it to be loud. Most bathroom fans were, but it wasn't. It was noticeable, and there, but as far as bathroom fans went, it was quiet.

He whipped a towel over his hair and body quickly, securing it around his waist, the absorbent material slouching on his hips before he pulled another off the shelf that held them and went carefully to work, drying me some before helping me to step out of the deep tub to do my legs.

"There we go," he said, coming up from his crouch, his knees popping and I think his feet maybe crackling.

I made a face and said, "Ouch."

"Sounds worse than it is," he said chuckling. "Just part of getting old."

"You can't be that old," I said, smiling at him.

"Well thank you," he said. "I'm thirty-eight."

"That's barely ten years older than me and not old!" I protested and he laughed.

"Well, it feels old."

I frowned and said, "You need to take better care of yourself then. If your body is protesting like that now, what will it be in ten years?"

"Dunno," he said with a reckless little shrug. "Guess we'll find out when I get there."

He winked at me and I smiled but I still rolled my eyes. He wrapped the towel around my shoulders, and I clutched it together with my hand and said, "I guess we forgot clothes."

"Nah, I didn't forget anything," he said and he led me out into the air-conditioned hush of his bedroom. He went to his dresser and opened one of the drawers, extracting a faded and cracked Voodoo Bastards t-shirt.

"Okay, how did she do this again? Bad arm first?" I nodded and he gathered the sleeve for my left arm into a ring and carefully slipped it over my hand, working everything carefully.

"Reminds me of that old board game," he said.

"Which one?" I asked, nervous and already bracing for pain if anything got jarred.

"The one with the tweezers and your pulling body parts out of the dude but if you touched the side, his nose lit up and the thing would make a god-awful noise and you lost or whatever."

"Operation?" I asked.

"Yeah! That's the one." He winked at me and said, "I thought you might be too young to remember it."

"They had one at one of the foster care centers I had to stay at. Missing most of its pieces so we only really had the one that we kept playing with over and over, or whatever. But when you're that bored, you'll make anything work."

He eased the tee over my head and I put my other arm through and it fell over me, butter soft and well-worn to just past my naughty bits.

He smiled at me and palmed my hip on my good side.

"We didn't have a lot of money on our face when I was growing up," he said. "My dad was a custodian for a local elementary school. Everybody liked him, but we were supposed to be poor so we had to act like it."

"Supposed to be?" I asked.

"My dad ran shine as a side hustle. Was pretty damn good at it. Master distiller. When I was a teen, some dude got into an argument with my pops about some shit and shot him right in front of me. He died. Mom and I had enough money stashed in the walls of the old shed out back that she can live mildly decently the rest of her days. The house is paid off, and I try to send her a little extra when I can."

He shrugged. "I spent my own fair share of time in the system. Not because of anything she did. Juvie type stuff. You know how it goes."

I nodded. I did. I had some students with ankle monitoring devices as early as my ninth and tenth grade classes. I felt like I was letting them down by not being able to return to teaching. My doctors had ordered at least eight weeks off and I knew I probably would push to go back sooner if I could, but I had to relent about it. My collarbone did need more healing than just a couple of weeks to make that happen.

"What now?" I asked softly, after he'd pulled on a pair of shorts and a band tee with the sleeve cut out a way down his ribs. He turned to me and sighed.

"Now, I tuck you in and give you your meds, and I go in and make us some dinner."

"I'm sick of lying around in bed," I tried to argue, but the raised eyebrow and imperious look he gave me said I wasn't about to get away with any shit under nursemaid Hex's careful and watchful eye.

"You got the TV in here with a hell of a lot better service than in the hospital," he said, leading me carefully to the bed by the hand. "And it's been a real long, real brutal fuckin' day for you. You need some peace and some good rest."

I couldn't argue that, as much as I wanted to.

"Tomorrow, we'll work on getting your stuff out there squared away as best we can and figure some other things out."

I nodded and let him tuck me into his big bed. He piled pillows around me and tried to make me comfortable, which was easier said than done with a broken collarbone.

"I'll be in the kitchen," he said. "Holler for me if you need anything, alright?"

"I promise," I vowed. He put the remote in my hand and kissed me on the forehead which *good Lord*, why did that do the things it did to me?

I watched him leave, sorry to see him go, but had to admit I needed a bit of a respite just to get my damn hormones under control.

I looked up at the television, sitting on top of the tall dresser in the corner and sighed. I wonder what streaming services he had available.

CHAPTER SIXTEEN

*H*ex...
I made us some steaks and some mashed potatoes, throwing a steamer pack of broccoli from the freezer into the microwave. I wanted something quick and on the easy side. The most time-consuming part of the whole process was the steak. I wasn't too thrilled with serving up instant potatoes but I wanted to get some food in her stomach so she could take her pills.

I loaded her meds into a shot glass and brought her a tray with a cold can of Coke out of my mixer stash. I didn't know what she liked to drink, so I'd have to remedy that.

I hadn't hesitated to bring her into my home and now, while I wasn't exactly having second thoughts, I was realizing there was still so much left to learn about each other. We were totally taking this whole thing backward by citizen normative standards.

That alone pleased me because fuck everyone's expectations on how anyone should live their lives.

I digress, though.

"Hey." She looked up from the middle of my bed and I set the tray I'd scared up into her lap after she struggled to sit up better one-handed.

She was hurting. It was way past time for a pill.

"I'll be right back with mine. You just eat. Don't wait for me."

"Okay."

She waited anyway, the little shit.

I got up beside her and set my plate in my lap and the beer I'd brought with me on the bedside table.

"God, I could use one of those," she said, eyeing the bottle.

"Meds," I said, chewing through a bite of broccoli.

She sighed and grumbled but cut herself a bite of steak and sighed happily.

"Get some of that in you and take your meds," I said.

"Oxy in there?" she asked.

"Yup, and you're going to take it," I shot back. "Fucking fighting me isn't going to end well so just do as I ask, please?"

She huffed an unhappy sigh and knocked back the pills. Wincing, she washed them down with the Coke.

"Melted?" I asked.

"Mm, explosion of foam – hard to get down, so yeah, partially."

I chuckled.

"Sorry, darlin'."

"Bleh," she muttered and hurriedly put another bite of meat in her mouth.

"How is it?" I asked.

"Good," she mumbled around the bite.

"Should have asked you how you like it," I said.

"Medium rare is perfect," she said, getting it down.

"Glad I over cooked it a bit." I smirked and she looked at me.

"Yeah, I don't like it when it moos when I stab it, but a little blood is just fine."

I laughed and said, "I'm just glad you like my meat in your mouth."

She snorted and choked. Bad timing. I'd gotten her when she'd taken a drink of her Coke.

"Oh, shit!" I got up and grabbed one of the damp towels we'd used from our showers out of the hamper and she thrust it against her face as she coughed.

"I'm so sorry!" I cried and stood by a little helpless as there wasn't shit I could really do.

"It's alright," she said, her eyes streaming. "It was funny."

"You alright? You hurt?"

"I'm good," she declared, taking in a wheezing breath.

"I'll try to be not as funny or something," I said, and she started laughing again and shook her head gently.

"You're too much," she said.

"I can be," I agreed.

"Thank you," she said and laid her head on my shoulder as I returned to my seat. I raised my arm and gave her a careful one-armed hug and we went back to eating, watching whatever she had on the television, which was, predictably, some sort of fantasy show. It was about a bunch of tween girl fairies in a fairy academy and all their bull-shit drama about boys and some big bad thing and their parents being some kind of assholes or whatever.

It wasn't my thing, but it made her happy and so I was all for it.

I cleaned up after dinner and loaded up the dishwasher. By the time all that was done, I was nursing my second beer and wrestling with myself on if I should do what I wanted to do which was stay in my bed with her, or if I should do the gentlemanly thing and put my big ass on my couch in the living room.

My phone went off on the kitchen counter, and I shook the water off my hands and dried them off pretty quick with a kitchen towel to see what was up.

It was the club's group chat.

Chainsaw: How's your lady?

Saint: Get outta my head, bro. I was just gonna ask that.

Bennie: Probably passed out. That was a lot of heavy shit for just getting out of the hospital.

La Croix: Will you let the damn man answer?

Axe: He will eventually if he's not busy tappin' that ass – which shit, man. You need to tap that ass. You didn't say she was so pretty.

Saint: Jesus Christ, Axe.

Axe: What? You know you were thinkin' it.

Collier: It's a far cry from fuckin' thinkin' it to sayin' it out loud, let alone taking the time to type all that shit out!

Axe: So?

Louie: He nut punches you the next time he sees you, it's your own damn fault.

Cypress: He ain't answerin.' Let the man alone.

Me: I'm here you chuckle fucks. Was just cleaning up from dinner. She's doing alright. Showered and comfortable, watching some girly-as-fuck show. Tired, hurting, but okay. Thanks for giving a fuck and checking in – and Axe, best not be thinkin' about how and when I fuck my woman. That's pervy as fuck. 😄

La Croix: Good deal. Glad she's doing alright.

Louie: You need help getting your place squared away, I got tomorrow off.

Bennie: Yeah, same. I ain't got nothing going on.

Cypress: I'm fishin'. Sorry.

Chainsaw: You want help with that bike of yours, holler. I'm not good with putting ladies' things away.

Collier: You can count on me.

La Croix: I can bring Alina by if you want.

Me: I'll let you guys know – party on for me tonight. Sorry I can't be there.

La Croix: It's no worries. You handle your business. We're straight.

Me: Thanks.

The boys all put in their two cents and the chatter sort of kept on to where I muted the notifications for the time being on the chat.

I left my phone charging in the kitchen and went back to my room where I found my Fable drowsing, her show still going.

It wasn't a hard decision. I got back into bed, set my beer aside, and cuddled my woman. She looked like she could use the contact.

CHAPTER SEVENTEEN

*C*orliss…

I woke that first morning, snug against Hex's hard body and it felt so… *natural*. Like the pieces had fallen into place, like I had finally found the *peace* I'd always searched for but hadn't quite been able to find… and it transcended anything I had ever experienced with any other person that had come before him.

We haven't even kissed was the first thought that'd crossed my mind and I wriggled a bit, worrying that maybe he was just helping, that he wasn't all that into me like I was him. His firm hand gripping my hip stopped me.

"Keep doing that," he said, his voice rough with sleep. "We're gonna have a problem, baby girl."

I froze and very carefully looked up at him over my shoulder. It didn't feel good, but it was worth it to see the heat in his gaze and the naked desire on his face.

"Sorry," I murmured, and he gave me a slow and almost predatory smile that quickened my heartbeat and made my blood rush just a little bit faster, raising a blush to my cheeks.

"Nothing to be sorry about," he said. "Just get comfortable. My neck hurts just lookin' at 'cha right now."

I giggled a bit and turned back into a much more natural position that didn't hurt and cuddled back against him. He gasped and slid his arm around me more securely, nuzzling behind my ear and breathing me in.

"Mmm, gimme just two more seconds of this, and I'll go get some coffee on and some breakfast going so you can take your pills."

That day I got the tour. He was pretty much in the midst of renovations. The kitchen was done, as was his bedroom and bathroom, and the guest bath out in the rest of the house… and now, he had turned to making an honest-to-goodness *bar* in his living room.

He told me his plans for the place which included vaulting the ceiling and making a nook space above the front bedroom, which he intended to make into an office. The back bedroom he intended to make into a guest room. Right now, that back room was piled with construction equipment.

"How long have you lived here?" I'd asked when a knock fell at the back door.

"Hang back here," he'd ordered, and he'd gone out into the sort of little mud room vestibule in front of the laundry nook and opened the back door.

"Well, hi," he said and sounded a little surprised.

"Cavalry has arrived," a male voice called out, and I drifted to the doorway to see what was going on.

"Hello," a redheaded woman said as two more of Hex's biker friends slipped in the back door.

"Hi," I said quietly.

"I'm Alina. I'm La Croix's ol' lady," she said, coming forward and holding out her hand. She kindly switched when she realized my left was done up in its sling brace thing and my right was the only one free.

We laughed a bit nervously as we shared an awkward right-handed handshake and she smiled at me.

"What're you boys doin' 'round here?" Hex asked, but he was smiling.

"Come to help you get this place fixed up for you and your lady," one of the men rumbled. I'd seen him yesterday. He was terrifying –

bald and covered in tattoos, his arms thick and built like a proverbial brick shithouse. He wore these contacts that made his eyes wall to wall midnight and the look was disconcerting to say the least.

"Y'all helped me summer before last," the pretty redheaded woman said. "It's my turn."

"Y'all hungry?" Hex questioned.

"You're offering, I'm eating," one of the men said, pulling his long, curly brown hair into a ponytail at the back of his head, a hair elastic stretching over his thick fingers.

"How you doing?" he asked me directly as he pulled his hair through the loop.

"Better than yesterday," I said with an attempt at a smile.

He sniffed and nodded. "I'm Saint. Sorry nobody thought to introduce themselves, situation was kinda all fucked up."

"Hi, I'm Corliss," I said, and I nodded. "It was very fucked up. This whole thing has been kind of a confusing nightmare but hey, it isn't the first time I've moved around via trash bags."

I lifted my good shoulder in a slight shrug and attempted to make light of it.

"Yeah, but it's the last," Hex declared and winked at me.

I forced a smile but if it was anything I'd learned? Life just didn't work that way and there was no predicting the future.

"You girls go on and do whatever hoodoo you do with organizing shit. You point, we'll follow through," La Croix said. Alina practically lit up, a soft smile curving her lips at the sound of his voice, even though she just stared off into space.

"You do whatever it is you need to do to fit her clothes in my room. Move my shit however you like," Hex said, and Alina gave a nod.

"C'mon, let these boys shoot the shit for a minute. This is more our territory anyhow," Alina said, and she took my good hand to lead me off down the hall.

"Okay." I let out a nervous little laugh and let Alina tow me into the living room.

She huffed out a breath and said, "Hoo boy! This was more than I was expecting, but that's all right. We got this."

"Thank you all for doing this," I murmured. "It's been…" I swallowed hard. "It's been a lot."

"Hey, it's no worries. I'm just glad I can pay it forward."

"Pay it forward?" I asked, as she started separating trash bags by what seemed to be content, bringing the ones laden with clothes toward the mouth of the hall.

"Yeah, a little over a year ago, I was right where you are now. These boys moving me, in a big damn hurry."

"Oh, wow," I said. "You mind if I ask what happened?"

"How much time have you got?" she asked with a grin.

I had to smile back. "Well," I looked around us, "apparently, I've got all day."

She chuckled and we got down to it but she didn't elaborate on whatever experience had led her into a similar situation as this. At least, not yet. My curiosity was most definitely piqued, but I didn't press or pry. I mean, we didn't know each other.

A little while into sorting things and making sure the bags with breakable objects were put up against one wall and were safe and the breakables would be as okay as they could get while we sorted through all the rest, Hex, Saint, La Croix, and a couple of others from the club came into the living room.

"Hey, there she is," the heaviest of them said. He wasn't fat, per se; he was just bulkier and had a bit of an extra layer of padding to him if that made sense. His hands were meaty, and he didn't look like someone you would want to punch you. His blue eyes sparkled, and his blond beard with just a hint of strawberry to it had liberal patches of white in its neat array.

"Chainsaw, meet Corliss. I call her Fable. Fable, meet Chainsaw, Louie, and Bennie."

"Hi," I said with a bit of a weak laugh laced with some embarrassment. "I'm sorry we didn't do proper introductions yesterday..."

"Aw, hell nah," Chainsaw said genially. "We didn't expect nothin' like that."

"You've got a lot going on," Bennie agreed. "It's all good."

"Babe." La Croix jerked his head and Alina was pulled to her feet as though by invisible strings to go to him. He put his hand to her waist and led her a short distance away to speak with her.

"You boys good with bein' at my lady's disposal for a bit?" Hex asked, and I raised my eyes to meet his.

"You're leaving?" I asked a little nervously, and he smiled like he wasn't quite happy about it.

"Just for a couple of hours," he said. "La Croix and I got some business to handle. You be alright?" he asked.

"Ah, yeah," I said, nodding carefully. "I've already imposed so much I—"

"Now stop," he chided. "None of that. I ain't do nothing I don't wanna do, right, fellas?"

There was a chorus of grunting agreements and I had to smile.

"Lemme finish up this breakfast and we'll get goin'," he said to La Croix, who nodded imperiously.

I smiled and Alina returned. The rest of the guys pitched in to help sort and carry things off, bringing totes in to help better hold and secure items until they could find their place. They talked about some of the plans that Hex had for the rest of the house over breakfast until it was time for him and La Croix to leave.

"Be back soon," he said, touching the side of my face and flicking his thumb in a light caress down my cheek. I nodded and then he was gone. I was kept distracted by picking through the sea of my belongings, sorting clothes, books, and photographs into neat little piles.

CHAPTER EIGHTEEN

*H*ex...

"She'll be alright," La Croix intoned as we mounted our bikes at the back of my house. It was all pavement back here, and I'd thought some on busting some of it up to have a patch of green back here. It was a little too sterile for my tastes, but the outside of this place was the last thing on my mind to making the inside habitable.

"Oh, yeah, I know," I declared. "Cornelius expecting our asses?" I asked.

La Croix shook his head.

"Well, this ought to be fun," I muttered.

We rode out to our sleazeball lawyer's place, and as predicted, it was a riot – for us at least.

"Aw c'mon now, fellas!" Bryan Cornelius looked none too happy to see us standin' on his front porch. "My house? Really?" he demanded, stepping back and ushering us inside quickly. He ducked his head out his front door and looked around. Ducking back in, he shut it firmly on the outside world.

"Now just what in the hell do you want on a Sunday?" he asked, turning around to face us.

"Relax," La Croix grated.

"You're on the side of the angels this time, buddy." I said and he looked up at me through his thick glasses, setting his jaw to the side as though he was thinkin', deciding to believe us or not.

Finally, he let out a sigh and said, "Uh-huh, what is it this time? Hopefully it ain't gon' lead to any more of my payin' customer's suicides."

He was talkin' about the city councilman from last year – La Croix's girl's best friend's daddy. He'd been a monster, sellin' his little girl out to the highest bidder until she'd gone on her own fucking program and turned full-on high-classed hooker. She'd flaunted the fact that she was just the whore that her daddy'd made her and had turned into a liability for the cocksucker. He'd had her killed, stuffed in a damn suitcase and dumped in the Atchafalaya Basin.

He didn't count on anybody carin' about her, but Alina? Alina never gave up on her friend. It was a dangerous game La Croix's girl found herself in, dropped in the middle of a damn chess board, only holdin' checkers pieces.

The fools pullin' the strings hadn't counted on our boy's obsession with the little redhead back at my place, and we'd wrought some good ol' fashioned street justice and had, by default, cleaned up some of the political garbage patch of this city.

"Not sorry," La Croix said with an impassive look, and I shot him one behind the lawyer's back, cautioning him to fuckin' behave.

"Not if that crazy bastard that hurt that teacher is your client," I said flatly to get us on the subject we'd come for.

Cornelius gave a low whistle and jerked his head for us to follow him deeper into the house.

"Can't say he is, and even if he was? I sure wouldn't take that case. Sounds like you got beef with ol' boy. What's he done?"

"That teacher's his ol' lady," La Croix said deeply, and I scowled at him again. That was a bigger leap than I was willin' to admit to just yet. I mean, I wanted Cor something fierce but what if she wasn't ready? I worried about that, about makin' a move too soon or whatever. Which is the only reason I hadn't yet, the ache in my balls griping about it somethin' fierce.

"Well, now, ain't that somethin' – the beauty and the biker." He looked me up and down.

I demanded, "Now how would you know what she looks like?"

"Ain't you turned on the news any?" he asked and I grunted.

"Can't say as I have. I've been spendin' my evenings at the hospital and purposely avoiding the news for her sake once I learned she was all over it." *Caught plenty of fuckin' Jeopardy, though,* I thought to myself with some fondness.

"So, what you boys want with me fer?" he asked, going around the desk in his den and sitting behind it, leaning way back in his seat with his hands behind his head like he didn't have a care in the world.

La Croix and I traded a smirk. The newly budding sweat stains in the pits of his royal-blue casual-Sunday polo were diming the lawyer out. He may appear cool as a cucumber, but he wasn't stupid. It was the "not stupid" part which is why we kept him on our payroll. He'd done right by one of our members back in Ruthless's days as president, and ol' Ruthless had something on him at one point. Now, La Croix and I didn't have a clue what that somethin' was, but we were better at bluffin' and intimidation. Ol' Bryan didn't know that we didn't know. So, we kept the lawyer on a tight leash that we loosened up on, earning ourselves more an' more goodwill with money and smaller asks like this one until the day we needed a big, more 'n slightly less-than-legal favor. Then we'd see about cashin' in and just how flexible Cornelius was within the confines of the law.

"You got connections," La Croix said.

"Just wanna know they ain't got 'im in a mental ward and what jail he's in, that's all," I said.

"For now," La Croix added.

"Hell boys, Google is your friend," the lawyer said, and he sat up and started clacking at the keys of his laptop.

He turned the machine around to face us, stood up and looked over the thing and hit a button. It started playing.

"*New developments in the assault on the Lakeside High School teacher that's shocked the city, Marianne.*"

The newscaster was standing right outside the local jail we was lookin' for.

"It seems Justin McDaniel has been found sane and competent to stand trial, so he has been moved to the Orleans Parish Jail for now and will be moving to the Orleans Parish Justice Center in the very near future as prosecutors advance their case."

Cornelius closed the laptop lid. "Now, just what are you fellas planning to do?" he asked and then held up a hand. "You know what, on second thought, I really don't want to know."

La Croix set down a wad of cash on top of Cornelius's laptop and said, "Stay by your phone the next few weeks."

The lawyer gave us a flat and unfriendly look and said, "Now even that's too much. I said I don't want to know."

"This conversation never happened, as far as we're concerned," I said, and he sighed.

"No, I reckon it did not... until it serves you somehow that it did." I felt my lips twitch with the familiar saying. I was pretty sure Cornelius and I had grown up in the same parts of East Tennessee.

La Croix and I traded a look, and both turned for the door.

"Y'all see yourselves out, then. Alright..."

We left the lawyers and rode back to the club, calling the rest of the boys in for church.

CHAPTER NINETEEN

*C*orliss...

The men left as suddenly as they'd arrived that morning and it was just me and Alina for a good portion of the day. I'd wondered aloud where they'd all got to and she said to me, "You'll get used to it. Club business is club business and it's not for us to know." She'd smiled then and crossed her eyes. I couldn't help but be a little discouraged at that.

"So, like, secrets?" I asked hesitantly, and she gave me a sweet look of understanding.

"No, nothing like seeing other women or anything behind your back. I mean, do they have parties at the club with a bunch of other women around? Yes, but this isn't that. There are things they get up to that aren't exactly legal by societies' standards and it's strictly forbidden for the women to know. It's to keep us safe."

I stared at the picture I held in my hands of my mother and me for a while. One of the few pictures I had of her of us together. I asked, "Well, that's deeply misogynistic, but I think my concerns lie more with... I mean... is it drugs?" I'd told her briefly of how my mother had died from her addiction, and Alina again gave me that sympathetic look.

"Maybe once," she said gently. "But…" she hesitated. "But between you and me?" I nodded and tried not to seem too eager. She smiled at me and continued with, "I don't know everything, but I think drugs played a role in the clubs near collapse a while ago. I mean, that's the impression that I get. It was before my time. Like *well* before it. Anyway, La Croix and Hex took over with the support of the rest of the club that was left, and now and they're trying to build the club back better but also in such a way that things can't or won't ever get out of hand like that again."

"It sounds like a lot happened," I ventured, hoping for a little more information about it.

Alina nodded. "Look, I know they look rough and that it's a little scary and mind blowing and just *a lot*, but I promise you I have never been treated so well by any man I have ever been with before. It's really *nice*, even with all the extra."

"Don't judge a book by its cover?" I asked, setting aside the picture of my mom, and picking up one of my favorite titles from the hodge-podge of items in the bag it'd come from.

Alina giggled. "Exactly."

We were going through the bags with breakables in them, unwrapping the glass things from the clothes that'd been hurriedly wadded around them, to see if they'd made it. I went through some more things and was silent for a time.

She sighed. "You know Hex? He adores you… you know that, right?"

I looked up a bit startled. "I mean, I guess that tracks," I said, stammering a bit and blushing. "He's done so much for me."

"Trust me, I've seen him party with the best of them and I've seen other women hang all over him in the last year and some change. Not a one of them held his attention the way he looks at you."

I sighed and said, "I guess there's a lot to learn about them and their life."

She nodded. "Just three really big rules that I've encountered," she answered.

"Oh yeah? I'm listening."

"One, club business is just that, club business. Don't ask and don't *ever* tell. Two, if the guys are in the chapel at the club, which is their meeting room, don't interrupt. Seriously, wait until they're done. And three, don't ask about their road name and how they got it. Not everyone is open about it or wants to tell that story. Like, some take it as a grave insult. Likewise, don't ask for their legal name, either. I've learned if you sit back and watch and listen, eventually, that comes out or shakes out. Or, you can just ask me. Three is at least the kind of stuff we can gossip about."

"I always wondered how Hex got his nickname, and I did ask once. He didn't answer me, just sort of dodged the question."

"Oh, yeah, I think I heard something about that. Something about a look he gets when he's beyond mad or pissed. Like he's straight up hexing a man with that one look. Their road names are more than just a nickname," she gently corrected. "I wouldn't make the mistake of calling it just a 'nickname.' Someone is liable to get their feelings hurt, and you don't *ever* want anything taken as disrespect. That's something they hold sacrosanct."

"I think I may have seen that look," I said, my mind stuck on the subject of Hex's road name, but I was definitely interested and taking mental notes on everything else she was saying. "Or at least a baby version of it."

"Yeeeah, the fact you saw that look and there wasn't immediate and bloody violence, means whoever garnered that look without immediate retribution is going to have a real bad fucking time for a real *long* time."

"What do you mean?" I asked.

"Hex is a clever man with a very long memory, honey."

"Guess it's a good thing he didn't look at *me* that way," I said.

"I don't think he could if he wanted to," she said. I frowned but couldn't help my smile.

"What is that supposed to mean?"

"It means," she said getting to her feet. "That I've never seen that man have it so bad for *anyone* like he does you."

"You keep saying that!" I said, and it sounded like a bit of protest had entered my voice. I mean, I didn't understand it.

"I know," she said. "And I'll keep saying it until it sinks all the way in."

I gave a frustrated sigh and said a little forlornly, "TMI, I know, but I wish I weren't so hurt that *he* could sink all the way in, if you know what I mean."

She laughed wildly and said, "You totally just reminded me of my best friend Maya. That was totally something she would have said."

"Would have said?" I raised an eyebrow. "I'm sorry…" I immediately followed up when Alina's sparkle dimmed.

"Ah, yeah, that's how La Croix and I met, actually. Remember that wild and long story I promised earlier?"

"I'm listening," I said, and I was.

…and that's how she really started to get into her story, and *wow*, it was awful. Like something out of a political action thriller movie or something. It was also *a lot* of food for thought.

"I don't understand how they could have such reputations when they're like this," I said quietly. I admit, I was troubled. I mean, they were *clearly* the good guys in all that she had to say, and I remembered the news reports about Councilman Bashaw's suicide and how it related to some big scandal surrounding the childhood sexual abuse of his daughter. I hadn't realized how deep or how sordid the whole thing was, though.

Alina sighed. "I fully admit, I was as scared of La Croix as I was intrigued by him in the beginning. But now, I don't even see the ink and the intimidation. How can I when he treats me so well?"

She was going to continue, but the back door to the house opened and masculine voices wafted up to us through the long hallway. Still, the look of pure love and adoration in her expression melted my heart a little. I couldn't help but feel positively green with envy. I mean, how long and how hard had I wanted that? How desperate had I been growing up, for a love like that and just to be… to be *wanted* by someone, by *anyone*.

That's when Hex came back in, his eyes searching for and finding me immediately. His entire posture relaxed once he held me safely in his gaze. Alina and I traded a look and stifled a giggle. I couldn't help it. I mean, there was no denying what she'd been saying in that moment, and I can't tell you how despite everything dragging me down, how my heart soared with that one look from him.

"What's so funny?" he asked, and I raised an eyebrow.

"A couple of hours?" I asked, and his smile turned apologetic.

"Club business can be like that, Fable. I'm sorry," he said.

It'd easily been four or five hours since he'd left, and honestly, everything was as neatly put away as we could make it. Alina and I were really just sitting on the living room floor against the wall, getting to know one another than actually doing anything super useful at this point.

"Alina," La Croix intoned and once again she went to him without a second thought, her movements graceful as she got to her feet and picked her way through some of the things surrounding us to go to his side. She leaned into him and looked up. He lowered his mouth to hers and gave her a kiss, and I think I could kind of see what she was talking about. I mean, the way they were, how tender he was with her, it was as if the scary tattoos and the weird creepy eyes – which I'd learned were *not* contacts – just sort of melted away.

You could see how much they loved each other, and it was a sweet and beautiful sight to behold.

Once again, my heart throbbed with a longing to have just that very thing, but my thoughts were interrupted by Hex crouching down next to me, slightly startling me out of my reverie.

"Hey, you alright?" he asked me softly.

"What? Yeah," I said and met his eyes, forcing a smile to my lips. He traced some of my long brown hair behind my ear.

"You don't have to lie to me," he said gently. "I saw that look."

"What look?" I asked. I genuinely didn't have any idea what he was referring to. "I was giving a look?" I asked.

He chuckled deeply and pressed his lips to my forehead and my eyes sank shut.

"I think you're tired," he said and he had me there.

"I am," I agreed.

"Okay, let me see these guys and Alina off and I'll come help you."

"Okay," I murmured.

I honestly just wanted to be alone with him. I *was* tired. Alina and I managed to get a lot accomplished. My clothes were put away entirely and just my random personal effects remained – books, photographs, trinkets – that sort of thing.

I was glad I'd managed to snag my good cookware and kitchen things. Those were mostly put away too except for the things that were piled in the sink that needed to be washed.

Hex helped me to my feet. I'd felt much better switched out of his tee and into a loose tee and pair of leggings of my own. More put together, and while not precisely my usual standard of presentable, I gave myself some grace on that and had convinced myself that the men of his club weren't perving on me. They were just being kind and didn't care what I'd been wearing when they'd arrived.

Funnily enough, I didn't take much convincing on that last part. I genuinely believed that was the case. They didn't care. They didn't make a big deal about any of this, and I could only imagine what some of the faculty at the school would say. I could already picture Mrs. Moreno, the junior and senior history teacher, clutching her pearls, exclaiming just how *scandalous* it was that I'd just been moved into the *janitor's* house and that all these rough-looking men had seen me that morning in nothing but his t-shirt. It hurt my heart a little.

Not for me, but for them. I guarantee you, had it been only the rest of the faculty at Lakeside at my disposal to move me out and give me someplace to go after all that had happened, I would have been on my own with nowhere to go and no one to turn to. I would be without my belongings, strapped into this medieval torture device of a sling brace hybrid thing, and trying to make the best of it on a cot at the homeless shelter.

I wasn't a battered woman, so I wouldn't be given shelter there... and maybe, just maybe, some church would take me in but at what cost there? A barrage of proselytizing when all I needed was some time to think and to heal and just process all that had happened to me.

Society was so quick to judge and look down on this man for being a *janitor* and a *dirty biker*, when he had been the only one there for me. The only one at my hospital bedside, the one to hold my hand and bring me flowers and… it clicked.

Everything Alina had been saying… Hex didn't say with words that he cared for me and that he loved me, as much as I longed to hear such things. No, he had been my friend and had shown up. He had done the work and proven time and again at this point, with actions and not words, how much he cared… with gentle touches and light forehead kisses and—

"Hey, what's wrong?" he asked when he turned from shutting the door behind everyone. It took me a second to realize I was shaking, and another handful of seconds to realize my face was wet. I opened my mouth to speak and shut it as I was swamped with a wave of gratitude for this man that words simply could not express.

"Baby, talk to me," he said as I put out my good arm and reached for him. I just dissolved into tears that I could neither call happy nor sad nor anything else. I think it was just all crashing down and I didn't honestly know what to do with myself.

"Hey, hey, hey," he chided, and I could hear the alarm in his voice as he wrapped me into a hug and held me close, but still oh, so, carefully.

I sobbed into his soft tee and the leather over his chest and let him soothe me completely, at a loss for words. He shushed me, rubbed my back, and kissed the top of my head until I could catch my breath and speak.

"Thank you," I said and the words were so tiny, so infinitesimal, when it came to express the gravity of what was in my heart.

"For what?" he asked, holding me out from him so he could get a look at me.

"Everything," I said helplessly, gesturing amorphously with my good hand.

"Talk to me, baby. You're scaring me," he said, and I sniffed and grimaced slightly at the dull and radiating ache taking over from my shoulder.

"Did you take anything while I was gone?" he asked gently, and I shook my head.

"Okay, let's get your medicine in you and go lie down. How's that sound?" he asked.

"Will you lie down with me?" I asked meekly and he smiled.

"Absolutely."

CHAPTER TWENTY

*H*ex...
     I got her into bed and fixed her a sandwich real quick, bringing it, her pills, and something to drink to her. She struggled to sit up and once I had her settled, I got into bed and tucked her into my side. She ate the sandwich and took her meds.

Cuddling her close, I asked her gently, "Now, you want to tell me what that was all about?"

She sniffed and tucked herself into my side a little closer and said, "I think I just got overwhelmed."

It was an answer, but it left me no less worried for her.

"A lot's happened in a real short amount of time," I agreed.

She shifted her head and laid it against my shoulder, burrowing in almost, and I had to smile. It was both adorable and made me feel like I was on top of the world, that I was becoming her safe place to take comfort in.

"How do you stay so calm, so cool about all of it?" she asked, and I had to chuckle just a little bit.

"Well, for one, it's not happening to me, it's happening to you. I'm just along for the ride now, darlin'."

"I mean, it's sort of happening to you, too," she protested. "I'm here and I've upended your life. It's turned into this thing where it's all about me all the time and—"

"Hey." It came out a little stern, but she needed a little bit of a reality check. "I don't know who it was that said, or treated you like you were nothing but a burden."

She scoffed a scornful little laugh. "Just about *everyone* that's ever had to live with me ever," she said, and the pain of that childhood trauma was real, radiating off of her like heat off a summer sidewalk, to the point even I felt burned by it.

"Yeah, well that was then, and this is now," I told her. "Those people that mind don't matter and I'm telling you I don't mind. I like you, Fable. You're a light in the dark, and even now, after all that's happened to you in the last couple weeks, you aren't worried about yourself. All I hear out of you is how you're worried about *me* and that has to stop. I'm fine. I *want* you here. I *like* having you here, and we'll get through this. Not like you've gotten through everything else because I gotta reckon, you've always done it alone. Well, not anymore. I'm here now, and it's not you against the world. It's us. For right now, until you decide you don't want it anymore, it's us."

She looked up at me, her eyes wide and made bluer somehow with how they were rimmed in red. She asked me, "Why haven't you kissed me yet?" I had to smile.

"Just waiting on you to ask," I murmured, and I lowered my lips to hers. She tasted like a dream and felt like silk under my lips. *God,* and when her tongue stroked against mine? It took everything in me not to put a hand to my already aching balls and double over with how swift and hard my cock came to attention.

We kissed for a while and when she drew back, it was with a whispered, "You're really good at that."

"You're definitely good at that," I praised her back. I couldn't help myself, I went in for more.

She lay back in the nest of pillows I'd built up for her on my bed and I *ached* to be inside her even more. Still, I knew she was too hurt for anything but the gentlest of touches and I couldn't swear to it that I could control myself completely. It was honestly best that I ultimately keep my dick in my pants.

She gave a whimper against my mouth, and I tore it from her. "You alright?" I asked, and it came out sounding gruffer than I'd meant it to, but I couldn't help it. She just had me that far up in my feelings.

"Yes," she breathed, and her blue eyes were glassy for an altogether different reason. One that made me smile.

"You have no idea how much I want you," I said, and she bit her bottom lip, an altogether alluring thing that just made my cock *throb* with desire.

"I want you, too," she said, and her hand found me stroking over the heat and hardness that resided in my jeans. I groaned and she wriggled her bad arm against her body, her good arm practically trapped beneath and between us.

I wanted to feel her body wrapped around my cock so bad but for now; for now, I'd just have to get creative, think of something that was *outside* her box.

I got up on my knees and said, "Lie back for me darlin'." She complied so beautifully for me, lying back, her hair spreading out in that way that *mm, yes.* She looked up at me with trust and desire. I hooked fingers into the waistband of her leggings and stripped them and her panties both down her legs.

She raised her hips and winced slightly when she put weight on her neck and shoulders. I was quick and then her bottom was meeting the covers on the bed and there was no trace of lingering discomfort on her face, just a raw desire, a want for me to do whatever it was I was gonna do and the perfect trust in me that whatever I decided, I was going to make it feel good.

Man, the powerful feeling that gave me. The intense, fierce need to deliver on the silent promise I was making with every bit of clothing I stripped from her, and every light touch I laid against her soft skin – *whew,* mm.

"Just relax for me, baby," I murmured, shoving her shirt up and out of my way, stripping my own shirt over my head to feel the backs of her thighs against my shoulders. I wanted to taste her. I wanted to make her come so hard and so bright she clenched her thighs around my head, and I almost passed the fuck out from my inability to fuckin' breathe.

She was au natural at the apex of her thighs, and *goddamn* did I appreciate that. I preferred it to clean shaven or even whatever little landing strip most of the club bitches tended to sport. I enjoyed fucking *women,* and when they did that shit, it made me feel like I was trying to fuck a little girl. I wasn't okay with that shit in the slightest.

I touched her, letting my gaze wander over her beautiful, sleek frame, as her hips raised unconsciously to meet my fingertips grazing along her sex.

"You're so fucking beautiful," I murmured. "So, fucking hot."

"Yeah?" she asked and there was a bit of her old spark in the word.

"Fuck yes," I growled against her stomach, kissing, and licking beside her bellybutton.

"Show me," she ordered.

"My pleasure," I shot back and delved one hand beneath her ass, grabbing a handful as I kissed my way to the apex of her thighs, prying her pussy lips apart with my fingers and finding her delightfully musky and already wet for me.

I teased her clit, looking up her body and locking eyes with her, keeping that look steady, unblinking, and just on the edge of predatory as I teased her clitoris with my tongue. A dangerously sexy game of chicken I was determined to win, and I did when I introduced my middle finger up inside her and her eyes slipped shut. I smiled against her body as her head fell back and she gave herself completely over to me and the feeling of me bringing her body up to a slow, rolling simmer.

She gasped, her breath coming in slow, even, sexy pants and I felt a surge of pride and joy when her good hand tangled in my hair and she half pulled my head, half ground her hips, putting my tongue *right* where she wanted it.

"Mm-hm," I encouraged her. I held my tongue out for her and drove my index finger into her wet and waiting heat, giving them some short thrusts back and forth to work her up into a more complete plea-sure frenzy.

She cried out, a keening desperate sound, her panting breaths the chorus, and damn did she sound wild. Wild and organic and as *free* as I'd ever heard her. She pressed her lips together and bit back moans in time with her exhalations, and I pressed my forehead to her lower belly and licked her furiously, turning my fingers up inside her to set her off like a fuckin' rocket.

She hit the sky and exploded with a cry, coating the ceiling and the walls in her glittering orgasm. I sat up just in time as the bear trap of her thighs snapped shut, and I got my other hand in there just in time to get my thumb on her clit, slicking through the commingling wetness of her pussy and my saliva.

She cried out sharply and laughed, giggling sweetly as she half tried to get away from me, but I wasn't having it. I was living for her smile and the way her pleasure was dashed across her face and chest in the most delightful pink flush.

Finally, she smacked my wrist repeatedly in this light smattering pattern that was *clearly* her tapping out, and I relented.

"Oh God!" she cried, finally able to form coherent words as she collapsed back onto the bed, her head lolling against the black pillow-cases and her chest heaving so sweetly in a staccato that proclaimed, *aw yeah, you did your job – good boy.*

Fuck that was hot.

CHAPTER TWENTY-ONE

*C*orliss…

I couldn't leave it. I couldn't let him please me this much and not do anything in return. He came up to lie next to me, his rough hand stroking tantalizingly over my skin as he propped his head on his hand and looked over the mess of me that he'd made in his bed. I lay and gasped, watching him watch me, and goddess, he was so achingly handsome, so beautiful to me in every masculine sense.

I sat up with a little trouble with getting my hand under me, and I eventually got to my knees, wobbling a bit. His hand whipped out lightning fast to grab my good one and to steady me. I said, "Pants. I can't do it one-handed."

"What's your poison, Fable?" he asked me.

I said, my legs trembling slightly beneath me where I kneeled on them on the bed, "I want to ride you. I need you to feel as good as I do."

"You sure you're up to it?" he asked, and I nodded as he shucked his jeans down his legs and off.

"Please tell me you have a condom. I'm on birth control, but the nurse warned me some of the medications I'm on can interfere with it."

"Absolutely, baby. Let me get one on for you."

He reached into the drawer of his bedside table and extracted one, tearing the foil packet with his teeth. I captured my bottom lip between my teeth and watched him. Holy goodness, this man was sex on a stick. Long and nearly purple with his desire, his cock was a thing of beauty. Not overly thick, but veined so lovely, and there was just something about watching his hands roll the latex down his shaft. So erotic and pleasing to watch a man make himself ready for you. I can't even describe the things it did to me.

He put up his hands for me to brace my good one against so that I could swing my leg over his lean hips, and he held himself up off his body for me.

I panted, his cock finding my entrance almost by sheer magnetism, and I tried to ease my way down on him slowly.

He gritted his teeth and leaned forward, panting himself, as though he were having trouble maintaining his composure and I *loved* that. Absolutely adored the effect that I seemed to have on him and marveled at the fact that me, little ol' me, in his eyes, was some sort of sexy siren or so it seemed.

My pelvis met his, and I swallowed hard and wished that we'd taken the time to get my tee off and out from under the bracing sling on my arm. It was hot and constricting. As I rolled my hips carefully, my hand braced against the swell of his chest, I wanted so badly for his hands to move off the tops of my thighs where he kneaded the muscles there and move to my naked tits. I fucking loved the thought of him pinching and rolling my nipples with his rough fingers as I rode him.

His cock was *perfect*, just shy of bottoming out against my cervix in this position, and just thick enough to press out against my walls and tease me somewhere past readiness, waking nerves inside of me that had lain dormant for entirely too long.

I whimpered and he looked up at me with heavy-lidded eyes and asked, "You aren't hurting yourself, are you?"

"Mm, no. I just can't go as hard or as fast as I want to."

He smiled. "Plenty of time for all of that, baby girl. I don't think

I'm going to be able to hold off for very long anyway. You feel so fucking good, and I've wanted this for so long."

Oh, fuck.

His words were an unexpected aphrodisiac and I rose and fell on him just a little bit faster, letting gravity take me down just a little bit harder and *oh, yeah!* Sparks of madness fizzled out from my core. I knew that just a little bit more of an ability to move, I could come again, like this, just by virtue of him being inside me.

"Shit," he grunted, his hands going to my hips and holding me down onto his cock as he sat up. He grunted, his body rising and falling as though he were panting, but he wasn't drawing breath. No, he was already coming, and I tightened my pussy up around him as he did. He cried out with the motion of my body around his.

I smiled and felt myself *glow* with every twitch I could feel from his cock inside me. That light inside of me growing more vibrant with every slight thrust he made beneath me, drawing me just that much closer to my own edge but not over.

"Mmm." He made the appreciative sound as he came back to himself and the sweep of his gaze up my body to my eyes made my pussy give a little throb of, well, possibly aftershock, but almost more like a preview of coming attractions.

"Fuck you're beautiful," he said.

"I'm so close," I told him, a slight fission of nervousness running down my spine.

If it'd been Mark, as of late, he would have just been, *"Sorry, babe,"* but not Hex. Hex licked his thumb, and delved it between us, pressing it against my clit.

"Use it while we still got it, baby. Come for me. I want to watch you."

Oh, shit.

I rolled my hips in that way that did everything for me, and Hex grunted, sucking in a breath between his teeth and letting it out slow, his thumb working magic against my clit and sending me spiraling, my body tightening.

"Oh God, there, right there, just like that!" I pressed my lips together and failed at keeping myself in check, crying out when the orgasm hit me. It was like slow motion, the pleasure barreling into me, tackling me, and dragging me outside of my body to leave me floating suspended for what felt like several drawn-out seconds but was really only a fragment of the smallest moment in time. It felt like time suddenly sped up, everything becoming a blur, as I jerked above him and came, slamming back into my body which quaked with the feelings that coursed through me.

I panted above him, smiling down at him, and loved that he lay beneath me, panting in rhythm with me, his eyes heavily lidded with the pleasure I'd given him, his body lax and languid as he basked in his own afterglow.

I wanted so badly to lean over him, to rest my head beside his, and to just enjoy myself, but my shoulder wouldn't allow that.

"You okay?" he asked me, and I tried to nod but winced.

"Yeah, nope. I think my body's done," I said and tried to hold my breath against the wave of pain that swept through me.

"Aw, shit," he said softly. "What do we need to do?" he asked.

"Um, I'm not sure." I laughed a little uncomfortably and knew that whatever I did, it wasn't going to be any kind of graceful.

I think I must have said something out loud to that effect because he laughed slightly and said, "I don't care about graceful. I care about getting you to a position that's comfortable for you without hurting you."

"Fair," I said, and with a calculated risk, I sort of just let myself keel over onto my good side, uncoupling with him and just sort of lying on my side, panting, but we were free, sort of.

"Um, hang on," he said, and he dragged the condom out of me with his fingers.

I couldn't help it. It was sort of the cherry on top of this ridiculousness. I started laughing at the absurdity of it all.

The best part about it was that he laughed with me, rolling onto his side, and kissing my hip, wrapping his arms around me, and laying his head on it. My good arm trapped beneath me, I couldn't do what I wanted to do, which was run my fingers through his short hair, which had been much softer than it'd looked.

"I think we need a shower," he said.

I said back, "I would nod to agree with you but I can't."

"Aw, sugar, I'm so sorry."

"Don't be," I told him. "I loved it, and honestly, I think I needed it."

"Happy to be of service," he said quietly after a few seconds of silence, where we allowed our breathing to ratchet down one or two more stages to normal.

"You feel so good," I said back, just as quietly. Maybe awestruck was the word.

"Okay," he said, getting up, and I missed his warmth as soon as he'd stood.

"Stay there, Fable. I'll get the shower going."

I watched him go into the bathroom and his ass was just as perfect as the rest of him. God, I loved to watch him either coming or going...

"HAVE you thought about what comes next?" he asked me gently.

"Hmm?" I mean, I'd heard him, it just took a second for it to process. I was drowsing against his chest, his one hand on my arm that lay carefully over him and the other buried in my hair at the back of my neck. He'd been massaging the base of my skull through my hair and the repetitive soothing rasping sound it made combined with his warmth and the feel of the tension bleeding away; well, I was almost in a state of hypnosis.

"You mean with us?" I asked.

"Not just us," he said. "I mean, with everything. You got a lot of doctors and physical therapy visits coming up. Then there are the lawyers and all the court shit."

I admit, I sort of froze.

"I... I hadn't thought about the trial and all the legal stuff, actually." I sighed and it was a heavy thing, laden with dread. "I mean, I've been trying very hard *not* to think about it if you know what I mean."

"I do," he said.

I swallowed hard.

"I was sort of hoping that because I don't remember anything that I wouldn't have to testify or whatever. I... I don't want to see him. I don't want to face the reporters or, or people saying stuff about me."

"Stuff about you?" he asked.

I licked my lips that felt suddenly dry. "You know, people have all kinds of shitty hot takes when it comes to things like this."

"Things like...?" he prompted gently.

"Things like... like what Mark said."

"Fuck him," he said vehemently.

"No thanks," I said, pushing up from beneath us carefully so I could look at him. "He wasn't that great, and I'd rather not repeat the experience."

Hex started to laugh but then stopped.

"You're serious," he said, cupping my shoulder gently.

"As a heart attack," I said. "Lately, if we got it on at all, the fore-play was non-existent. I'm not exactly sure when he started to treat sex with me like it was a chore or a challenge to overcome but yeah... that's sort of how it was."

"Shit," Hex said softly, and he caressed my face gently.

"Yeah," I said, and it was sad. I mean, it'd *hurt*; in more ways than one. Oftentimes, Mark hadn't even tried to make me ready. He'd just go for it and would make some comment about how it felt good because I was so tight, when on my end, it felt like he was trying to force his way in, and my body was just *I don't like this!* But I'd just grit and bear it because I already felt like he was unhappy with me, and I just wanted him to love me again.

The confession was out of my mouth before I even knew it and Hex sighed, stroking a hand over my hair. He said, "I promise you, here and now, I will *always* fuckin' communicate with you. I will *never* do that to you. Shit, Fable, I'm so sorry."

"It's okay," I said, sitting up. "I think I need to go back into my sling, now."

"Yeah, you mind if I just put your sling on and nothing else for now. I like the feel of your skin against mine."

I smiled and said, "I'd like that."

"Okay." He chuckled and helped me back into the bracing contraption of straps and buckles. He kneeled behind me on the bed, adjusting straps, and I tried not to shiver when his fingers grazed my skin. I loved the sensation but it also half tickled.

"Let me ask you something," he said quietly.

"Anything," I said.

He was quiet for a moment then cupped my good shoulder with his hand and without letting me turn to look at him, he asked me, "If there was a way to shut the whole thing down... the trial I mean, would you want that?"

I snorted and said, "God yes. I hope you don't think badly of me, but I really wish he was dead. I feel like it's the only surefire way he'd never hurt anyone again." I sighed.

"I don't think badly of you at all for that. I wish I'd killed him when I had the chance."

"You thought you were beating a fourteen-year-old kid," I said.

"Now it's your turn to think badly of me. I tried. Believe me. Only reason I really stopped was because you were bleedin' so bad and I didn't want to lose you." He kissed my shoulder, and I leaned back into him.

"I don't think badly of you at all. How could I? You saved me." I closed my eyes and said, "I wish I could remember. I feel like I'm letting the world down that I don't. Like if I only remembered, it would remove all doubt and... well..."

We lapsed into a silence, the both of us thinking so hard and so loud it was like if I reached out, I could maybe touch his thoughts like gossamer hanging in the air and likewise, I was sure the same applied to me.

"I'm going to ask you again," he said after a time, and his voice was steady and had a gravity to it that made me think I had better think long and hard about my answer before I gave it.

"If something could be done to shut down this whole trial, would you want that?"

I didn't have to hesitate at all. "Yes," I said unequivocally.

"You know what I'm askin', don't you?" he asked.

"If I am to understand things correctly," I said. "This falls under 'club business' yeah?"

"Alina's been talkin'," he said but he sounded pleased.

I turned carefully and looked up into his eyes.

"If you're asking me to sign the death warrant on the man who attacked me, do you just want ink or blood? Because I'm good with either, Hex. I don't want to do this. I don't want to have to march into that courtroom day after day and listen to the lies and the bullshit all in a bid to get him off. I don't want to have to run the gauntlet of reporters asking me questions about this thing I can't remember and honestly hope to every god that there ever was that I never do. I don't want to watch the sordid true crime documentaries about me, and I don't want this one thing becoming my whole life. This one moment in time, arguably one of the worst things to ever happen to me, become my everything for any length of time. I'm scared to death that my legacy won't be the students I've helped, or that I've inspired. That it will be this – this – this *thing* that happened to me. I can't tell you how much I don't want it to be."

"Say no more, Fable," he said, pressing my head to his lips then to his chest. "It won't be. I promise you. But this conversation never happened. Okay?"

"What conversation?" I asked somewhat miserably.

"That's my girl," he murmured.

He carefully pulled me down into the bed with him and we cuddled close beneath the blanket, cozy and warm in the air-conditioned hush of his little house, the ceiling fan turning lazily above us from where it was suspended from the vaulted ceiling.

I honestly didn't believe that anything could or would be done to stop my having to go through any of the things that I was sure was to come surrounding my case. The nice thing was that I didn't have to think about it anymore for now. For now, I could just lie safe and warm and protected with Hex, until the morning came, and he had to go back to work and all of that.

I still had no idea what life was going to look like from here, but I could live it one day at a time for now, like I was taking toddling little baby steps. It was nice to have Hex to hold on to. He was a level of security that I'd honestly never known before.

CHAPTER TWENTY-TWO

*H*ex...

I didn't know why I'd felt the need to... I don't know, *get permission* from my Fable when it came to the asshole who'd hurt her. Maybe it was because I wasn't sure if she still had faith in the system or whatever. Maybe I was second-guessing whether she'd want her day in court. At any rate, the decision had already been made yesterday in church, before she and I had even had the chance to talk. The plan had been laid, too. Now it was just a matter of getting through the week to put it into action.

I got up the next morning and I felt bad about having to leave her. But it was a Monday morning, and another day, another dollar needed to be made – for now, anyhow. Didn't know how much longer that would be a viable option once I got done doing what had to be done.

I kissed her goodbye, pulling the blankets up over her to make sure she was warm enough, and she barely stirred.

I left the coffee pot on and set out her meds in a shot glass next to a bowl of instant oatmeal. She just needed to add some hot water.

The day dragged, and I texted back and forth with her when I could. She said she was spending the day curled up in bed, reading, and I liked the thought.

The day dragged on by, and when I came home, it was an odd feeling sitting out there in my truck, knowing for the first time ever that I had someone I was coming home *to*.

I was tired and didn't know what I was about to do for dinner for the both of us. When I went on in through the back door, it was to discover that she'd already had dinner handled. She looked up from the stove all unsure, covered up awkwardly by one of my tees stretched over her arm which was still braced underneath it and I chuckled.

"You been naked up in here all day? Because I really like the thought of that."

She blushed hard and said, "Um, yeah. I could take it off, but I'd never be able to get it back on right by myself so…"

I went over to her and leaned down to kiss her, and she kissed me back.

"I'm sorry," I murmured against her mouth. "You were sleeping so good, I didn't want to wake you."

She smiled and said, "It was okay for today, but if it's alright with you, I would like to get up and get dressed tomorrow."

"Absolutely," I told her and her whole being just sort of lit up.

"What you got going on in here?" I asked, peeking into the pot.

"Spaghetti… nothing fancy, you just had the supplies. I figured you might be hungry, and it might be nice to come home to some dinner."

I gave a low whistle. "Look at you go," I said.

"You're just in time," she said. "Can you get the jar of sauce open so I can add it in here?"

I opened the jar for her, and she added it to the meat and awkwardly chopped onions and garlic frying in the pan.

"I'm gonna go rinse off," I said, smacking a kiss to her temple.

"Okay," she said, but she was concentrating on things going on in front of her.

I went in and took a hot shower but made myself quick about it in case she needed help.

It was nice having dinner with her that night. It was nice coming home to her drowsing on the recliner end of my living room couch on Tuesday night, although it wasn't nice discovering she'd gone all of

Monday and most of Tuesday with no pain meds aside from some fucking Tylenol. The reason I'd found her like I did on Tuesday night was she'd finally knuckled under and had taken one of her opioids, and it'd made her sleepy. So, Tuesday I showered with my lady, tucked her into our bed, and I'd ordered out so neither one of us would have to cook.

Wednesday, I came home, and she was in tears, and that freaked me the hell out. Apparently, it was a combination of a missed doctor appointment neither one of us even knew that she had, and the detective on her case, calling numerous times, trying to badger her into remembering things that she just couldn't. Pressing for details that she had no way of recalling and wanting to come over and meet her in person.

She'd gotten herself all worked up about it, worried that I would be upset if she knuckled under and let the pigs come to my door.

I'd consoled her, told her they could come around all they'd like, but only if she was comfortable meeting with them.

She said she felt like she had to, and that the detective had been agitated with her and had called her uncooperative. I was pissed, but there wasn't anything I could do about it yet.

What I did do was call her doctor as soon as they opened the next day to get her straight with that. They had an opening, so on Thursday I took off work early with Curtis's blessing to take my girl to the doctor, where we got the good news that everything seemed to be healing up nicely and received the referrals she'd needed for physical therapy and all that crap to get started on the next phase of her healing.

We went to the club that night for dinner and to see if we could connect with Alina to make sure she could get Fable to her appointments since my girl wasn't comfortable driving yet. Her car was also still at the school. While she was comfortable and entertained by Alina and the rest of the guys, I took Louie with me to go grab it and bring it back to my place.

"You ready for Friday night?" Louie asked me on the drive over to the school.

I grunted an affirmative and he nodded. It was going to be a long fuckin' weekend, but the week wasn't done yet.

"You think Cy's kin is gonna pull through?" he asked me. I could tell he was as nervous as a long-tailed cat in a room full o' rockin' chairs.

"If Cypress says his kin can get us in with that rat fuck mother-fucker, then I believe it'll happen. You ain't doubtin' Cy now, are yah?"

"Not Cy," Louie said shaking his head. "Never Cy."

"Have a little faith, brother," I said.

He nodded as I pulled up behind Corliss's old Toyota and jumped out with her keys in one hand and his cut in the other. I kept him blocked with the truck from the school and the old surveillance cameras that I knew were trained on the parking lot. They weren't the greatest quality, but still. I wasn't worried about them seeing me or even Louie, just anyone having any questions should they be able to pick out what was in his hand as he got in.

He started the little car no trouble. I pulled out and away, and he fell in behind me. I went home, he pulled into the drive, and I picked him up and ran him the few blocks back to the club, slipping back in and leaning down to kiss Cor.

"Where did you get off to?" she asked me, and I was pleased to see she was smiling. Seems the rest of the boys and Alina had kept her spirits up in my absence and I was grateful.

"Oh, Louie and I went on down to the school and brought your car home for you, for when you get to feeling like you can drive it," I said, and the corners of her mouth lifted that much more.

"You think of everything, don't you?" she asked. I slid into the seat beside her, my thigh along hers, and gave the top of her knee a squeeze.

"I try, baby. I try," I said.

She tucked into my side, and we enjoyed the rest of our Wednesday night, cuttin' up with the boys and having a ball, tellin' stories and the like.

Thursday night, the plan went into motion. I got home, took my shower, and had some dinner with my lady when she brought up the fact that Alina had invited her out to see her business over the weekend.

I played it cool, leaning back in my seat and sayin,' "You mind if I take you on out there tonight?"

"Tonight?" she asked.

"Yeah," I said simply, and let myself drink her in, patiently waiting to see how this was gonna go.

She set down her fork and asked, "Club business?"

I nodded and she sighed quietly and leaned back in her seat. Her smile was both wan and brittle, but she was brave and good about it. She said, "Yeah, tonight sounds good."

"Might not be able to pick you up until Monday or Tuesday," I told her gently and she nodded.

"That should be okay. I don't have any appointments until Friday."

I nodded and said, "Finish your dinner for me, baby, and we'll go pack you a bag."

"Alright," she murmured, but I could tell that her appetite had fled.

"You alright?" I asked a few moments later when she'd been too quiet for too long.

"I'm worried," she confessed. "About you. Promise me you'll be safe."

I chuckled and shifted in my seat.

"Safe as can be, I promise you," I said.

She nodded slowly but still wrestled with it; I could tell. I helped her pack some bags – one with clothes and the like, one with some books and crafting shit that I had no idea what it was or how any of it worked, and finally, her laptop.

She'd set her worry aside for the time being and now was asking a million questions about where we were going and what it was like. Questions that I just laughingly put off with a "You'll see," and a "Just wait 'til we get there, darlin'."

She was adorable. Right before she got up into my truck, she captured my hand with hers. I looked her in the eyes in the dim light of sunset and she had such a sincere look in them.

"Thank you," she murmured.

I bent and kissed her. It was as sweet and true as the first time every time she let me do it.

"You don't have to thank me for nothin' any time I do it," I said, and she smiled. It was almost serene.

"That's precisely why I do," she said. With a little smirk, I jerked my head in the direction of the open doorway. She climbed up into the truck and got herself seated. Even though she didn't need it, I stepped up on the runner board and belted her in. I liked caring for her, and it was probably a thing I would continue to do.

She smacked a kiss on my cheek before I could step back down, and I loved the sound of her giggle.

I drove us out to La Croix's family place on the edge of the swamp out there, east of the city. The headlights swept his shadowy figure standing under the big ol' tree in the house's side yard, the Spanish moss hanging over him, his black eyes glittering in the sudden illumination. I felt my Fable stiffen momentarily, her leg muscles coiling under my hand where it rested atop her thigh.

"Well, that belonged in a horror movie," she said flatly, and I laughed.

"Leatherface eat your heart out?" I asked and she shook her head.

"There was this movie with Denzel Washington a long time ago, where he was like this cop or something, chasing this killer, but the killer was a demon, jumping from person to person, using their bodies like puppets. He would always know it was the demon because it would sing the Rolling Stones, 'Time Is on My Side' with this eerie smile." She shuddered. "I don't know why, but it just reminded me of that. That movie wasn't supposed to be like a horror movie in the traditional sense – more like a thriller or crime drama with a supernatural element, but it scared the absolute *shit* out of me."

"I'll have to watch it sometime if you can remember the name of it."

"I *think* it was *Fallen*, but I can't be sure," she said.

"Hm, well, that's what the internet is for." I shrugged and shut off my truck. La Croix was fording the grass of the yard which was getting tall. His daddy usually never let it get this way.

I got out and cocked my head and asked him, "Your old man doin' alright?"

La Croix's expression was impassive when he said, "He's finally on his way out. He's in there dyin' slow."

I shot a look across the hood of my truck and at the dimly lit window of the living room of the old house.

"I'm sorry to hear that, man," I said. "My condolences."

"Don't waste 'em," La Croix said, and he immediately dropped it when Cor popped her door open.

He beat me to it, going around to offer a hand to help her down. I shut the door to my side of the truck and wished that La Croix's daddy had been half the man my daddy'd been. I felt right sorry for my club brother. I hated this for him, but I knew it'd rankle him something fierce if I made a thing out of it, so I dropped it too.

La Croix was greeting Corliss pleasantly, and I worked on gettin' her bags out. La Croix took them with a nod of thanks from me and I went and put a gentle arm around my girl and led her to the dock.

"You ever been out on the swamp?" La Croix asked from the boat as I handed down her bags to him.

"No, never," she confessed with a bit of a nervous laugh.

"At night, it's somethin' else," I told her.

"Different kind of beauty at night," La Croix said, holding up a hand to steady her as she held mine to step down into the boat, her hand leaving mine to take his as the shallow aluminum skiff wobbled slightly.

I appreciated that he treated her like precious cargo, as good as he would treat Alina. I couldn't tell him how much.

"You're in for a treat," I told her, getting down into the boat behind her and pulling her between my knees and against my chest carefully.

La Croix moved around behind us to take a seat at the stern, looping the emergency stop around his wrist and pulling the ripcord to get the motor started; steering us carefully into the night-darkened swamp that was so alive with frog and insect song.

CHAPTER TWENTY-THREE

*C*orliss...

It was the sort of terrifying out here that was equal parts exhilarating and deep primordial dread.

The guys kept most of the fear away by talking, telling me different things about the swamp, training the spotlight from the boat out into the dark and pointing out the pinpricks of eye shine from the alligators just above the waterline. Talking about things like how Cypress was a professional alligator hunter when the season came around and how it was easier but more dangerous to hunt alligator at night. So dangerous, it was outlawed in Louisiana. You could only hunt them during the day.

They also talked about what else lurked in the shallow waters we traversed. About different turtles and a fish called Alligator Gar, and how the latter made damn good Gar cakes. Sort of like fish patties mixed with vegetables; formed and fried in oil. It sounded good, actually.

The talk of Gar cakes morphed into talk of food in general and of the legendary cookouts that were put on by the locals whenever a good enough occasion arose. Of course, some of those occasions were purely made up for the hell of it just as an excuse.

It was nice listening to them as the dim lights of the shoreline receded and the only thing that held back the impossible dark ahead of us was the boat's dim spotlight.

Through it all, the pressing dark and the foreign hoots and calls emanating threateningly from that dark, I felt totally and perfectly *safe*. Safe in the circle of Hex's arms, as though he was my personal protection spell from, well, everything out there – be it nature or city life.

I perked up when we turned an invisible corner sometime later and there was a light up ahead, shining back at us from the deep swamp night.

A rectangle of light appeared as we approached what appeared to be a small house on a barge, and a woman's delicate frame was backlit by the light within it.

La Croix let out a whistle and a whistle came in return from the barge. As we drew nearer, Alina's smiling face greeted us.

"Hello!" she called out.

"Hi!" I called back and La Croix smoothly arced us out and around, and slid us right along upside the barge, stopping on a dime, with practiced ease, at the ladder over the side.

It was only two steps up onto the barge, and I made it well enough, if a little awkwardly with one arm strapped to my side.

Hex got up with me and caught the bags that La Croix tossed up. Alina took one, I took another, and Hex turned with the third over his shoulder as La Croix hoisted himself up and tied off the small boat.

"Welcome home," Alina said, passing us up to kiss La Croix as he stood firm on the barge's edge.

"Go on, now," he ordered deeply and she followed me and Hex into the house.

"You'll be back here in the guest room," Alina said, leading us back to a door just past the small kitchen in a nook of a hallway on the right. Across from the open doorway to the small bedroom, there was a closet door with a stacking washer and dryer.

"How does this all work?" I asked impressed.

Alina smiled with a feral grin and said, "I had the same thought the first time La Croix brought me out here. This is his place," she said.

"I'll give you the grand tour in the morning. For now, would you like some tea? It can be a bit chilly out on the water at night this time of year."

"Oh, yes," I said. "I would love some."

Hex set my things down beside the bag I'd brought in on the bed and took the bag Alina had from her, doing the same.

"Alright, babe, I have to go," he said.

"So soon?" I asked.

He gave me an apologetic smile and said, "I have to work tomorrow, so yeah."

I felt my shoulders drop. Alina said something to La Croix around the corner in the kitchen and he answered in the affirmative.

"Alright," I said and forced a smile.

We went out into the main part of the house and Hex turned to me again and leaned down to kiss me. I kissed him back, blushing a furious pink. My knee-jerk reaction was to stop things quickly because that was what I was used to – an almost ingrained response from Mark, who if I lingered too long, would get bent out of shape about it and all but accuse me directly of being embarrassing. I still wasn't used to being around other people with Hex, let alone two people who watched us so intently – La Croix impassively, and Alina with an open, happy, beaming smile.

"I'll see you Monday or Tuesday," Hex declared, and he looked to La Croix. "Thanks for taking care of my lady."

"Thank *my* lady," La Croix intoned. "I'll be at the club most of the weekend."

Hex nodded and La Croix broke off from our little group and headed for the door with him.

I looked to Alina who winked at me and said out loud, "Pick your poison, honey. What kinds of tea do you like?"

"Oh, um, what do you – *wow*." I blinked in wonder, and my heart went all happy and a little gooey at her countertop. The entire backsplash was lined wall to wall with jars of loose-leaf teas. Everything from white, to green, to reds, to blacks – herbals and spices mixed in some and each jar labeled beautifully with these antique looking labels, in a flowing and lovely script, with the name of the contents on each.

"This is *fantastic!*" I declared. "I'm a little jealous." The front door shut behind the men and the screen clacked in its frame shortly after.

Alina touched my arm and said, "They'll be okay, I promise. I get it though. It's a bitch not knowing what they get up to."

I bit my bottom lip between my teeth and turned back to her when the boat motor started up outside. She smiled at me and the sounds of the water coming to a boil in the electric kettle filled the small space with its low ceiling in the kitchen and the vaulted space out from underneath it over the living room.

"Did Hex do this?" I asked, looking out into the living room and the warm glowing golden wood climbing the front wall and crawling up the ceiling.

"Uh, yeah. How'd you guess?" she asked, turning to take down a pair of mismatching but beautiful teacups from one of the cupboards above the low hood over the stove. She set them down into equally mismatching but no less gorgeous saucers and I smiled.

"He's got the same thing going on in his bedroom back at his house – the wood, and the ceilings. It has his flare."

"You want to see impressive, you need to see the bathroom down here and the shower upstairs." Alina pitched a low whistle. "I love it out here."

I eyed the kettle, which was still going to take a bit, and said, "Why don't you take me on a tour?"

She smiled and said, "Bet, follow me."

We started downstairs with the room next to the guest room but up front, just off the living room. It was sizable, certainly bigger than the guest room, but it was likewise gorgeous. The walls were painted a deep, rich, forest or hunter green accented in gold. There was a big, heavy, old antique apothecary desk that had scrollwork sides and back that were paned with frosted glass. The top of the desk a bunch of odds and ends – herbs and flowers in jars full of liquid that leeched their colors into the fluid, some forming crusts and crystals within.

Alina glowed with pride and swept out a hand, saying, "Welcome to the beating heart of Swamp Witch Watercolors," she said. "I started playing with extracting my own essences and things from various items to make handmade watercolors a while ago." She picked up a big brown bottle of an oily, viscous liquid and pulled the cord on a banker's light, sitting back center of the desk. It illuminated a white glass plate taking up a good portion of the middle of the desk, and there was a glass flat-bottomed upside-down mushroom thing sitting on one corner of that.

"I extract the colors and break everything down to a powder then add this binder and mull it until it's rich and smooth," she said, setting down the bottle. "Then I scrape everything into these little pots with their magnets on the bottom and bam, you can drop them into anything, really. An old makeup palate, a mint tin, and you have a watercolor palate that's customizable."

"That's really cool," I said. "How did you get into all that?"

She smiled. "I paint."

"Really?" I asked.

"Mm-hm."

"Can I see?" She smiled, and it turned her whole face beautiful, like an elfin princess or something out of a fairytale. She turned to the closet door in the room and went to it. Inside were shelves and racks, and she took some of her paintings out.

They were beautiful land and cityscapes, and I absolutely loved them.

"These are phenomenal," I told her.

"You like them?" she asked.

"Absolutely!"

We chatted about it some more when there was an audible click from out in the rest of the house.

"Water's ready," she said, sliding some of the thick watercolor paper sheets back into their places.

"Ah." I followed her out of her modern witchy office and the art on the walls let me know just how pagan she was. I felt even more at ease than I had before. It was another thing we had in common it seemed.

"So," she said. "What's your poison?"

I went to peruse the teas, as she made her cup. The aroma wafting to me made me straighten and ask, "What did you pick, because that smells divine!"

She wrinkled her nose with this impish smile and slid the jar in my direction, the label on it reading *Bourbon Street Vanilla Rooibos*.

"You're here all weekend and then some. You can try it all," she said, and I grinned.

"Fair point, but I'll start with this one!"

She laughed and made a second cup, and we retired to the living room for a while to chat books and crafts and things.

It felt good to make a friend.

CHAPTER TWENTY-FOUR

*H*ex...

"You gonna be straight, having Fable around for a bit?" I asked when we got into the swamp a bit.

La Croix grunted. "I don't like that I can't go in with you," he said, and I sighed.

"I know it, brother, but we knew we were destined to keep us separated when we took the roles we did within the club. Heavy is the head that wears the crown, but we can't have the pres and the VP in shackles side by side. Just ain't how it works," I said.

"I know it," he said. "Still don't have to like it."

"I don't like it either. Been a fair few minutes since I had any kind of brush with the law to take my freedom, and I can't say as I'm lookin' forward to it."

He just grunted, and we were silent the rest of the ride to the boat launch at his daddy's place. I got out of the boat and stretched, tying the line, while he rid himself of the cord to the kill switch from around his wrist.

"You headin' into the club?" I asked.

"Nah." He shook his head and then jerked it into the direction of his daddy's house. "I try to take the night shift while he's out and I don't have to listen to his bullshit," he said.

"Good plan," I said and nodded. "Wish like hell that you had a daddy like mine in your life. I'm sorry you didn't."

He grunted and shrugged, then said, "I got a good brother out of the bargain. A whole lot of 'em. I have the love of a good woman out there," he said, turning to look out into the tangle of trees and Spanish moss out in the water and mud of the swamp.

"You and me both," I said. "Anything goes wrong, and I get locked up for longer, you take care of my woman until we get it sorted out?" I asked.

"You know I will," he said.

I nodded.

"You make me your call. I'll get the lawyer involved."

I nodded. "I'm counting on it," I said.

We bear hugged, pounding each other on the back, and then he struck out across the high grass of the yard, and I got into my truck.

There was a lot that could go wrong tomorrow night and through the weekend. A lot. But I chose not to dwell on it too much. I preferred to keep my eye on the fuckin' prize, which was gonna be McDaniel gutted and bleeding, gasping like a landed fucking fish at my feet while I watched the light leak out of his eyes right along with his blood across whatever floor happened to be handy.

The first hurdle would be getting in with him. The second hurdle would be killing him. The third and final hurdle would be getting away with it.

Of course, I had plans for all that. I always had plans, and I had plans for *those* plans in case they fell through. Still, we would see.

My house wasn't that big, but oh what a difference a near week made. It was as though the very walls echoed the ringing silence back at me with her absence, and I was glad that it would only be the one night with me in here alone.

I went to bed, I got up, and I went to work as I ever did. I went through the motions, talking to staff, talking to the kids who talked to me or who I recognized as the outcasts and loners. The ones who were smart as heck, and far too grown for their ages. That's how I accidentally came across Tomeka Ross, standing at the bank of second-floor windows overlooking the faculty back lot, quietly crying and trying to keep to herself.

"Hey, now. What's this?" I asked, leaning my dust mop I'd been swiping through the hallways up against the nearby wall.

"I just noticed Miss Legare's car is gone," she said. "Does that mean she's not coming back?"

"Oh, hey, she's coming back, honey. Just a matter of time," I said. "A friend of mine and I picked up her car and took it to her just last Wednesday. She needs it to get to her doctor appointments and such. Surprised you knew which one it was."

"She's the reason I keep coming to school," she said.

I felt my shoulders drop, and I said, "You know Miss Legare and I are real good friends. I see her out there from time to time. You want, you go on and write her a note or a letter. I'll make sure she gets it."

"Really?" The ninth grader looked up at me and there was hope in her brown eyes, her round cheeks stained with wet. I shook out my clean bandanna from my back pocket up under my coveralls and handed it to her.

"Really," I promised her. "Why don't you keep that, write your note, and come find me later. I'll be around. Okay?"

She nodded and said, "Thank you," and tried a smile. I smiled back and reached out and barely tapped her shoulder with a light bump.

"Anytime, I know she misses you guys, too."

"Some of the boys are so *mean* about it."

"Well, you just point 'em out and I'll have a chat with 'em about whatever it is they're sayin'. See if they're comfortable sayin' it to me. If not, then they maybe need to rethink it before it comes out their mouth, yeah?"

She nodded emphatically.

"She's one of the good ones, Mr. Johnson," she said, and I smiled that she even knew my name.

"Yeah, she is," I agreed.

We parted ways. She came and found me at second lunch and delivered her note, which was thick, like four pages folded in quarters. I held it up in a gesture of "I've got it" and put it up in the breast pocket of my flannel shirt up under my coveralls. She nodded and looked like she felt better, which was all that mattered. Still, I was a man as good as my word and I'd make sure my Fable got it. I'd respect Miss Ross's privacy and keep whatever it was between her and my girl.

I went home at the end of the day, took a hot shower, and headed on out back to the garage, opening it up and sighing when I laid eyes on my bike. Man was she a sight for sore eyes. My project bike sat forlorn and wanting attention next to her.

"I ain't forget you, baby," I told the stripped bare machine that was going together piece by piece. "I just need to give your big sister some attention." I went over to my baby and sat astride her, tipping her up onto her two wheels and twisting her key, thumbing the starter switch, and letting her come to life.

I ain't been up on two wheels for too long of a spell, and I was looking forward to the ride tonight – knowing the one I was about to take just a few blocks on over to the club wouldn't even serve as one of them fancy horse-doovers appetizers.

I rolled her on back out of the garage, her engine chugging like she was cranky I ain't rode her in so long, and I had to hand it to her, she weren't wrong.

I rode to the club to find everyone there and gave a nod to Axe and Saint. I went to La Croix and handed the note from Corliss's student and told him about it. "You mind makin' sure it gets to her sometime this weekend?"

"Louie," La Croix called, and Louie came jogging out from behind the bar.

"You mind doing me a favor, man?" La Croix asked, and Louie gave a crooked grin.

"Anything for you, boss."

"When Cypress goes out to check on the girls, why don't you go on out there with him and make sure Hex's woman gets this." He handed the note to the kid. La Croix then turned to me and said, "I'm stayin' my ass right here in the city in case shit goes sideways."

I nodded and I could appreciate that, so I didn't argue the point and just let it go.

"Fancy a fuckin' beer?" Axe asked.

"Two birds, one stone," I agreed and winked at him.

"Hold up," Cypress declared. "You ain't goin' without me."

I raised an eyebrow.

"I got a bone to pick with these motherfuckers," he said, and he looked pissed.

"What's that now?" La Croix demanded, crossing his bulky arms over his chest.

"Some of them motherfuckers were poaching our lines," he said, and I felt my eyebrows go up.

La Croix grunted and I held up a hand. "No, this is good. This is fortunate," I said, and all eyes turned toward me.

"Might we can kill *three* birds with this one stone," I said.

"How's that?" Chainsaw asked, but I could see he was already halfway there, and Bennie, who was a smart little fucker, was already nodding. He was pickin' up *right* what I was puttin' down.

"We go in, we got our colors, and we open up this can of whoop ass based on Cy's family honor. They know not to poach his lines. They learn to stay the fuck outta our territory, and we get our weekend staycation courtesy the city. Our objective is met with the added bonus we got some cover to keep the heat off the club some – or at least keep it to a low simmer based on the fact this fight wasn't a rivalry type of bullshit they gon' want to keep an eye on but rather a family honor sort of thing."

The boys looked thoughtful. "Sounds good to me," Cy said and honestly, the biggest added bonus is we'd have Cy throwin' hands on our side.

That motherfucker was built like a brick shithouse and fought on the side, doin' that MMA bullshit. Won himself and the club some tidy sums doin' it, too.

"Do it." La Croix bestowed his blessing like I knew he would the second he dropped his arms to his sides.

"Now if there's nothing else," I said. "I'd really like to get this party started."

There were grunts and nods of agreement, Saint, Axe, Cy, and me heading for the door.

"Fuck some shit up!" Chainsaw called after us and I waved him off over my shoulder.

We rode out and it felt good to get my knees in the breeze, leading our boys down to the edge of the city, well within the bounds of where we wanted to be, to be taken to the jail we wanted to be taken to.

We'd been having trouble with a club called the Bayou Brethren getting a little too comfortable, hittin' up this bar inside our territory. The disrespect hadn't come until we started gettin' word, they were gettin' just a little *too* comfortable in callin' it theirs and pushing people out that they didn't like. Like they owned the fuckin' block the bar was on.

We'd been chill about it as we had some other shit goin' on behind the curtain with squaring up with some fuckin' dealers that were shaving our cut by shaving their numbers out in the quarter. They wanted to run their business in our territory, they needed to square up with us. They mostly dealt in weed and Moll-E so we weren't too pressed about them existing; however, the crack, meth, and heroin trade? They were getting too damn big for their britches and one of the warehouses down at the docks was fixin' to burn if they didn't straighten their act out and keep it movin'.

We were becoming less tolerant of their bullshit every day, especially when they had a bad batch out there, makin' some of the crescent city's poorer citizens very dead.

Somethin' that hit different with some of our crew after that whole thing with Louie and his momma last year.

We were working toward a better and brighter future for the lot of us – one where it would be possible for some of us who wanted one, could pursue a family. With women who loved us and young'uns underfoot. I mean, I didn't know how that all would shake out for us. I wouldn't mind a son of my own if it was in the cards. A boy to raise like my daddy done me, out in the woods, huntin' and shinin', keeping the old ways alive for a future generation. Wouldn't be possible if I didn't secure the here and now, though.

We rode in formation, two by two, Cypress bein' the wounded party up by me, as we led the way to ol' Swamp Daddy's, the bar that'd been commandeered just inside the city limits by the Bayou Brethren.

We pulled up out front, backing our bikes out across the lot and starin' down a row of six out in front of the bar.

We locked up the important shit in our saddlebags and hard-sided cases, and I gave ol' Moonlight, my Harley-Davidson Road King I bought new back in 2013, a pat. She was a beauty. I'd dropped a pretty penny into giving her a good ol' custom paint job a few years back. A nice glossy black that I'd had overlaid with a fine mist of blue-white shifting pearl luster that was mighty fine when sun or streetlight hit it just right, like moonlight caught in the paint to go right along with her name.

Subtle, like. I liked subtle… except for tonight. Tonight, me and the boys? Subtle we were not.

"Well boys," I said, re-fastening the Velcro on the backs of my fingerless riding gloves. "Last chance if you wanna pussy out. I'd understand it, I reckon."

Axe grinned with a savage glee. "Not a fuckin' chance."

Saint cracked his knuckles and Cypress rolled his shoulders and cracked his neck.

"Away we fuckin' go, then."

There were some good ol' boys out front, country born, and corn fed; likely from over the Texas border with their cowboy hats and boots, their wrangler jeans and rodeo macho swagger, thumbs hooked behind their belts and hands framing their belt buckles bigger 'n their fuckin heads.

They had some goddamn sense in them, though when one pulled his cigarette from his lips and flicked it out into the parking lot, givin' me a nod of respect and tellin' his counterparts, "Well boys, I think we ought to call it an early night." One of them thought to like to protest, but another one of them boys smacked him in the shoulder and gave a respectful nod in our direction.

"Good idea," Saint declared as we passed them.

Axe added, "Y'all have a nice night now, y'hear?"

I reached for the door handle to the bar and dragged the door open. We were immediately assaulted by some good ol' Creedence Clearwater Revival and the smell of beer and the sweat of a hard day's work – or in one or two of these motherfucker's cases, Cypress's hard day's work and their ill-gotten gains from it.

A bunch of the genial chatter inside ceased the second people caught sight of our colors, and a few people even took an unconscious step back as we sidled up to the bar in line with the six Bayou Brethren that were already bellied up to it.

"Whiskey," I ordered from one of the bartenders. She was rode hard and put up wet, I tell you what. Her face pockmarked from drugs and prematurely aged. She looked sixty, the teeth in her mouth too perfect to be anything but dentures. She was skinny, too – too much of what I had to hazard was amphetamine or heroin use in her past. Her brown eyes were clear, though – so maybe in recovery. You couldn't always tell. Still, while she looked sixty, I doubted she was a day out of her early forties, maybe even late thirties.

"None of that bottom shelf shit." I stopped her when she reached for the house shit or whatever. "Gimme the Knob Creek," I said. Their selection fucking sucked and that was the best they got. Jack was my usual go-to, bein' a Tennessee staple, but I wasn't in the mood tonight and they didn't have the Sinatra Reserve.

"Make it four and make 'em doubles," I called.

She turned her head like "alright buddy" and brought out three more glasses, and asked, "Rocks?"

"Nah!"

She nodded and poured them neat and slid them one by one to me. I passed them back to my boys and slid her more than enough to cover the drinks and a generous tip. She didn't say anything. She and the old guy with the gut, working behind the bar didn't make eye contact with any of us. They knew. They knew a visit from us with a pack of Bayou

Brethren in here wasn't no fuckin' social call. Not when the Brethren had been all but fuckin' regulars lately.

"To what do we owe the pleasure?" the one standing closest to me asked. He'd brought a cigarette out of his back and was tapping the filter against it to pack it down further.

I sniffed and set my empty glass down on the bar, swallowing the fiery nectar down to put a fire in my belly.

"Got a name, son?" I asked. The dude had to be older 'n me. I wasn't tryin' with comin' with anything resembling respect here.

He sniffed and let out a barking bray of a laugh. One he cut short.

"They call me Chicory," he said and moved the toothpick from one side of his mouth to the other before taking it out.

Chicory wasn't no young buck, but I damn sure got the impression he was big for his britches.

"Wish I could say it was nice to meet you Chicory, but this here ain't a social call. The fact I even have to ask you who the man in charge out of the lot of you is says all it needs to about this situation."

"Oh yeah?" he demanded, and his bravado was about to get him in far more trouble 'n he an' his was already in.

"Oh, yeah," I said. "Now you ain't the highest rankin' official in this little menagerie you got goin' on in our territory, so I suggest you learn right quick just who is in charge of this show before we have to spank your ass and learn you some fuckin' manners."

He straightened up, raised an eyebrow and tried lookin' down at me from where I leaned on the bar, which probably might have at least looked more impressive if it ain't for the fact we were the same damn height.

A hand fell on Chicory's shoulder, and he was moved back, a man my age stepping sideways past him and putting himself in front of him.

"And you are?" I asked.

He crossed his big arms over his chest and looked down at me from his three inches or so of added height, and said, "Tonight, I'm the man in fuckin' charge."

I barked a laugh and let it roar.

These dumbfucks were abso-fuckin'-lutely clueless, and it showed.

I felt Cypress looming at my back and read the name flash on this asshole's cut.

"Well now," I squinted, making a show of it. "Hatchet. I do believe you might wanna walk that statement back a pace or two."

"Oh yeah? Why's that?" he demanded.

I straightened up and went toe to toe with this upstart mother-fucker. "Because I'm the VP of the Voodoo Bastards, boy – and you're in *my* fuckin' house, drinkin' my fuckin' booze and the way I hear it – some of you boys are dirty fuckin' poachers, stealin' food off my boy's line and money out his pocket. Now, we been mighty fuckin' generous, lettin' you all call Swamp Daddy's your home lately but, bitch, get one thing fuckin' straight in that inbred swamp critter skull of yours. When you're on *our* turf, *I'm* your fuckin' daddy."

His nostril's flared and predictably, he swung on me. But he was at a disadvantage with his bulk, and I ducked and came up on the inside of his swing with a mean-ass right hook right into his fuckin' ribs. A pure fuckin' money shot that had him grunting and taking a step back.

It was like the world held its collective breath, the energy of the bar shifting and crackling as citizen patrons rose and went for the door, and the bartender that'd served me and mine started shrieking some shit, but it was too late. It was fuckin' on, and the Bayou Brethren and the Voodoo Bastards clashed in an all-out free-for-all.

It was a free-for-all they were gonna fuckin' lose and they did, the cops storming the place and throwing me and my boys down on tables and against the bar. I grinned savagely in the face of one of their boys who was glaring murder at me from inches away as we each struggled against the cuffs going on. Then I was jerked up and back by my colors and marched for the fuckin' door.

Mission fuckin' accomplished, I thought to myself. *And away we go.*

My only regret at this point was that'd I'd let my passion for the club get the best of me and I'd made it more about the club than the poachin'. That was alright, though. Me and my boys knew what needed to be said when the questions started comin.' We could make it about the poachin' first, then follow it with the ol' razzle dazzle of "fuck you, I want a lawyer."

It was an old refrain, a well-loved song and dance.

Fuck you, ain't sayin' shit', I want my fuckin' lawyer, was a biker's greatest hit.

It was about to get sung like a chorus as soon as we hit the station.

CHAPTER TWENTY-FIVE

*C*orliss...

Friday, when I got up, I realized it was just me and Alina and that La Croix hadn't returned.

I was equal parts relieved and unnerved by that.

"So, it's just you and me, huh?" I asked as Alina slid a mug of black tea at me to start the day with.

"Oh yeah," she said. "I'm used to it by now. Some of the boys will be along tomorrow to check on us and run us to town if we want. Personally, I don't need anything. Do you? If you do, I have the sat phone and could give La Croix a call."

"Oh, no," I said. "I'm good."

It was sunny and cool despite all the natural light pouring into the place from the windows. I got the *real* tour in the full light of day, and I had to say I didn't think such a thing was even possible. We were in a house, built on a barge, one hundred percent sustainable and self-contained and one hundred percent off the grid. It was a modern marvel. I was so impressed I forgot to be concerned that we were out in the middle of nowhere with nothing but a satellite phone with which to call if there was any kind of emergency.

Alina and I talked amicably, and each got a shower and dressed. I had to admit, I absolutely adored the bathroom.

I managed with minor difficulty to shower on my own and Alina, bless her, offered to wash my hair in the sink if I needed. I managed to do it one-handed, but boy my good arm was exhausted by the end of it and felt like a wet noodle.

She helped me dress where I needed and helped get me out of and back into my sling, but overall, I was proud of myself that I'd been mostly self-sufficient with minimal aid.

I found out Alina loved to read as much as I did, and we went out on the barge to soak up some sun until it got a bit much and we found ourselves under the awning off the side of the house. The furniture out here was nice and weatherproof, and it was a comfortable spot for reading the day away and sipping iced tea which we did.

We fixed lunch and dinner together, and I laughingly failed at making a pound cake for breakfast the next day. Alina tipped it out of the pan onto a plate at my say-so, only to discover it hadn't been done in the middle – that the toothpick I'd inserted to check it had lied!

We salvaged what we could out of that for the next morning and with the sun dipping low, popped some popcorn and watched some television – the spooky things still available, although I'd missed Samhain or Halloween.

We talked about tarot and mysticism, witchcraft and spell jars, and I felt lighter, happier, and more… I don't know… *seen,* than I had in a good long while.

"Thank you for inviting me out here," I said with a gusty sigh as the night grew late, and I grew too tired to stand it any longer.

"It's been my pleasure," she said and smiled warmly. "I've missed having a girlfriend. I mean Dorian and Marcus almost count, but not really."

I giggled. She'd told me about her gay best friends who were getting married soon, and I'd said we had to catch one of Marcus' shows.

Of course, his name being so similar to Mark's had led me down that dark rabbit hole of talking about my last relationship. Alina could relate. Her last relationship before La Croix had ended on similarly bad terms.

Cheaters sucked.

We went to bed, me to the guest room and Alina trailing up the stairs to the loft area, and I sighed with contentment as I switched out the bedside lamp.

∽

THE NEXT DAY, we heard the sound of an approaching boat as I watched Alina mix a fresh watercolor out of a powdered extraction that she'd made from marigold flowers.

"Shit, shit, shit. Can you go out and meet them? I can't leave this like this."

"Of course!" I said, and I went for the front door of the house. I stepped outside onto the barge just as the motor wound down and Louie hopped to the ladder and shimmied up the few rungs to tie off the boat.

"Well, hiya!" Chainsaw called from back by the boat's motor.

"Hello!" I called. He handed Louie some grocery bags and climbed up after.

"Brought some stuff to make a good ol' lunch. Where's Alina at?"

"Oh, she's mixing paint and couldn't leave it," I said, letting them into the house and calling, "Alina! It's Louie and Chainsaw!"

"Hi guys!" she called from her office. "Gimme just a minute!"

"No worries, girl! I'm here to take over the kitchen!" Chainsaw called back and headed for it.

"No problem," Alina called back. "Have at it!"

"Hey," Louie said, turning to me after he passed the goods to Chainsaw who was literally getting down to work with what was in the bags.

"Hi," I said.

"Hex wanted me to give you this," Louie declared and handed me a quartered sheaf of folded notebook papers.

"Oh, thank you," I said.

"You're welcome," he said, moving past me to go see what Alina was doing.

"Hi!" she called jovially when he entered the office, and I went to sit on the couch and opened the papers in my hand.

"You alright, Fable?" Chainsaw called out and I looked up, racked with guilt.

"Oh, yeah, um, it's from one of my students. Alina!" I called.

"Yeah?" she called back, leaning back in her seat, Louie standing aside so she could look out the door of her office at me.

"Can I get on the internet?" I asked.

"Absolutely!" she cried. "Everything okay?"

"I think I've upset some of my students," I said. "I haven't checked my email and apparently they've been emailing and not getting an answer. Some of them are feeling a little abandoned."

I felt *awful*, and I definitely felt the need to rectify the problem immediately.

"Go ahead, honey, take your time," she said and then she said something to Louie who jumped like he hadn't thought of that.

He came out and asked, "Where's your laptop? I'll help get you set up at the dining room table."

"Oh, it's in my briefcase in the spare bedroom. Thank you."

"No problem," he said.

He came back with my computer and set it up at the table for me and I sat down. This would be the first time I'd switched it on since… well, *since*.

I held my breath as it went through its booting up process and let it out slowly as I keyed in my login awkwardly with one hand.

Louie keyed in the internet password for me, and Alina warned me it would be a little slow, but it did just fine. I opened my in-school email program, and I was *not* prepared for the absolute *flood*.

By the time they all finished loading, I had one hundred and ninety-four emails and most of them were from my students.

I choked up. I don't know what made me think that I was so easily forgotten, but I'd just been shown that it was they who felt I'd abandoned *them*. I felt so guilty about that. Their feelings were certainly as valid as mine, even if they were slightly unfair. If there was anything I'd learned, life wasn't fair and you were going to make mistakes. It was what you did when those mistakes happened that made the difference.

I sniffed and ordered my email from oldest to newest, scrolled through the pages of read but stored messages, and with some trepidation, opened the first unread message dated the evening of the day I'd been assaulted.

I read, I hit reply, and I started to slowly peck out a response one-handed.

"Here," Louie said. "You're gonna have to spell things but move over. Let me type. You'll be at this all weekend if you try and do it like that."

He pulled up a chair beside mine from the other side of the table, and I moved over.

"Thank you," I said.

Alina came out and took over after her paints were all settled to dry and harden, and Louie was grateful. Things did move much faster then, without me having to correctly spell even some of the simplest words. I had a fear that the educational system had failed poor Louie. As a man, the level of struggle he was experiencing with reading and writing shouldn't have been a thing.

It was a mark of what a good man he was that he put all of that aside and was willing to help me anyway. I did suspect, however, that I maybe could help him, too. Still, by the time I had dutifully answered every email, I was then duty bound to begin the work of reading the few things I'd been sent as attachments and provide feedback.

The student who had written me through Hex was an outcast among her peers. She was, in my estimation, neurodivergent to a point that she could mostly mask and function normally, however she had enough of an aura of otherness to her that her peers could be brutally cruel with their bullying.

She was highly intelligent, and very sensitive. While everyone wanted to proclaim her this unfeeling weirdo, that simply wasn't the case. If anything, Tomeka Ross felt everything so profoundly it was overwhelming and frightening to her, and it was something she tapped into *beautifully* with her writing. For a tenth grader, she had such an amazing grasp of language and writing, and I was doing everything that I could and then some to foster a belief in herself with her creative writing endeavors.

I felt as though I had failed her in particular, over the last three weeks by not opening my email and checking it. She'd sent me so many messages asking when I would be coming back, each becoming more distraught than the last until they'd simply stopped altogether.

I was grateful to Hex for thinking to bring me the note. Tomeka had mentioned that Mr. Johnson had told her it was okay, and it broke my heart how many times she'd written she was sorry. As though it was somehow her fault I wasn't responding. As though she was afraid, she'd angered or upset me.

I had a feeling she dealt with a lot of anger and upset at home, and it killed me that I had tapped what was clearly some major fear of abandonment issues by my lack of diligence and care.

It was something I was determined to rectify immediately.

We'd lunched on some delicious po' boy sandwiches I'd whipped up while something fragrant simmered on the stove for dinner later that night.

I discussed some things with the other adults at the table and worked through some solutions regarding the deep anger and mistrust I'd accidentally fostered in some of my students with my inattention and inability to respond in a timely manner.

One of those students, I referred the emails from him to our school administration, looping the principle, the guidance counselors, the school resource officer, and the school's social worker into the picture and forwarding all of his emails to me to them.

I didn't feel particularly good about it, but the adults at the table I was sitting at all agreed, that while the kid would see me as a narc, and no one liked a narc, there was a time and place for everything, and handling the level of inappropriate vitriol in his emails was above my paygrade as a lowly teacher.

Chainsaw was particularly upset at the contents and said he'd like five minutes with the little shit for a lesson about respect.

Louie seemed to have a different view. He seemed to think that the kid wasn't getting any attention at home and that even negative attention was better than none at this point in his life. I was inclined to agree with that view.

Still…

"After what happened, this is just plain scary," I murmured.

Louie looked sympathetic.

"Boys are different from girls," he said with a shrug. "I did some similar stupid shit when I was that age. It's a miracle I didn't end up in juvie or expelled. Then again, I dropped out before I could be expelled, so there's that."

"Trust me, I understand it's hard growing up with an addict as a mom," I said. "I've been there."

Louie perked up a bit at that. "Me too!"

I gave him an empathetic look. "Mine was heroin," I said.

"Mine was more meth." He shrugged, and I caught a glimpse of that terrified wounded inner child and I felt my own wounded little girl reach out a hand, just wanting to be friends.

"I think you're right, though," I mused. "I think girls just try to stay in their lane and do everything to unmitigated perfection, in hopes of getting the attention they crave. At least that's what I did."

Louie nodded and then shook his head. "Yeah, not boys. I think when we can't get the attention we're looking for or crave at that age, we try something different and just go wildin' out until somebody sees us… but, at least for me, it didn't work out that way. Like I got a bunch of attention, alright – but they still didn't see me, you know?"

I nodded. "They didn't see me either," I said.

I sighed and Chainsaw leaned back in his chair and said, "Well, fuck, didn't this devolve into a group therapy session or some shit?"

Louie laughed. Alina got up and went into her office and came out burning some sage, wafting it around the lot of us. I smiled at that.

"I feel like I need to put out some hematite, or some smoky quartz around my computer before I open it up next time."

She laughed and said, "I have a big chunk of snowflake obsidian. I'll go grab it."

"What the hell does all of that do?" Louie asked.

"They're stones that banish or absorb and process negative energies," I explained.

"Oh." He looked thoughtful. "Well how do you know if it works?"

"Some stones will fracture or break after they've given all of what they've got, some will lose their color, and others are just tried and true. But I guess what it boils down to the most is faith," Alina said, coming back from her office and setting chunks of hematite, snowflake obsidian, and smoky quartz on the table, ranged out around my laptop. She set the smudge stick of green sage down in an overturned abalone shell, the smoke still curling and lingering in the air around us. I breathed deep and smiled at the hint of lavender for calm and rosemary for strength in her mix.

"I'm making tea," she declared. "You boys want some?"

"Nah, I'm good," Chainsaw said.

"You got that orange spice stuff?" Louie asked.

"Yeah, I've got you," she said with a wink.

"Some white tea with something fruity would be lovely," I said.

"I have the perfect thing for that," she said. "You like pear?"

"I love it," I answered.

"Coming right up."

We sipped tea and talked about other things, things that weren't as heavy, and circled back around to some charity ideas to help local kids that the club could be involved with.

I had no idea that they did things like toy runs and rides to raise funds for things like food banks, etcetera.

Something clicked in my mind, and I spoke up, saying, "What about raising money to pay off student lunch debt?"

Chainsaw frowned at me and asked, "Do what now? Lunch debt? What's that?"

I explained, "Low-income families are eligible to a point, for free and or reduced lunch costs at school. Some of the low-income families *still* can't afford to pay for the reduced lunch and some families make just enough to not be eligible for reduced lunch or free lunch, but can't afford school lunches for their kids or to send them with lunch."

"What happens when a kid can't pay or gets behind?" he asked.

"Well, they sometimes have the lunch confiscated at the end of the line, and it gets tossed. They're given a cold processed cheese sandwich, an apple, and a milk and that's that—"

"Holy shit, that makes no goddamn sense!"

I nodded. "I know."

"Yeah," Louie said. "I was that kid more than a few times until I got lucky enough to qualify for free lunch. It was embarrassing as hell. The other kids already gave me hell for my unwashed clothes and the fact I only had the one shirt for all of fifth grade. Having your lunch tossed in front of *everybody* was the worst."

"That's some bullshit," Chainsaw muttered.

"So, if Corliss and I plan it, and get it all figured out, would you guys do a run to clear the school's lunch debt and put money on the books for these kids?"

"Fuck, it's a good idea," Chainsaw said.

"I'd do it," Louie said without hesitation.

"Okay, then." Alina looked pleased. "I think we have a cause. Let's figure out the details."

I leaned back in my seat and looked from one to the other of the men and woman at the table with me a little shocked.

"You're serious?" I asked.

"Absolutely," Alina said without hesitation.

"That's the shit I'm talking about and why I hate the fucking government so damn much. They talk a good game but to throw out perfectly good food and hand a kid some shitty processed government bullshit because of their parents' failings or whatever? Come on! We can't do much but this is a cause I can get behind. We just need to figure out what to do."

"Crawfish boil?" Louie asked. "Twenty bucks a head, all you can eat, at the club, at the end of a ride that anybody that wants to ride with us can for like ten dollars a head?"

"There's plenty of RUBs that'd like to get in on that," Chainsaw said.

"RUBs?" I asked.

"Rich Urban Bikers," Alina supplied. "Weekend warriors of the biker world."

"Ah." I nodded.

She got up and went to the kitchen and came back with a notepad and a pen to jot things down.

Chainsaw got up and went into the kitchen to check what he had going on the stove, calling from the kitchen, "Could do a poker run."

"I'm sorry. I am so behind on this grading curve. What's that?"

It turned into a joint plotting session and crash course for me in biker speak and the world of a motorcycle club, but it was fun, and so very worth it. I wondered vaguely what Hex was up to. I hope whatever it was, he was having a good time.

CHAPTER TWENTY-SIX

*H*ex...
   The four of us were stuffed into the back of a van for transport to the booking facility. There was some random guy back here with us in street clothes and the four of us traded a look.

Axe asked, "The fuck you back here for?"

A little wide-eyed, and entirely too clean and un-roughed up, the guy tried to sell us on some bullshit story that he was a patron at the bar and had just started swinging when the swinging started. That he didn't really know why he'd been picked up.

I snorted, the rest of the boys just as skeptical, and rather than chat, we shut the fuck up – and I mean all the way up. Ignoring the dude and his leading questions about us and what we'd been doing in the bar.

We could smell bacon, and we didn't want no part of it.

At the jail, we were processed for a wide variety of charges. Seems the boys in blue decided to just throw everything at the wall, wanting to see what stuck.

Assault and battery, drunk and disorderly, destruction of property, inciting violence; you name it, we caught it.

Funny enough, though, and not gone unnoticed by me, we were the only ones *to* catch it. There wasn't a Bayou Brethren boy in sight. As soon as we went into processing for our mugshots and shit, the old boy in the back of the van with us had his cuffs taken off and said to me with a shrug, "It was worth a try."

I glared at him and spit on the sidewalk in his direction. Fucking asshole.

I used my call to phone La Croix to put things in motion. I told him to call the lawyer and to make sure that the lawyer got the damn footage from the security cameras at the bar. That Hatchet had swung first and that somehow, we were the only ones locked up. Cut and dried, this was clear targeting of our club and our boys and probably good grounds for misconduct and a dismissal, should they try to stick any of the charges to us, lookin' for jail time out of it.

Of course, La Croix and I were old hands at this shit, and we knew that these cocksuckers were listening to the call, so we spoke in a lot of code and round-about ways to get my meaning across and shit in motion on our end.

La Croix grunted in assent just as the line clicked off, my allotted time to speak up.

They tried to grill us and get us to slipup. We sang our same ol' song of '*Fuck you, I want my lawyer,*' and finally, *finally,* we were booked into custody for the weekend, after all the fun and excitement that was a strip and full cavity search, which honestly? I just thought about my Fable, of the one time we'd managed to enjoy one another, of the view of her riding my cock above me and it worked like a fucking charm. Nothing like popping a boner on a good ol' boy guard to make the motherfucker uncomfortable.

Did I have the potential to get my ass whooped for it before I got out of here? Yeah. Did I care? Nah, it'd be worth it. Plus, we still had our ace in the hole out there by way of Cypress's kin.

"Looks like they put Saint with Cy right next door," Axe said.

"Top or bottom, buddy? I ain't got a preference."

"Top," he said, and I threw some chin and took the bottom bunk.

I sighed and couldn't help but picture my girl's smile. Was I uncomfortable up in here? Hell yeah, but it would be worth it to spare her some pain.

"What now?" Axe asked.

I said, "Now, we get some rest, and we wait. This'll happen before the weekend is out. We just gotta be patient."

"A little convenient we're in here and the Bayou Brethren ain't, isn't it?" he asked.

"Yeah, I'm still thinkin' on that," I said honestly.

I had an uneasy feelin' about all of it, but I didn't have all the pieces yet to make a full picture of what it was that was going on. All I knew was I smelled a rat, but it wasn't our boys. No, this was something else, an interloper. Still, as my old man used to say, *priorities.* And our priorities as of right now were to hang tight and make sure this motherfucker got perished. Then it was getting the fuck up out of here come Monday, be it posting bail or on our own recognizance.

Saturday we were roused early, headed through to the cafeteria, and were served some slop that was supposed to be grits alongside grainy powdered egg substitute and sausage I was pretty sure didn't contain any real meat.

The four of us sat together and Cypress said, "My kins is on shift today. They got McDaniel in a separate pod, but we're gon' be escorted to the showers. We're supposed to stay behind, and he'll be brought in."

Cy, who was sittin' next to me, passed me a shiv. I stuck it in my sock, makin' like I was adjusting the ill-fitting jailhouse shoes.

"Good deal," I muttered.

We went back to eating, which I passed on it to be sure, and went about the rest of the day as normal.

I kept it cool and calm. It was after lunch when we was called up. We were escorted to the shower, and we waited after we were done. Sure enough, the rest of our unit was escorted out but when we got to the door, the last four in line, the guard stepped in front of us and put a hand up.

"Stay here. He's on his way," dude said.

"Thanks," I grunted.

He shook his head. "My cousin's kid is in one of that teacher's classes. Really loves her and is real broken up about it. I'd do anything for that kid. She's got it hard enough with her mamma havin' the cancer. You do what needs doin' and put a hurt to that bastard. Don't mind if you kill 'im. I don't think anyone in here would mind overmuch."

The guard locked eyes with me and gave a curt nod. I had to imagine the ol' boy who'd hurt my girl hadn't made any friends in here. Not with the guards and not with the other inmates as he was in segregation.

We went into the shower and waited. The shower was the only spot where there were no cameras, and I wondered briefly if this weren't a setup because there damn sure were cameras *outside* the shower room.

I looked to Cy who looked dead certain, and I put my trust in the man.

The door opened behind the shower wall then shut, and McDaniel turned the corner. He spotted us and took off running back to the door and slid in the water on the slick tile, his whole body fetching up against the door. He wasn't a big guy, which was what'd lent to his passing as a fuckin' teenager. He pounded on the inside of the door, the guard on the other side standing against it, blocking the window glass with his broad back. He'd seemingly had gone deaf because he didn't move a muscle.

Cy and Saint got a hold of the guy and dragged him back around into the shower.

"How long we got?" I asked.

"Fifteen at the most, five at the least, definitely don't go beyond ten," Cypress told me.

I looked to Axe who stepped in, drew back, and kicked the guy in the nuts as hard as he could. The man collapsed onto his stomach. His dark wheat-blond hair, that was too long in the front, fell into his eyes as he cradled the family jewels and struggled to breathe.

I stared down at him coldly and told him, "We had more time, we'd rape you. Each takin' our turn until your asshole was bloody and gaping and you begged us for more just to keep us from killin' you sooner."

Axe grinned and I knew that crazy bastard would do the work of the three of us to make that level of terror and pain a reality. He wasn't gay, but he'd buttfuck a dude just for the power trip. That's what got him hard and kept him there – the power.

I crouched down and brought the shiv around where McDaniel could see it.

"Make no mistake, you're gonna die in here," I told him. "Unlike what you did to that woman, *my* woman, I'll take no real pleasure in it."

I put an arm under his chin like I was gonna help him to his feet. The shiv probably felt like I was kneeing or punching him in the back until the burning pain set in. I went for maximum damage, punching holes in the major organs I knew I could get to – kidney, liver, guts, and finished off by punching a hole in his neck. Not really going for a quick bleed out with that. No, I wanted him to die slow. This was more a die slow by choking to death on his own blood, thing.

I washed myself quick, rinsed the shiv, and the door opened just as we were through. We left him there, bleedin' and choking,' and sure to die at any moment. We were handed towels outside the door and were escorted into the sort of locker room to pick up fresh new socks, shorts, jumpsuits, and tees. We shrugged our feet into our shoes, and we were taken back to our cell block. A lot of stares greeted us, but no one wanted to make eye contact.

These fellas weren't stupid. They knew some justice had just been served. They knew we held power in here, that we were in control, and that we weren't to be crossed.

The four of us broke apart, two of us joining a checkers game, Saint and I takin' a seat at the table where cards were bein' dealt.

"What're we playin'?" Saint asked.

A shaky fella said, "Texas hold 'em."

"What's the bet?" I asked.

"No bet. We just play with the chips like they worth somethin'," another big guy said. "Real friendly like."

"Bet, deal us in," Saint asked, and we went about quietly playing cards until the alarm sounded and the frenzy ensued of getting us all back in our cells. I caught Cypress's eye and he gave me a nod, and we all went into lockdown.

Word flew down the whisper network fast that the man that'd hurt that teacher was dead and I have to say, that jailhouse dinner never tasted finer, and I never slept better than I did that night... well, except for when my Fable was in my arms.

Still, I was anxious all through Sunday, although to look at me? I was cool as a cucumber. The day dragged, and I do mean it moved slower than molasses in January. And Monday? Monday we were called for transport to the courthouse where we met up with Cornelius.

"You boys mind telling me just what in the fuck?" he asked when he got us in a room.

"Had some business to handle," I said, and he put a hand over his mouth and rubbed his lips thoughtfully.

"Yeah, well, all of *that* aside – they sure are tryin' to git 'cha on some trumped-up charges for this li'l ol' bar fight." He looked through a file in front of him and said, "Tell me everything, and I do mean *everything,* about what happened on Friday night."

We told him everything, and he'd gone and gotten the bar surveillance. He'd see what the what when it came to the bond hearing in a bit, and was keeping that video in his shirt pocket for any eventual trial if there was one.

This wasn't going to go how law enforcement envisioned it going, but then again – we had beef enough with the Bayou Brethren at this point and it was bigger 'n what they were going to be able to handle if I was thinkin' what I was thinkin' on that front.

"I think they got something on the other club, promised 'em some kind of sweetheart deal if they helped trap us by causin' beef," I said.

"Yeah, well, where's your proof?" Cornelius asked me.

I gave him a crooked grin and said, "Get us out of here, and we'll get it."

"I don't want to know," the lawyer said. "I don't *even* want to know..."

THE LAWYER DID what we paid him to do and got us out – on our own recognizance, no less. Our trial date was set for next month, but Cornelius already had so many holes poked in their shit it wasn't even funny. He didn't even need to see their evidence to do it. They didn't know we had a copy of the bar's surveillance, and he was betting they weren't even going to try to admit it into evidence.

"The only thing worse than how corrupt the NOPD is, is how lazy they are, boys. Enjoy your freedom and try to stay out of trouble, yeah?"

He'd been uneasy at Axe's mad grin. Truth be told, I had been too.

Some of Cy's family had come to pick us up and take us back to the club, namely his sister. She'd been pissed at him, but that was just her love language – at least that was the running joke within the club. Nah, she was good people.

When she let us out the car, it was to La Croix waiting and scowling something fierce.

"What's up, P?" Saint asked him.

"Had a hell of a time getting your bikes outta impound," he said. "Cops had 'em towed outta the bar's lot before we could get there. We got 'em, but Axe, Cy, yours got some damage."

"What?" Axe looked pissed. Cy just looked discouraged.

"Saint, Hex, yours look alright, but yeah, come on an' have a look."

We went in and it wasn't too bad, but it wasn't pretty either – some serious scuffed chrome on Axe's bike and a whole ass dent and fucked-up paint along with some fucked-up chrome on Cy's.

"Son of a bitch," Cy muttered.

I told him, "Don't you worry about it. We'll get it handled. The important thing is that shit still runs."

Everything seemed to run alright, and I took my ass home. I show-ered for real with my own soaps and shit and got myself dressed in fresh clothes. Out of paranoia, I swept all my shit – both personal effects and bike – for any tracking devices and fuckery, and shot a text out over the burner lines for the boys to do the same. I started some shit up in the laundry and checked out the window at the sky which was already dusted with rose as things headed on toward sunset.

"Fuck," I muttered.

I got in my truck and headed for the bayou.

I wouldn't spend another night away from my Fable.

CHAPTER TWENTY-SEVEN

*C*orliss...

I tried calling Hex from the sat phone once or twice on Sunday but there was no answer. Well, not just no answer, but it went straight to voicemail, like the phone wasn't even turned on. I worried about him, and I could tell Alina was empathetic but that she too was a little concerned even though she'd been able to reach La Croix just fine and he'd sworn everything was all good.

It was a relief when on Monday night, we heard an approaching boat.

We both went out onto the barge and there was a weak spotlight out there, sweeping the swamp and waterway ahead of two figures in a boat.

It was La Croix and Hex, and I was so relieved.

"I was getting so worried," I cried as they approached.

Hex chuckled and said, "It's all good, sorry, Fable, weekend didn't go *entirely* as planned."

"What happened?" Alina asked, taking and tying off the line he tossed her as La Croix brought the shallow aluminum boat up alongside the barge.

"Hex and a few of the boys ended up in jail," La Croix called back simply.

"*What?*" I cried.

"I'm starving, can we talk over somethin' to eat?" Hex asked, taking me into his arms as soon as his boots hit the barge deck.

I held myself to him and looked up. I didn't bother to disguise the worry in my eyes. He leaned down and kissed me and it was wonderful. I melted, and I couldn't help myself. Hex had become my haven and I felt so many things it could get confusing sometimes.

"Come inside," I murmured and so we went in.

Alina and I had decided on easy for dinner and had a family sized lasagna in the oven and were in the midst of preparing a salad to go with it when the boys had come home. They took seats at the dining table. Alina pulled a couple beers from the fridge and popped the top, handing me one for Hex. I brought it to him and he took a drink, pulling me into his lap.

"So, what happened?" I asked.

"Cypress had a run-in out in the swamps with some poachers. A few of us went on up to Swamp Daddy's for a drink and the poachers were there. A fight broke out over it, and we all ended up in the clink for the weekend," he said and I bit my bottom lip.

"You can go on and say the rest," La Croix said.

Hex raised an eyebrow, and Alina and I traded a look.

"What's the rest?" Alina asked.

"The poachers belong to an MC outside the city, the Bayou Brethren. They're harmless for the most part, but they been takin' up more and more of their leisure time inside the city limits. Just keep a watchful eye out for now. We don't think there'll be more problems but could be a little bit of a turf spat in our future."

"How bad is this?" I asked Hex, searching his face. He smiled up at me, but the smile didn't reach his eyes when he said, "It's fine. We've encountered this type of shit before. I'm sure we will again, but we'll get through it."

I nodded slowly and murmured, "Thank you for telling us. I know this falls under the purview of 'club business' and that it could be bad for you for saying."

La Croix lowered his beer and shook his head. "We took it to a vote to disclose. We don't trust these fools to have any honor among thieves so to speak. They've already proven they don't by poaching lines. We don't think they're a threat, but you girls can't watch for a danger you know nothing about. The club decided better safe than sorry."

I took my time to process the information and finally nodded and said, "But you think it will be okay?"

"I know things'll be alright," Hex said, and he turned his mouth up for a kiss, one that I gave him gratefully.

"I'm so sorry your weekend was ruined," I murmured, and he smiled.

"Can't win 'em all, and besides – jail wasn't all that bad. I got to share a cell with Axe. It was like bein' back at summer camp when I was a kid."

Alina snorted and I had to laugh too. "Now I *know* you're telling tall tales."

We had dinner, and I could tell that Hex was tired. Even though I just wanted to go home with him, when he quietly asked me, as we lounged together on the couch, if we could crash here and head back in the morning tomorrow morning? I couldn't say no. I was just happy to be with him.

I told him about all the emails which I had spent the weekend combing through and responding to, and he told me a little bit about what jail had been like, saying it was mostly boring more than anything.

"Do-do you think it will make you lose your job?" I asked and he chuckled.

"I'm not worried about it," he said. "I don't think they'll shitcan me for the arrest, but a conviction? Yeah, I'd lose it for sure, then. But I'm not going to get convicted. I doubt it will even see the inside of a courtroom."

"How come?" I asked.

"Cops played dirty. Took us in but didn't arrest a single one of the poachers from the other club. Security footage is gonna show they threw the first punch, and we were just defending ourselves."

I reached up and touched the bruise at his cheekbone that climbed around the outside of his eye, but somehow didn't give him a whole shiner.

"It'll get thrown out," La Croix said with a yawn. Alina shifted on his chest slightly and snuggled in.

I smiled, happy for them, and for myself.

"I hope it does," I murmured. "School wouldn't be the same without you either," I said to Hex. I was referencing some of the things the students had said about me in their emails, begging me to come back soon. Some were lamenting how boring the substitute was, and that had made me smile.

I was making a difference, in only my second year of teaching, and it was all I had ever wanted. The moment of realization was made more perfect when Hex kissed my forehead, sliding his hand up and down my back in a light and soothing pass.

"Mm," La Croix grunted. "I'm taking my woman to bed," he declared.

"You are, huh?" Alina asked, all smiles.

"Fuckin' right I am," he said, giving her ass a little swat. She laughed a throaty and full-bodied sound and clambered off him and the recliner they were in.

"We're headed that way, too," Hex declared. "After I get my woman in the shower. I took one when I get home but, man, I still feel like I got that place on me."

I felt my face crumple into lines of empathy, and I got up carefully, holding down my good hand and saying softly, "Come on."

"Have fun, you two," Alina said as she and La Croix trailed up the stairs to their bedroom in the loft.

Once in the bathroom, Hex shut the door behind us and turned back to me, coming to me to kiss me with purpose. I kissed him back and melded to his front and said, "I want to try again."

We'd made love only once before, and I'd paid for it the next day. It'd been worth it to me, though Hex had put a moratorium on going any further until I was more healed. I wasn't sure what a difference a week would make, but I was keen to find out and desperate to feel him against my skin, moving inside of me once more.

"We'll see," he rumbled against my ear as he kissed along my jaw.

I put my hand to his chest, and he drew back to look at me. I looked up at him solemnly and said, "I need you inside of me."

His lips twitched into a pleased smile, and he didn't even come close to rejecting me again, simply saying, "Okay."

He kissed me slow and sweet then, his hands careful and gentle as he started working at our clothing, to take it off. He'd left his jacket and cut hanging off one of the dining room's chairs. That was less that we had to go through, although Alina had to tell him to take off his coat and to stay awhile earlier. It was as though he'd worn it like armor, and now, the way he kissed me... it was fraught with the kind of energy that said he was home and desperate to erase something he'd seen or that he'd done. I couldn't imagine that was something a simple bar fight would bring on.

Then it clicked.

I leaned back, cocked my head, and said, "You did it on purpose, didn't you?"

He cocked his head in the opposite direction of mine, mirroring me subconsciously, and a slow smile filled with an amused pride spread his lips.

"Say what's on your mind, baby."

"You went to that bar. You got in that fight..." I swallowed nervously. "And you did it on purpose. You *wanted* to get arrested. You did what you said you were going to do, didn't you?" I asked.

He searched my face and all but confirmed it when he said, "Nobody hurts my girl and lives to talk about it, or to hurt her some more by making her go through a bunch more bullshit that she doesn't want or need."

There was a darkness in my heart that rose to the surface. It was a darkness that I knew had always been. The same darkness that had left me sighing with relief at my mother's passing. The same darkness that had made me glad for it, in knowing that she couldn't or wouldn't let me down ever again. The relief that'd flooded my veins like its own sordid drug that I wouldn't ever have to be disappointed, or scared of her, or hurt by her, or worry about what one of her boyfriends would try and do ever again.

It was the same sense of relief that flooded my veins now. I know it wasn't something that was healthy or good for me, and it was definitely toxic… but I couldn't help myself from falling absolutely head over heels in love with the man in front of me for doing it.

I pulled him to me with both arms, ignoring the sharp pain in my chest and shoulder from my protesting and still healing collarbone as I pulled him to me, and breathed out, "Thank you," before dragging his mouth to mine.

I was the fabled princess in that moment, and he was my brave knight, my prince charming, who had slew the dragon.

I know that it was likely awful of me to feel this way but damnit, I would spend the rest of my days making it up to the universe. I swore it. I would be good in every other way, but I would embrace this and revel in this moment. The monster was dead, and I wouldn't have to face him again. I wouldn't have to face the stuff of nightmares and that was so precious to me.

"Careful, your arm," Hex growled against my mouth when I pressed to him too tightly and wound up making an unconscious mewling pain sound into his mouth.

I put it back down, where it needed to be, and said, "It's fine."

He tipped back from me slightly and said with the first real vulnerability I'd ever seen in his eyes, "So, you don't think I'm a monster?"

"No, you're my knight in shining armor if you're anything. You slew the monster," I said honestly.

He smiled and said, "On my trusty iron steed." I bit down on my laugh. I didn't want to disturb Alina and La Croix.

"Take a shower with me," I murmured. "Make love to me and leave that place and all of that shit behind for a while."

He smiled at me and said, "Fucking hell, I love you."

I was warmed from the crown of my head to the tips of my toes, and I would have said "I love you, too," except his mouth was on mine all over again and with a renewed sense of desperate urgency.

No, not urgency – *joy*.

As much as he was the one person, the thing that made me happy? I was the thing that made *him* complete. I felt it in that moment soul deep – that we were each other's person, and I felt my heart soar, I mean really soar, for what was likely the first time ever. I felt it take off unfettered. It wasn't weighted as it'd been with Mark, wondering how long things would last until the other shoe dropped. Desperately trying to win his love and affection back when he grew bored. I had no fear of that with Hex, because he was a man and not a child, and I needed that. I needed that and I desperately wanted to be that for him, too.

He undressed us, got the shower going and got us into it. It was beautiful, and I had to believe it was also his work or that he had a hand in its construction, but all of those thoughts fled under the touch of his hands on my skin and the way his tongue thrust against mine, tangling and twisting, slipping along mine in this tantalizing way. I don't think I'd ever kissed a man so skilled with his tongue, and I remembered keenly just how much I'd enjoyed it elsewhere.

I pressed my thighs together as he backed me into the warmth of the shower spray and moaned into his mouth as he slicked his hands with soap and ran them over my skin. Sensual and slick, I loved how he touched me and it just served to get me even more excited.

"God, I want you in me," I moaned against his mouth.

"No condom," he grunted.

I giggled against his mouth and put my lips to his ear and said, "Worth the risk this time."

He groaned and drew back and said, "You get knocked up, I'll be happy either way, boy or girl, but, woman, you give me a son and I will love you forever."

I laughed and threw caution to the wind and said, "If it happens, it happens."

He put his mouth against mine all over again and made me swallow my gasp as he pressed me against the cool stone tiles of the shower wall.

I kept my bad arm tucked to my side, and my good one, I wrapped around his shoulders.

His touch made my body glow and I couldn't help but wriggle against him, trying for more skin contact as he smoothed his hands over me and stepped closer, pressing me against the wall as we kissed in the warm shower spray.

"I don't want to accidentally hurt you," he growled, and I smiled.

All I could think to say was, "Then don't."

He laughed a little and pulled me to him, away from the wall, and turned me around by my hips.

I pressed my hand against it, and rounded my back, thrusting my hips out, practically begging for a more intimate touch. He made an appreciative noise and ran his hands down my back and over my hips.

"Just like that, baby. Stay just like that," he said. I bit my bottom lip and arched my stomach down, thrusting out my hips just that little bit more for him.

He ran the head of his cock up and down my pussy lips, and I groaned with need, thrusting back just the little bit that I could, to encourage him.

He moaned and pressed inside of me. It was all I could do to keep myself up with how weak in the knees that it made me.

"Fuck, yes." His breath, cooler than the steamy shower, caressed my back with a hint of the whiskey he'd drunk, and it gave me the shivers in all the right ways. I pressed against the wall, and he started to move, and *oh yes,* right like that. That felt so good.

Was it graceful? No, not even close. Do you think either of us cared in that moment? Absolutely not. Not when it was getting the job done so well.

He rode me from behind, snaking an arm around my waist to run his fingers back and forth over my clit. It unfortunately shortened his thrusting that much more, but that was okay. He was relentless and was sure to get me there, regardless.

I panted and concentrated on the feel of him, closing my eyes and moaning even as he groaned against my back, pressing his forehead against the base of my neck as though he was concentrating very hard on not coming too early.

I don't know how long we were like that, but I do know it probably felt much longer than it actually was. It was driving me crazy, not being able to enjoy each other fully because of my stupid arm. Still, as frustrating as it was, I would take what I could get, and right now, he was giving it his all with as much restraint as he could muster to protect me. That was something so sweet and so wonderful and so *everything*, I mean, literally everything that I had ever wanted that I grew emotional.

I felt this wellspring open up in the center of my chest, even as the orgasm came out of seemingly nowhere and *rocked* me. Absolutely rolled me, drawing me tight around him and sending me out into the atmosphere in rippling rolling waves of pleasure. I felt him drive into me and grunt, holding me around my middle and pulling his arm tight around me as he came with me, and it was a beautiful moment.

He slipped from me, and I straightened after a few breaths. He drew me back to him with both arms and cuddled me close as we stood under the warm patter of the shower's spray and both panted, catching our breaths.

"Damn, I don't last long enough with you," he complained, and I smiled.

"You last long enough, lover, and that's what matters," I said, leaning my head back against his shoulder and tipping my mouth up to his for a kiss.

I felt so whole and so cherished, so *safe* in Hex's arms, that I wouldn't trade it for anything.

CHAPTER TWENTY-EIGHT

*H*ex...

  Waking up with her in my arms the next morning after what had to have been the best sleep of my fuckin' life was like a goddamn dream, only better, because it'd been real.

She'd been sore, and not in the right places, her collarbone giving her fits and makin' her hurt somethin' fierce. It could have been the sex, but it also could have been the changing weather. We'd managed to get to the dock just fine, the four of us, after buttoning up the houseboat but *damn*. We were soaked, my lady shivering with cold.

I made it a point to turn on the radio for the drive home, to the AM station and the local news network.

"Why don't you put on some music?" she asked me after only a little while, and it helped that that was when it happened.

"Justin McDaniel, the twenty-three-year-old man that was posing as a ninth grader in order to assault one of the teachers at Lakeside High School was killed Saturday afternoon in an apparent suicide at the Orleans Parish Jail. He was set to begin trial for the rape and assault of a female teacher at the school in the coming weeks. The district attorney's office released a statement this morning, saying that while they're disappointed that the teacher wouldn't receive the justice

she so richly deserves, they hope that this brings her some kind of closure and that she can heal more swiftly without a trial hanging over her head..."

I switched the radio off and she looked at me a little wide-eyed.

"Now when the cops reach you, it won't be a lie when you tell them you heard it on the news first."

"Suicide?" she asked.

I shrugged. "Police coverup at its finest. They don't want to lose face and have to admit they couldn't catch who shivved that mother-fucker in the shower. Honestly, why investigate? Nothin' of value's been lost, and it would just be an expensive investigation to cost them a lot of money, only to have to spend even more money to house the guy that did it, when absolutely no one is sad that I did."

She swallowed hard, and I reached over and put a hand on her knee. She put her hand over mine and gave it a squeeze and said, "It doesn't seem real, you know? That that's it. There is no more and it's really over."

"I hear you," I said. "But that's the way it is. The news only cares about it so long as it rakes in the ratings. The guy was just a disturbed individual that made a bunch of people in authority look real fuckin' bad." He sighed and said, "I know you'd like to think it's over, baby, but it's not. Their next step will be to do everything in their power to keep you from suing the shit out of the school and the district as you probably should be."

She sat back in her seat.

"Sue?" she asked. "I mean, do I even have a case? Wouldn't that make me lose my job?"

I shook my head.

"Hell no, they'd be stupid to fire you for anything. Not only would that put them on the hook for retaliation and wrongful termination, but they also don't want to make themselves a straight-up villain in this saga when they just look incompetent as fuck right now."

She looked thoughtful and when we got closer to the city where I knew that cell service cleaned up, I told her, "Why don't you go on and restart your phone and see if you've missed anything."

Sure enough, she had *several* missed calls – not only from the police tryin' to reach her for a meeting but also from several ambulance chasing lawyers lookin' to cash in. I told her to ignore the latter, but that I did think it was a good idea to lawyer up. I wanted to ask Cornelius for a good civil attorney. Someone a hell of a lot more trustworthy than what was blowing up her phone.

She was going to call the cops back and agree to have them meet with her, but I wasn't too keen on them coming to the house. I didn't want them putting two and two together with me there. Not that I thought they were competent enough to do it – most of the time not so much – but why tempt fate?

I sound boarded my thoughts and concerns off my Fable and she said, "Easy enough. I'll agree to meet them at the station tomorrow, or when they come to the house, you just won't be there. Go to the club or something."

"Good plan," I agreed.

"That or I lawyer up first and have them meet me at my lawyer's office."

I nodded. "I like that idea better, but I suppose that any of the above will do."

After I got us home, I called Cornelius and got a referral to a good civil attorney, and we contacted them.

The next day, my girl met with her and the cops, who were indeed trying to notify her of McDaniel's death. They went to her lawyer's office to speak with my girl, at my girl's request, and said they'd been cool about it. She said she'd thanked them, and that she'd heard on the radio on the way back from a weekend spent out with her friend in the bayou for her mental health. They bought it. She said they were very kind and understanding and didn't give her any shit for having them meet her at her attorney's, and that was all I cared about.

It was a load off my shoulders as I was at work and couldn't be waiting in the wings as much as I'd like while she handled this. Not gonna lie, that low-key'd like to drive me nuts.

As for me, I'd gone into work and gave ol' Curtis the skinny on my troubles over the weekend, although I heavily edited some things. I just told him I was out with some buddies of mine and things got outta hand between them and some other fellas, and I got picked up.

I figured it was better to tell on myself than have it go down any other way. I was pulled into ol' Mrs. Donal's office for a sit-down and she was none too pleased, though her disposition softened when I told her it was purely self-defense, which was the truth, and that I would be happy to do whatever she thought was best.

She told me to keep it quiet and that we would have to wait and see the outcome. That if I was convicted that it would have to be an automatic dismissal. I told her the truth, that I didn't see that happening, and it was a wait and see from there, which was alright with me.

She did let me use accrued sick leave to cover the Monday and Tuesday I missed, so at least there was that.

As for the rest? Well, Cor and I tried our damnedest to settle into a new sort of normal, which was hard to do with as much renovation as the house needed and my sudden desire to make this house into the home I'd always wanted and that she'd always needed.

It was like my Fable was the missing link, and I was suddenly inspired to do so much with the place. I wholeheartedly wanted her input every step of the way.

Corliss did what she could during the day with cleaning and keeping up with her physical therapy and doctor appointments. It became a full-time job, jockeying between labor and industries and workman's comp claims and her regular insurance to get everything covered, but her lawyer assured her, everything was going to wind up paid. Her credit wasn't going to take a hit and that she'd have a tidy sum to do with what she pleased by the time she was done with everything.

Corliss, true to her fashion and her ways, didn't care about the money. She just cared that this wasn't going to hurt her return to the classroom and that she would be able to continue teaching.

Weeks went by, and I spent every evening I could working on the living room and making that nook above the office while Cor did what she could to help, and mostly just sat nearby reading and spending time with me, keeping me company while I worked. It was nice.

Her period came, and I was pretty grateful for it but also a little let down. I wanted a child with her, but I also understood that this was more than a little soon to be thinkin' about that. I needed to calm my shit when it came to that until such a time was right.

That first week back was a short one and a blur that blended into the next, which blended right into the next. Shit was honestly just a whirlwind.

I wanted Cor with a fire that was unmatched, but with her period coming on, her arm in the shape it was in, and how she'd hurt both times after we'd been intimate, I learned to deal with the abstinence really damn quick.

That was until the day she came home from physical therapy as I was working on fixing some dinner at the stove and *two* arms wound around my waist.

"Whoa-ho, look out now!" I cried as one hand drifted to the front of my jeans and massaged me through them. It took a minute for me to register what was going on and when it did, I straightened and turned in the circle of her arms to look at her.

"Well, I'll be!" I declared and her giggle was everything.

"Hi," she said and held up both of her hands. "Look, pa – two hands!"

I laughed at her stupid joke and pulled her laughing and giggling into my arms and said, "One, I don't do that daddy shit, and two – om nom, nom!" I attacked the side of her neck with my lips over my teeth and listened to her shriek with glee.

"Oh, my God!" she cried, laughing, and her laughter was infectious.

It was everything in me to *not* switch off the stove and to drag her into the bedroom to do more than just cop a little oral or commit some mutual masturbation which is what we'd pretty much been limited to with her body's need to heal.

Instead, I backed off for now, kissed her soundly, and we celebrated with a nice pasta meal and a glass of wine with dinner, now that she'd been off her medicines – specifically painkillers for a while now.

We were doing the dishes together, her rinsing, me loading the dishwasher when the mood shifted. Something in me just broke as I took in her profile at the sink, all graceful sweeping lines and smooth skin just calling to me...

There was a reason I called this woman Fable that had nothing to do with her reading habits. She was a dream come true, legendary in her beauty, wit, and intelligence and a fable made real in my eyes. I had no idea how to go about expressing it with words, but touch... touch was a whole other thing, and I ached to touch her the way she was meant to be touched.

We kissed, and my hands on her ribs, smoothing down that to-die-for hourglass shape she had going on, flaring subtly to her hips, I walked back, luring her in the direction of the bedroom.

She followed me, her hands on my chest, gripping my tee in needy fistfuls, drifting along before me as I walked backward and holding to me as though she would die if she let go.

Her mouth on mine was phenomenal, her taste so sweetly divine. She was true ambrosia, and I relished in everything about her as she was a feast for my senses.

I worked us out of our clothing slowly and felt a thrill that this was finally happening and something I could do with her.

She cuddled close in the slight chill of the room even as the heat kicked on momentarily to get the house to seventy. It was a cool forty-two out there for the south, the daytime high for this time of year below the average high of sixty-something, but all mundane thoughts of the weather and any notice of the chill to the room disappeared when she wrapped sure fingers around my cock and stroked over its sensitive head.

"Oh, fuck," I moaned, and I threw my head back and stood still, just focusing on the feel of her hand around me, stroking over me, the warmth of her body so close to mine. I looked down into her blue eyes as she looked up at me with this impish smile. Once she had my attention, very slowly, very deliberately, she got down on her knees and took me into her mouth.

I very nearly spontaneously combusted right then and there.

I watched her suck me, gently pulling back her hair and playing with it, luxuriating in the silken strands between my fingers even as her hot, wet, velveteen mouth very nearly made my soul leave my fucking body.

"Shit, babe, slow down," I panted and the little shit? She just smiled around my cock with those blue eyes of hers looking up at me and I lost my fucking mind.

CHAPTER TWENTY-NINE

*C*orliss...

I pushed him to the back of my throat and swallowed when he came, he looked down at me, completely undone and I could tell he was pleased, but also... not, but at the same time that it was okay. How could I tell all of this? By the hard look in his eyes offset by this sexy as hell smirk that almost undid *me* just by the look of it.

I backed off and wiped my lips and he reached down a hand to help me to my feet. I got up, and he turned me and with a hand to my chest shoved me giggling and half shrieking with laughter onto the bed. Diving over the top of me and pressing me into the mattress.

"You're just going to have to suffer my wrath for making me come so quick," he growled, and I giggled.

"And what does that look like?" I asked playfully.

He kissed me soundly, and I loved that he didn't care or make a big deal about my just having his dick in my mouth. He worked his way down my body, making me gasp as he took one of my nipples into his mouth, pinching and rolling the other between forefinger and thumb, rolling it between them to a wonderful and tantalizing effect. Sensation blooming in my chest and washing down through my body and almost feeling like it made contact with what was going on down below.

The look in his eyes as he watched me heated my blood that much more as I lay back and with a pleasured smile touching my lips told him, "Do your worst!"

He popped my nipple from his mouth and with a rakish grin that I knew was on his lips despite my closed eyes, he said, "Challenge accepted, darlin'." God, the way his smile touched his voice… it was a turn on in and of itself.

His lips against my stomach, taking his time to work his way down my body had me practically writhing under him with anticipation. I couldn't help my sudden gasp as he kissed my pussy lips, gently teasing them apart with his tongue, making this sound like I was the best thing he'd ever tasted. He sucked my clit into his mouth to gently capture it with his teeth, pleasing it with the tip of his tongue in that way that had me losing my goddamned *mind* less than three seconds into his sweet torture.

I moaned, gripping his hair, tangling my fingers in its short strands as best I could, pressing his mouth to me, and he growled against me. The bass thrum of the sound sending shivers through me that was half thrill and half base primal prey instinct. It was absolutely sensationally delicious the way he played that fine line of thrill and fear with me and I absolutely adored it.

I adored everything he did to me, but still… it was as though something were missing and this time was the first time that felt different. Like the fetters were off and we were both one hundred percent free to test each other's limits up to and including crossing some lines and that? Oh, I wanted that. I wanted so much to see how far we could go. How far he would take me now; and I trusted him implicitly to take me such wondrous places that I lay back and simply let him do his worst, which I already knew would be the very best.

"Hex," I breathed, my tone taking on a note of begging as he worked me up slowly with his mouth, taking his time. He just chuckled darkly against me and wouldn't be swayed whatsoever to going any faster or any harder with me no matter how I panted or begged and it was a joyful sort of infuriating.

"Oh, my God! Don't make me beg!" I cried, and he chuckled

against me again, a sort of little boy glee despite the very adult position we were in and it was a delightful sound. I was about to smack him when he introduced fingers inside of me, curling them toward the roof of my cunt, pressing down on my lower stomach between my pelvic bones to bring that special spot to his fingertips inside me.

The combination of the rough pads of his fingertips against that textured patch of nerves so close to the surface inside me, and the feel of his hot velvet tongue against that sensitive nub at the apex of my thighs on the outside?

"Oh, shit! Oh, fuck!" I collapsed back and arched, everything feeling as though I'd opened up and I mean opened beyond anything physically. This was so good, so hot, wet, tight, and wonderful that it was damn near a spiritual awakening of some kind.

"Hex!" I cried, so close, so on the verge of something intensely splendid it was frightening – I was almost afraid.

"Just relax and let it happen, baby," he growled against my body. "I've got you."

I trusted him completely and let go and I swear by all things that are holy, if what he did to me was meant to be the devil's work or whatever you could send me straight to Hell and I would go happily.

He made me come so hard and so swift after he quit playing, that I thought I would never come back from wherever we went when the sex was so toe curling and great you lost vision and forgot to breathe.

I got back with it to him grinning down at me, kneeling up between my thighs as he rolled the condom snug around his thick base. I panted, dragging my breath into lungs that somehow didn't feel like mine anymore as he wrapped one of his strong arms at my lower back. I was limp as he hauled me up some and it forced my back and my abs into this delicious stretch that felt so good it bordered on pain.

He fitted his cock at my sopping entrance and didn't hold any mercy this time as he plunged into me balls deep.

I wrapped my arms around his shoulders and slid down his body fitting him inside me as snug as he could fit. I settled over him and he wrapped strong arms around me to hold me to him in a position that would otherwise be awkward.

"Gon' take it nice an' easy for you baby," he said and somehow rolled his hips just right in a way that made me gasp as I looked down into those warm brown eyes of his. I put my lips to his and we kissed as he made love to me slow for a little while and let me calm down some from my last orgasm.

The way he managed to shift beneath me in counterpoint to the way I rode him when I could finally feel my legs enough to do it was nothing short of pure magic.

He was warm and solid against my body, my arms tight around him, and I found myself coiling tighter and living for his touch, the way he kissed me, the way he held me, the way he let me take control of the pace and the wild magic between us for a while, only to flip the script once he'd deemed it enough.

I loved how he man-handled me, how he lifted me seemingly so easily to retake control, dropping me back onto the mattress, driving himself deep, hooking an arm behind my leg to drive deeper still. The feel of him so far inside me scrambled my thoughts to the point it was like an old television, the picture being sucked down and into the depths of the old tube except for me it was down, down, so impossibly far down into the warmth, safety, and pleasure he provided that I simply twined my arms around him and gave in to whatever it was he wanted to give me with perfect love and perfect trust.

He did not disappoint.

He struck an even, deep, slow rolling rhythm that curled my toes and rode deliciously over that spot inside me and I felt as though he plucked at the very fiber of my being, unraveling me slowly but surely into little more than the dust of the stars we were all born from.

"God, you feel so fucking good," he growled, and I felt myself glow from the praise.

I turned his face with a light touch of my palm and thanked him wordlessly with a kiss, a kiss he returned just as truly, madly, and deeply as he made love to me and being like this, with Hex, was nothing short of magic.

He cast a spell on me, for sure, but certainly not one of his namesake's varieties. How could being hexed or cursed feel so damn good or make me so damn happy?

~

I WAS DROWSING against his chest in that hazy exhausted state of being well fucked. My body was deliciously languid but also slightly sore which promised to be worse in the morning if I didn't get up and stretch.

"Suppose this means you've thought about going back to the class-room, then?" he asked, his voice slightly rough with being on that edge of just getting ready to fall asleep.

We lay close in the dark of his – *our* bedroom, I amended firmly in my mind. He'd been on me quite a bit lately to stop asking permission to do little things around the house, reminding me often that I lived here, too and that wasn't changing. I guess I just needed to get used to the notion that this was a permanent place for me; not something shifting and ever-changing like I was used to.

We'd talked about that a time or two, but I always shied from the topic of my mental and emotional damage as soon as things got just a little too uncomfortable.

Surprising to no one, least of all myself, his question struck a bit of a nerve…

"I know I have to go back, but I also know I'll never be quite ready for it," I confessed, and I felt him move beneath me, to look down at me. I cuddled in closer so that moving around wasn't quite the best option for him and made a bit of a pouting noise. He chuckled slightly at the sound of my pout at his having moved, but the desired effect had been achieved, he stilled and his hand smoothed over my nude back beneath the sheet, warming it.

"Talk to me, baby," he said quietly when the silence had become too protracted. "You remember something?"

"No," I said softly. "And truthfully, that almost seems scarier and more fucked up than if I had…"

He grunted in slight agreement, as though what I'd just said made perfect sense to him, and he kissed my forehead.

"I'm glad you don't," he declared, and I smiled and snuggled a little tighter into his side.

"I think I'm more afraid of remembering than I am of the missing memories sometimes, then others I... I don't know. It's like this pervading sense of dread to go back, you know?"

"Dread because you're low-key afraid it's going to happen again?" he asked. "Or more about the kids makin' fun of you or tryin' to give you a hard time about it?"

I thought about that for a minute. I mean *really* thought about it.

"Maybe a little bit of both?" I hazarded to guess. "I mean, I don't really know how I feel about any of it and I don't really want to explore it all that much. I just wish I could bury it; you know?"

He gave me a little squeeze and kissed my forehead and said, "I know."

I settled against him and told the truth, "I'm so grateful for you."

He chuckled lightly and said, "You know, I'll be there, right? Every day, makin' sure you're okay."

I hadn't thought of that... and even still... "But what about...?"

I didn't need to finish; he knew exactly what I was talking about. His court date was coming up for the bar fight he'd been in and even though he seemed unfazed, I worried...

"Don't you worry about me, baby girl," he said. "Things are gonna be fine."

He gave me a squeeze and kissed my forehead once more and the tension just drained out of me, his touch pure magic in that regard.

"Get some sleep, baby. We got time to figure it all out. One thing at a time, you know?"

I nodded, and he made sure the blankets were tucked up around me.

"I love you," I murmured just before I fell asleep. The only answer I got was a tender kiss to my forehead and a tighter hold on me.

I loved that, too.

CHAPTER THIRTY

*H*ex...

"Dismissed!" the judge said curtly and banged his gavel. Cornelius smirked at the prosecuting attorney and gave him a wink.

"Not very sporting like of me, but that sumbitch had it coming," Cornelius muttered as he put a hand to my back to follow the rest of my boys out the courtroom.

Out in the hall, hands were shaken and out of the corner of my eye I saw Corliss raise her chin and rise off the bench in the hall. She was insistent on bein' here, but I'd asked her to wait outside. She looked apprehensive and Cornelius, eagle-eyed as he was asked me, "That your lady?"

I nodded, and he cocked his head.

"Ain't she that teacher?"

"Shut it," I growled warningly as she approached.

"Well?" she asked nervously.

"Dismissed, all charges dropped," Cornelius bragged before I could say anything.

Her shoulders sagged with relief and her arms went around me. I put an arm around her shoulders and she leaned into me.

"For as much as we pay you, you need to keep it that way," La Croix said, wandering up with Alina on his arm from where they'd been sitting with my girl.

"Oh, ye of little faith, my friends. Oh, ye of little faith..." Cornelius chuckled and shaking his head wandered up the hall no doubt to work on something for somebody else.

"He seems nice," Corliss said without a hint of irony.

"He's alright," Saint said begrudgingly, already working his tie loose.

I couldn't wait to get out of my monkey suit myself but it was almost worth wearin' the damn thing just to see my girl's reaction. Mostly that she couldn't keep her hands off of me.

I'd made a joke about cleanin' up nice when I needed to, and the heat in her gaze had made my slacks tight in the crotch region. Made me want to clean up just for the hell of it, see what she could do with herself, and take her out for a night on the town.

It was definitely something I was looking forward to, but first... first I wanted to do this Christmas charity thing she'd turned some of the boys onto.

I didn't exactly know the particulars. She'd put her head together with Chainsaw and Alina back when she'd stayed out in the swamp and they'd come up with something about clearing the lunch debt for the kids at our school. It'd caught like wildfire with a lot of our boys having some experience growing up food insecure themselves and it'd damn near been unanimously voted on to make it our thing this year and maybe every year if we did well enough.

Bennie was in charge of the books and he'd said things were lookin' good. I'd been a little preoccupied with makin' sure that we were gonna get off the hook with these bullshit charges and more 'n that? We were explorin' to see if we had grounds for a suit somewhere in there against the NOPD I didn't have high hopes of that goin' anywhere, though. Still, it'd be nice. We had an active suit going, just about anything they tried to do for the next minute while that was gettin' resolved would look like retaliation.

There was still a lot in the air, but that was alright. With the holidays right around the corner, Christmas a comin', things were slowing down some to let us all breathe and take a minute to focus on a thing or two at a time instead of everything all at once.

"Let's get the fuck outta here and out of these damn clothes?" Axe asked and La Croix nodded.

"Meet up at the club in," he checked his watch, "two, two-and-a-half hours."

"You got it," I said with a nod and I was a little jazzed. That was enough time to get home, and either get naked with my woman or to take her on what was bound to be the second greatest ride of her life – I'd still had yet to get her on the back of my bike and God *damn* did I want to.

The weather out there was cool, crisp, and maybe not the best for a ride – but it was also sunny and dry, and she'd do alright as long as she had some gloves on and the like.

We chatted for a few with the boys as we made our way out of the courthouse and finally broke off to make our way over to my truck. I tucked her up safe and sound in the passenger seat and made my way around to the driver's side.

"So, what now?" she asked and I smiled.

"Now we go home, get a change of clothes, and I take you for a ride."

A small smile curled her lips, and she raised an eyebrow, asking mischievously, "Oh? What *kind* of ride?"

"You're a woman after my own heart," I said with a laugh, pressing the button and starting up the truck.

Her laugh was high, clear, and bright as I pulled us out of the spot I'd backed into and headed for home.

It was everything in me to keep my hands off of her, to keep things from going further which was hard as hell with the way she kissed me and undressed me. She had this way about her – the way she looked at me, no matter how many times she saw me strip or she was the one doing the stripping she unwrapped me like a present and looked at me with this rawness this gratitude, like *she* was the one that ought to be grateful.

Wasn't that some bullshit?

I wasn't worthy, and I knew that… but I'd try to live up to as if I were every fuckin' day to the end of time.

I'd do anything for her. Her smile soothed my soul and her laugh healed parts of me that I hadn't even realized were broken. I didn't know how else to put it, but one night La Croix and I got to talkin' and some of this got to spillin' and it was an eye-opening experience, that was for sure.

There were times you'd like to forget that La Croix was just a man. Certainly, it was easy to forget he had any type of feelings… but that night I'd caught a glimpse of just how deeply that man felt about his woman and had some realizations about just how much I felt for my own.

Did she have some habits that drove me nuts? Sure. Like how she seemed to apologized for literally everything, even when there wasn't a thing to be sorry about. Or how she *still*, after months of living with me, would ask me stupid shit like permission to do this or that to the house.

It was to the point of ridiculous – but some of that had eased off with the completion of the loft above the guest room, just off the living room, the one I'd gifted her and said to make it her own.

The one she'd stared up at, a blank canvas – hers to create a space to do with what she wished, and she'd tried so very hard not to cry when she asked if she could make it a little library. A cozy nook and reading space for herself. I told her she didn't have to ask me shit – that that was what *'hers'* meant.

She'd calmed down on asking permission for things and asking if X, Y, or Z was alright with me but then the barrage of "what do you think of this?" or "what do you think about that?" had started. While they still would like to needle me – it wasn't half so irritating with the way her eyes shone with excitement as we scrounged and thrifted and she got on with Alina making some magic up there and turning the space into something I couldn't even begin to tell you. It certainly was something magical. She even found a corner desk thing for her laptop and grading and such.

I was dragged out of my thoughts when I dragged a tee shirt over my head and her hands on my flanks stopped me.

"What's up?" I asked, looking down at her, and she asked me, "What's *your* hurry?"

I smiled down at her and reached up from my side to palm her cheek and run a thumb over her smooth skin.

"Well, I figured why we had the time, even though it's short, it was high time we took you for your first ride."

Her squeal of excitement was damn near earsplitting as she leaped up and flung her arms around my neck. I laughed, I mean, how could I not, and returning her hug I held her close for a minute and told her, "Go on and get dressed now. Jeans, boots, all that like I showed you."

"Okay," she said but had to kiss me soundly before she complied.

I slipped my wallet in my back pocket, and threaded my worn leather belt through its loops, watching her scurry around the bedroom like the most adorable little creature you'd ever seen. Like an excited ferret or something, which I know, I know, not the best thing in the world to compare your girlfriend to an excited ferret but that's seriously what it reminded me of. That kind of cute that forced a smile so big onto your face that your damn cheeks hurt.

"Dress on the warmer side, darlin' it's a bit on the colder side out there," I reminded her and she nodded and pulled a pair of leggings out of her bottom drawer to layer up under her jeans.

"That's my girl," I praised and the smile on her lips and the glow in her cheeks meant I'd hit the mark with my praise.

I helped her into the chaps I'd bought her, and into the jacket; treating her as the special cargo she was but to anyone on the outside looking in? I probably looked like an overbearing or protective asshole bundling her up against the weather.

The sudden image of a kid in a fat snow suit flashed in my mind with those three haunting words any parent dreaded to hear once they got them all bundled up... *"I gotta pee!"*

"What's so funny?" Cor asked me as she turned back around and shrugged the jacket into a more comfortably and evenly distributed weight across her shoulders.

I told her, "I feel like the parent in just about every Christmas or winter movie ever bundling their kid up in all the layers and I'm just waiting for you to say you gotta pee."

She laughed and shaking her head said, "I definitely don't have to pee but I think I'm so excited that I might."

I laughed and ushered her out of the bedroom.

We finished by wrapping her lovely throat in a warm and stylish autumn colored scarf she'd made for herself. One in that eternal loop or whatever.

She looked so good; I was going to hate to put the helmet on her – I'd gotten one with a full-face mask to protect her best, I just hated to cover up her beautiful face.

We went out to the detached garage, and I threw open the door. She practically danced in place, very nearly vibrating with excitement.

"Okay, you remember everything we talked about?" I asked.

She nodded eagerly, and I stopped short and looked at her, eyebrow raised, silently reiterating my expectations when it came to any conversation about safety. To her credit, she didn't roll her eyes but I could tell it was a near thing.

"Yes," she said, settling down.

I tilted her head and with a slightly amused smile she ran through the safety bullet points. I couldn't help but smile at that and leaned forward to palm the side of her neck and run a thumb along her jaw, kissing her sweetly.

"That's my girl," I purred against her lips and I felt as well as heard her gasp slightly. The thing that made me smile more was the leap of her pulse against my fingertips, her heart warming up for the race it was about to endure once I got her out for the ride.

Hell, I couldn't remember a time I was as excited for a ride, myself. It felt as though I was fully bringing her into my world, that this was it. The final stepping off point, and I did everything to slam the door on my vague worry of *what if she hates it? What if the ride is too much for her?*

I thumbed the switch on my bike to start it up. I guess we were fixin' to find out.

CHAPTER THIRTY-ONE

*C*orliss...

    I was nervous more than anything else, but I hoped that Hex didn't notice and just took all of my fidgeting as pure excitement. I felt my heart very nearly seize up in my chest when the bike fired and roared to life. It was somehow louder than I expected. I hated how the mask of the helmet fogged when I let out my pent-up breath, but that quickly cleared and I figured out for myself that if I breathed a certain way, it didn't fog nearly as badly or at all.

I got on behind Hex when he waved me toward the back of the bike and wrapped my arms around him, scooting forward so I was snug against his back. He shouted something, but I couldn't make it out so I just nodded and gave a thumbs up, hoping that was the right answer – I mean, I had a fifty-fifty shot, right?

He gave a nod from beneath his shiny, beetle black half helmet, put on his sunglasses, and turned forward again. I held onto him tighter when he put both hands on the handle bars, and then we were moving.

I felt my heart leap in my breast and the bottom drop out from my stomach as we rolled down the driveway, swooped out onto the street and he *really* made the bike roar to life. The intimidating machine lurched forward beneath me, and where I was once annoyed at how *loud* the motor was, now I was grateful as it muffled the terrified bleat that escaped me as I clutched onto Hex harder.

I couldn't hear him laugh, but I felt it, and it made me laugh too as I realized we weren't going all *that* fast.

He wove through the city streets with practiced ease and took us on a circuitous route that eventually took us down along the river before he looped us back toward the club. We'd been out for what felt like forever but really couldn't have been more than forty-five minutes to an hour.

A bunch of the guys whooped and cheered as we rolled into the fenced-in yard of the club and Alina, standing near the picnic table where La Croix smoked a cigarette that looked hand rolled and suspicious, smiled at me as I waved feebly from behind Hex.

I waited for him to double tap my leg like he said he would when he needed me to get off, and I minded the pipes like he'd told me to, because they were hot, before I stepped back giving him a wide berth for him to back into the place among the long row of bikes already parked against the inside of the fence.

"Well, how was it?" Alina asked when I got the near suffocating helmet off my head.

"Terrifying," I answered, and she raised her eyebrows as if that was the wrong answer. I laughed some. "Exhilarating, too," I confessed, and she broke out into a smile.

"Now that's more like it," she said. "I can't remember if it was Thompson or Kerouac or who the hell said it, but they said something about the ride being like starring in a movie versus being in a cage is just like watching it on TV."

"It's the difference between living and watching others live, that's for sure," La Croix said. "And before you ask… I don't know who the fuck said it either, but Hunter S. Thompson is a poser piece of shit."

He rose like a leviathan from the sea off that bench and stalked toward the club's front doors bellowing, "To order!" then he called back over his shoulder to us, "And for once, you ladies are invited."

I looked to Alina puzzled and whispered, "Is he in a bad mood?"

She grinned at me and shook her head with an impish smile. "Not at all. That's just how he is – and he was *really* upset when he found the copy of *Hells Angels: A Strange and Terrible Saga* by Hunter S. Thompson in his house. He threw the book overboard and told me if I had questions that I needed to ask him or Hex, but that was enough of that bullshit."

I made a strangled pained noise and put my hand over my chest. "That poor book!" I cried and Alina threw her head back and laughed.

"I somehow knew that'd be the first thing you'd have to say about it," she said and throwing her arm over my shoulders, she steered me in the direction of the club.

Hex fell into step on my other side and asked me, "What happened now?"

"La Croix is a monster!" I mocked.

He simply snorted and asked, "What else is new? What'd he do this time?"

"Murdered a book," Alina chirped.

"Threw it overboard and watched it drown," I said solemnly.

"Okay, now I'm curious. Why'd he do that?"

"It was by Hunter S. Thompson," Alina said.

Hex snorted and called out, "Hey, La Croix!" La Croix looked up. "Beer's on me, buddy."

La Croix simply frowned. "The fuck you talking about?"

"Tossing a Thompson book into the swamp."

La Croix lifted his chin, his otherworldly tattooed forehead smoothing out into the now familiar lines of his stoicism.

"That's where his shit belongs," La Croix grated.

I looked to Alina quizzically, asking without saying anything out loud and she winked back at me. It had become our signal over the last couple months of *this is best talked about with a bottle of wine just between us girls.*

I smiled, and she bit her bottom lip to try and contain hers and we filed back toward the chapel with the boys.

They all took their seat around the table and Hex and La Croix drew us down into their laps. This was only the second time we'd done this, but our presence and the presence of the boys playing with their phones meant that this was what Alina and I had dubbed *Church Lite,* or the *Diet Coke of Club Business.* It was a glimpse, for us, of how the club operated as a whole but none of the serious talk the boys didn't want or need us to know.

Our presence here pretty much guaranteed that this was about the *Feed These Streets* campaign that was the brain trust of Alina, me, and Chainsaw, who had asked and been granted the temporary position of Road Captain for just this event – something Cypress had been all too happy to hand over to him.

The plan was to sell tickets at some of the biker bars around town, and other local spots. We had sponsors in the fisher folk and hunters with donated game and other things for the big feed at the end of the long ride through the city. Permits had been gotten and things were coming together for the first day of winter break so the kids from the local schools could participate.

I wasn't back in a full teaching capacity, but I had suggested and had been granted coordinating volunteers from Lakeside High School to help in the effort and already this whole thing had grown monumentally and it was a beautiful thing.

The club's big giant industrial kitchen would be open and the grills and boiler burners would be fired up. People from Cypress and La Croix's parish and bayous would man the kitchens with supplemental support from the high school kids. Food would be prepared while the motorcycles decorated in holiday and Christmas themes would roll through the city streets on a predestined parade-like route.

At the end, everyone would get a hot meal, there would be music and dancing, a competition for people to vote on the best decorated motorcycle and even a few fair games and cheap little prizes to go with them.

The talk around the table was joyous and carefree, but I couldn't help but have one nagging, niggling little doubt that just would not be ignored.

"What if…" The table fell silent, and I felt myself turn red with all the attention on me. "What if the Bayou Brethren turn up and try to cause trouble?" I asked. "I know we, uh, didn't exactly have a good last meeting with them and there may be some," I swallowed hard, "hard feelings?"

Hex smiled up at me from where I sat in his lap and winked at me, holding up his hand thumb and pinky out, to his ear and mouth like a phone handset. An indication to the rest of the guys to remember that their phones were present and to remain as diplomatic as I had just been with my question with their answers.

"Fuck 'em," Chainsaw said with a wink.

"There'll be a police presence. It's required for an event this size," Hex said with a warning look across at Chainsaw who was silently laughing.

"Speaking of all the money going out, how's it lookin' for money comin' in to make this whole thing a thing?" he asked and looked over to Bennie who had a laptop open in front of him likely with an Excel sheet open. Bennie lived and breathed his spreadsheets and ledgers. Numbers seemed to make him happy the way words touched my soul.

"We're actually doing surprisingly well, close to breaking even on the food ticket sales and the ticket tier to participate in the run has already pushed us over into the black."

"That ain't including any of the sponsorships or accounting for any of the extra food tickets or what we do with the carnival games and shit the day of, right?" Axeman asked.

"No, there's plenty of room to increase profits here," Bennie declared.

I took in a deep breath and let it out slow.

"It sounds like we're doing good and we're as ready as we'll ever be," I said.

Saint raised his chin some and asked me, "And what about you? You ready to go back to work?"

I was supposed to return to the classroom three days before winter break, allowing me to get my feet wet, then have just a little more time off before fully taking the plunge after the return from winter break just after the new year.

"I'm as ready as I'll ever be," I declared with a bit of trepidation.

"You'll do great," Hex said with assurance.

I smiled. "We'll see."

~

ONCE HOME, it was full dark and just getting darker out there. I always found the days too short and the nights far too deep and long in the wintertime.

"Hey, come take a hot shower with me," Hex breathed into my ear, cuddling up to my back, arms around my waist.

"Mmm," I groaned. "That's so tempting."

"But?" he asked.

"But it's getting late, and getting my hair wet is gonna be a no-go."

"Ahhh, I'll be right back," he declared, and he went on in further toward the front of the house, ducking into our bedroom.

I chuckled and hung up my new leather jacket on its peg by the back door and started working my way out of the chaps which were still like learning a new language or something to me. Like I could see how it went and had the basic grasp on the whole concept but left to my own devices I would probably do something embarrassingly wrong.

Like some well-meaning sod trying to tell a pregnant Spanish speaking woman to push when really all that was coming out of his mouth was calling her a whore. You know, that whole overplayed trope in just about every medical drama ever on television that was cringe but still... Lord and Lady, you couldn't help but laugh at it because as problematic as it could be with its whole stereotyping and everything it was still so very funny.

Hex came back around the corner marching up to me with purpose and produced... the ugliest damn shower cap I have ever seen out from around his back, still in the package. I burst out laughing and he grinned at me.

"Huh? Ahh, yeah?" He held it out to me and said, "Sometimes you just gotta be smarter than the problem, am I right?"

"Sometimes I think you will literally do just about anything to see me naked," I declared, still giggling and taking the thing from him to look at it.

Okay, so when I flipped the package over, the shower cap inside wasn't nearly as bad as the picture on the package which was some kind of snake print. This cap was actually just a uniform pale pink... which on second thought was *almost* as bad.

"Come take a shower with me," he said softly, a gentle cajoling to his tone. I looked up and as much as I wanted to just crawl into my pajamas and up into my book nook overlooking the living room.

I smiled up at him and said, "You drive a hard bargain, Mr. Johnson."

"Well, you know the best way to get rid of temptation, Miss Legare..." he murmured, stepping closer, hands to my hips, half drawing me in even as he was half drawn to me, like a moth to flame. That was the thing about Hex... he treated me like I was the light of his life and the sentiment shone in his deep brown eyes like flecks of whiskey gold, sending shivers down my spine every time I glimpsed it.

"See," he murmured seductively. "You're cold."

I felt my breath still in my lungs as he took that last tiny step to put our bodies close, a scant half inch from touching completely, the warmth radiating from him so very inviting.

"You know that shiver had absolutely nothing to do with temperature," I whispered.

"Trying to teach me science?" he joked faintly.

"Law," I whispered. "The rules of attraction."

He smiled but didn't quite laugh as he lowered his mouth to mine and there could be no illusion of my being cold left. Not with how my blood heated and rushed through my veins.

His lips moved against mine so darkly sweet. The touch of them soft, but the way he loomed over me something so threatening, so menacing, but not to me. Never to me. For myself, I could feel the danger and menace radiate from him, but it was as though I were safely cocooned within its bubble. If he were a dragon, I was his precious thing, his horde, and I loved that feeling. I loved feeling his aura around me. The sensation of his energy a very real and almost palpable thing.

For the first time in a long time… hell, maybe if ever, I not only felt seen by the man cradling me in his arms, but I genuinely felt as though I was the absolute center of his world, of his very universe, and that was a heady and intoxicating thing. One that I wanted to swear by all things that were holy, that I would *never* take for granted.

It was too precious a thing for me to disrespect like that. To squander by taking it for granted.

I broke the kiss reluctantly, and asked, my voice trembling, "I thought you were going to take me to bed."

"Shower?" he asked playfully.

"Bed," I murmured, and he chuckled. "Shower in the morning," I added, and he outright laughed.

"Whatever my lady wishes," he said and walked back, taking me with him to the night-darkened bedroom.

The dark I had been so sad to see just a little while before became a tantalizing and wonderful thing as we groped and kissed and explored by touch. Disrobing each other one piece at a time without the benefit of our sight was a uniquely wondrous experience filled with whispering gentle touching punctuated with awkward giggling from time to time.

Our mouths clashed, tongues lashing against one another, his warm hard body pressing to my softer one and I swear, I lived for the sensation of his body against mine. I reveled in his warmth. It was better than any fire and warmed more than just my skin, deeper than muscle or bone. This man warmed my very soul and took me places in thought and sensation I never knew existed and I honestly hoped against hope that I did something similar if not the very same for him.

"Oh, fuck," he moaned as I wrapped my fingers around him, pressing the shaft of his cock into my palm, before stroking him root to tip.

"Fuck, I love that you get so hard for me," I whispered, and he chuckled so very deep and darkly from the darkness that the hair rose on the back of my neck and something primal in me stood like a meerkat, stalk still and waiting for what was next. Even still, my hand never stopped its stroking, his precum sticky and lubricating the path it took, even as I stood there right before him, pressing my thighs together and *knowing* without feeling just how wet I was becoming.

I couldn't help myself, my pussy giving me a throbbing little ache of need to have him there, up inside me.

"I want you so bad," I murmured.

"Yeah?" he growled and the angle and the pitch of his voice changed ever so slightly. I pictured him standing there, eyes closed, hands where I could feel them, one on my hip, one on my ribs, traveling toward a goal of palming my tit.

I pictured him, eyes closed, chin tucked, head turned like a predator listening, hearing out in the wood for its prey to make even the slightest movement, the slightest sound before…

"Fuck me," I begged. "I want you to drive this cock so far inside me, so deep, it hurts and I want you to do it until I either beg for mercy or beg for more."

His hand seized my breast and jerked me forward into his hard body. His other hand traveled up my back from my hip and tangled in the back of my hair. My head was jerked back with just that slightest edge of biting pain in my scalp and his breath came hot in my ear, sliding down the side of my neck, my nipples tightening as he ground out, "Be careful what you wish for, little Fable, or you might just turn into a cautionary tale."

I think my insides turned to liquid fire.

"Fuck, yes… please…" I begged, and I worked my hand a little faster, gripping a little harder.

His hand covered mine and stopped my rhythm.

He didn't say anything, he just turned me around, to the side and hand still in the back of my hair for the control it provided him, he pushed me toward the bed. I felt the front of my thighs hit the edge and then he ordered me, "Bend over, put your hands on the bed, and hold on tight."

I did as he commanded, and waited, face down and ass up and listened as he groped through the bedside table. I heard the crackle of the condom wrapper, the wet plastic sound of him rolling it onto his cock, but then there was a little more, a slight plastic thunk and a click before he slid the drawer shut.

"Oh! Cold!" I cried, shooting up slightly, but he barked out, "Head down, ass up! I won't tell you again."

I put myself back down as he touched whatever cool gel to my pussy entrance. I moaned as he unnecessarily lubed me up, I was hot and already so wet. I could tell not only by the feel of him gliding over my entrance but also by the wet *sound* of him petting along my pussy lips.

I moaned and pushed back into his hand but he took it away and said, "Don't move." I swallowed and nodded and realized he couldn't see it only *after* his hand cracked into my right ass cheek.

"Oh, God, yes!" I cried and bit my bottom lip, drawing in a ragged breath.

"Mm," he hummed in appreciation. "I'm going to fuck your pussy good and deep, just like you asked, baby but I'm gonna play with your asshole too, this time. Okay?"

"What?" I asked, slightly confused. I mean, I didn't realize he was into that and honestly? I'd never tried it.

"I didn't stutter," he said, shoving into my cunt with a grunt. I thrust my hips back to meet him and nearly had my legs go out from under me.

"Nope, up on the bed, get up there. On your knees," he commanded, and it took more than one try, but I did it.

"Good girl," he declared, and he laid into my left ass cheek with a stinging slap.

I yowled and rocked back out of pure instinct which just drove me onto his cock to where he bottomed out against my cervix.

I panted and then sucked in a great big breath when more of that cold gel was pressed against my asshole with the tip of his finger or his thumb.

"Oh, goddamn," I uttered because surprisingly? Surprisingly, that felt *good.*

"Yeah?" he asked. "You like that?" He moved his cock intentionally then, and I felt my pussy clench around him keeping him there nice and deep as I bit my bottom lip and a guttural sound of almost protest left my chest. Protest at the thought that when he'd moved, he was going to pull out. I didn't want that. I wanted him there, deep in my cunt. I loved the feel of his thick cock opening me up, filling me, stretching my walls and driving me wild.

I thrust back against him for another delicious shock of almost pain traveling like electricity along every nerve in this pulsing shockwave out from my middle to strike at the inside of my skin and while it felt good, so very good, it wasn't quite enough to be mind blowing. It wasn't quite enough to send it washing back to my core along the same path, it was like I needed *more* but I didn't know what more was…

"Mm, more!" I begged, and he asked playfully, tantalizingly, "More?"

"More!" I managed to eke out.

He asked, "More like this?" He thrust forward, gripping my hip and pulling me back on one side to where I cried out again and clenched around him.

"Or more like this?" he asked and his warm finger was gone and a cold, smooth piece of metal pressed at my asshole and I mean pressed, just starting to breech the opening. I hissed out, and he backed off before starting again, going just a little further with it this time.

"Oh my God!" I cried and cringed away from the slight burning sensation in my asshole.

"It's not that big, baby girl. I know it feels like it, but it's not. You can take it for me. Come on."

I bit my lips together, and heart pounding, breath sawing in and out of my lungs, I pushed back ever so slightly on his cock and onto the rapidly warming metal taking it a little bit further.

"Ah!" I cried as the pain increased and his voice, encouraging me, overrode everything.

"That's it, darlin', almost there, it's almost all the way in, push out for me baby, take it all the way and I swear to God, I'll fuck you like you begged me and then some."

Shit yes, I wanted it. I wanted everything he was offering and then some but most of all I wanted to make him proud. I cried out as my asshole stretched uncomfortably and then with a sort of plop, whatever it was, it was in and my ass was sighing with relief and with both hands to my hips Hex made fucking good on his promise.

He absolutely *railed* my pussy into next week. His thrusting wild, rough, hard, and deep. I folded myself down face first into the mattress and bit the comforter to muffle my screams as the paces he put me through at my request were enough to damn near make my soul leave my body.

My last coherent thought before I just gave myself over to the delicious mix of pleasure that was gilded at the edges with pain was *be careful what you wish for...* but it was a glib thought. I just hoped he was enjoying this as much as me.

CHAPTER THIRTY-TWO

*H*ex...
I was sweating, I didn't care. The steel bejeweled plug I'd bought for her and had just put up her ass made her already tight pussy almost excruciatingly tight as I did what she asked and fucking railed her. Fuck, I was high as hell on the sheer power of dominating her, and the trust she put into me to do her right. I listened to her cries, to her ragged breathing, and it was as though everything was heightened. My sense of her so complete that we were no longer two beings but one, two cogs that were the lynchpin of the whole machine's operation, well-oiled with sweat and desire spinning away and doing its thing to take us both down a long dark road where only the two of us mattered.

I liked that. I loved being inside of her, I loved that she took my love and my toys, and my dick so fucking well. She was such a magical fucking creature, beautiful and otherworldly like a phoenix. Something rarer and not nearly as oft talked about like a unicorn.

One thing was for fucking sure, my girl was fucking *fire* the way she gripped my dick and trembled beneath me and around me.

I could feel her edging closer and closer to a wild orgasm and I couldn't help myself, I had to talk her through it. I had to encourage her. I wanted to feel her come around my dick so bad. I wanted to hear her that scream of pleasure claw its way out of her long and lovely throat and I wanted to feel her pussy flutter and twitch and I wanted to feel her milk my cock dry because I knew. I knew as soon as she went, I would follow.

It would be as it would be for the rest of our fucking lives if I had anything to say about it.

Where she would go, I would fucking follow. Her menacing shadow, her protector, her savior if she would let me – just as long as she kept this up, just as long as she bowed low, opened herself up to what I had to give and would continue to take me as I was.

"Come on, baby, that's it. Mm-hm, you got it. Just like that, darlin', just like that. Why don't you give me what I want, baby. You go on now, you come around that cock. You fucking scream as loud as you want and you fucking come all over that dick, come on now!"

Oh, shit...

She wailed, screamed this beautiful cathartic thing, made some feral noises I had never fucking heard come out of a woman and it set off every predator victory instinct that I had inside me. A rush of the good chemicals flooded my brain, swiftly rushed along every nerve, through every vein, screaming through my body screaming all the signals to *fire* and boy fuck howdy did I shoot my load. I mean, I was still shooting, collapsed on top of her, as her pussy twitched in counter-point to every now blank that I fired off inside the condom.

"Ah, fuck!" I repeated, and it took me a fair few seconds that'd like to feel like whole ass minutes to realize I was even the one that spoke the words.

"Oh, God!" Her voice cracked as I shifted on top of her and my cock shifted inside of her. The sweet, delicious oversensitivity zapping me into a silent, quiet, submissiveness of my own to the dominance of the moment and the unspoken and unordered whims of my own body.

"Ah, shit." I forced myself out of her and couldn't care that I left the condom behind as I managed to awkwardly roll off to one side so I wouldn't crush her. She immediately sought refuge from the feelings her own body wrought in my arms and I sheltered her gladly, giving her a safe a place as any to ride out the tempest of her own body chemistry.

"If you can survive a fuck like that, you can survive anything," I said when my own panting had calmed down. I kissed her forehead soundly and said, "That's my good girl. Holy fuck, you made me proud with that one."

She looked up at me, her hair mussed her wide blue eyes glassy, and at my words fell the absolute fuck apart. I mean full-on frantic cathartic sobbing, and I felt my heart leap in my chest, my arms closing around her in action before I could even think to command them to do it and I crushed her to me and held her tight through the storm, trying to keep my panic to a minimum until I could sus out just what the fuck set her off and what the fuck was going on.

I mean, was this a good cry or a bad cry?

I knew sometimes rough fucking like that could bring on a whole heap of emotions someone wasn't at all prepared for, but that was why I was here. That was my fucking job as the man in charge, the one in control.

"I'm sorry!" Her voice was high pitched, frantic, and filled with confusion and panic.

"Shhh, shhh, shhh, none of that now, no apologies, baby. You didn't do nothin' wrong. I've got you."

"I don't know what's wrong with me!" she wailed.

I chuckled lightly and said, "Shh, it's okay, I've got you. Nothing's wrong with you."

She sobbed and I just told her, "Let it out," and let her let it go.

"Shhh," I soothed a minute later, when the sobbing had subsided and the faucet turned off and settled into a drip of just the odd sniffle or so.

"Just talk to me, baby. When you're ready and not a moment before, okay?"

She sniffed and huddled into me. "I'm okay. I'm okay now," she said, and I leaned back just enough to take in her red-rimmed eyes and beautifully blotchy face. I know it was called ugly crying but Corliss

Legare couldn't do ugly even if she fuckin' tried. It just didn't matter; she was always crazy beautiful to me.

"Do you know what that was all about?" I asked gently, and she shook her head, mute, swallowing so hard her throat nearly clicked.

"Okay," I said calmly and with all the patience I knew she needed. "What happened, can you describe it?"

She sniffed. "I came, and everything just felt…" she swallowed, her voice trembling a bit as she said, "everything just felt so good, and I remember thinking to myself just how much I love you and it was like it hit me just here," she put a hand over her heart in the center of her chest, "this sense of incredible, I don't know… of, of, of *loss*. It was crazy! Just out of nowhere, it was like I could *feel* every single little grain of sand trickling through the hourglass and I just… I felt like our time was just so insanely, crazily, limited and that at any moment you were going to wake up and look at me, and…" her voice cracked and she started to cry again and I shook my head. She didn't need to say it out loud. I knew what it was… *and it would be over.*

"Easy, baby. Deep breaths, okay? I'm not going anywhere."

I held her tight and she clung to me, and my own mind chased itself into some serious damn circles trying like hell to figure out where this panic attack was coming from and if I had given her *any* indication that I didn't love her like anything less than my moon and my fuckin' stars… and the answer to me was honestly clear as day.

"This don't have nothin' to do with me, and I know that, so don't you be afraid of hurtin' my feelings none," I told her, smoothing her hair gently with my hand. "You just speak your heart and speak your mind and I reckon we'll sort some of this out somehow, yeah?"

She sniffed and nodded mutely and I had to smile some. "An' if you don't want to talk about it, well I reckon that's fine too."

She sniffed and rubbed her nose with the back of her hand and looked up at me.

"Everyone I've ever known has left me," she said. "Left me and didn't want me… I guess… I guess I got so used to it, I convinced myself that I didn't need anybody and that I was okay by myself but something about you… about what we just shared? The thought of losing you, of you just someday walking away? I... I... I lost it. It hurts more than anything I—"

I pressed her face into the crook of my neck and wrapped my arms around her so tight and swore with every bit of myself, "Never gonna happen, baby. Okay? Better or worse, sicker or poorer, hell or high water – I'm your ride or die. I'm not going anywhere and neither are you. We're just two peas in a pod."

She laughed a little brokenly but cuddled in tighter, her body relaxing, the tension of the last vestiges of her panic leaving off and falling away.

"I'm—"

"Shh! None of that. No apologies. I told you, I've got you. I'm right here and I'll *always* be here. That's how this shit works and fuck anybody else who's got shit to say about it. You get me?"

She sniffed and nodded and looked up to me.

I kissed her and held her tight and said, "Now I do believe that's one insecurity I've fucked all the way out of you tonight. What's one more? You ready?"

Her high gale of laughter made the rain turn back to sunshine in our hearts and in the dark of our room and I had to smile.

Somehow, I knew a bad joke would get her to smile and take the last of the pain away... for now. I also knew there were more issues, more land mines lurking and I would traverse that field with absolutely no fear. There wasn't a damn thing that would turn me away from her. Not a one.

I CAUGHT a glimpse of her through her classroom window. She was sitting alone at her desk and looked a bit frazzled. I went to try the handle and come in – but she had it locked. She'd never done that before, and while I absolutely understood why she did it now, it still worried me. Her head came up at the sound my attempt to get in the room made and she smiled, her stiff posture easing and I could tell – she wasn't alright. Being back was taking a toll on her. It just remained to be seen if it would be something she could work through or not.

I waved her back down into her seat and keyed my way into the room and let the door swing shut behind me. No need to lock it when I was here.

"You doin' okay, Fable?" I asked her.

She sighed and said, "Yeah. Just... it feels weird, you know?"

I shrugged slightly and asked, "Anybody giving you problems?"

She looked uncomfortable and said, "A couple, but nothing I can't handle."

I smiled and dropped into the seat across from her desk and cocked my head.

"How are you really? First day back and all..."

She smiled. "Tired. Like *really* tired. I forgot how mentally and emotionally exhausting this could be and that was *before*... well, you know." She shrugged and I nodded.

"You eat lunch yet?" I asked, and she checked her watch.

"Shit," she muttered softly.

I had to chuckle. "I thought so."

I pulled a tinfoil wrapped Shrimp Po' boy from the brown paper sack I'd carried in from our favorite place. She stared at it a second and then looked up at me.

"You... I could kiss you," she declared and started unraveling the sandwich.

"I'll take a raincheck on that tonight; I'll tell you what." I pulled up a drink thing of sweet tea and put it on her desk and slid a straw to her.

The look of gratitude in her blue eyes made the effort of having this delivered from across town worth it.

"Have to keep my girl fed," I said quietly. "Can't have her wasting away on me."

She smiled from behind her sandwich as she chewed and winked at me. We were keeping our relationship on the down low when it came to the school for now.

We ate in silence and she looked up at me finally and asked me, "Do you really think I can do this?"

I looked at her and the worry in her eyes and the fear etched in every line of her being? I could read her like a book…

"I think you can do anything you put your mind to, baby," I told her. "Now as for *do you think I'll be disappointed if you can't?* No. No, I wouldn't. You're not built like me – you feel and are passionate and are all softness and light; everything that's wonderful in this world. The shit that's happened here would take a toll on anybody but if there's anyone in this school that can handle it and work through it, it's you. I don't reckon it's gonna be easy – but I believe you can."

"Thanks for the pep talk," she said. "I needed it. Everybody, for the most part has been so nice – just a couple of students that are trying to get a rise… I think it's the other faculty that's bothering me the most. They're treating me like I have leprosy or the plague or something."

"That more 'n anything is what chaps my ass. You've already been through so much and that on top of it is some bullshit."

She snorted delicately. "I don't disagree with you there," she said, and then followed up with a soft, "I just wish I knew why."

"It's because you're suing," I said, swallowing the bite of Po'boy I was talking around the moment before. "Some of them are pissy thinkin' it's going to affect the budget and their bottom line – like they wouldn't have been hollerin' for a fuckin' lawyer themselves the second they came out of anesthesia." I didn't care that my tone was derisive. Fuck these motherfuckers for making anything harder on her in the absolute slightest. Self-serving sons of a bitches.

"I hadn't thought of that," she said and looked a little stunned like she'd been hit by a revelation. "I was hoping things would be different, you know?"

"How do you mean?" I asked.

"I don't know… just *different*, you know?"

"No," I said and set my Po'boy down and wiped my mouth with a napkin.

"I think you just haven't really caught up to the fact that *you're* different. A thing like that, whether you remember the details or not, fundamentally changes a person. You may not remember the sordid details as it happened but you still went through a hell of a thing with a long recovery; mending broken bones and some deep physical trauma to your body changes you too. I think the thing that's bothering you is that you've been so deeply changed by your experience you deeply feel like everything's changed and the fact that all these people are wandering around like nothing has—"

"Yeah." She perked up. "It's like living in the twilight zone. I mean, I'm back and people are glad but at the same time it's like I never left except for the silent shunning by the faculty and everyone has this false brightness or… whatever."

"Alternate timeline?" I asked with a smile.

"Another dimension," she said, and it held enough unhappiness despite her smile that I ached to hold her.

We sat in silence for a bit and I asked her quietly, "So, what do you wanna do tonight when we get home?" I was asking in a bid to distract her from her first day back struggles but instead of keeping it G or PG like I expected her to do, she dipped her chin, gave me a crook of a mischievous smile and with a sultry look and a raised eyebrow, and asked me, "What do you think?"

I laughed, outright then and shook my head and said, "My darlin', I do believe you are insatiable."

"For you?" she asked innocently. "Always."

I bowed my head smiling to myself, and dare I say? The woman somehow found the right combination to make *me* blush.

CHAPTER THIRTY-THREE

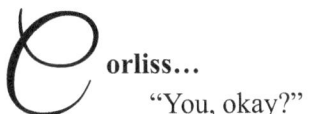 orliss...

"You, okay?"

"What?" I looked up from the absolute *vat* of greens I was stirring over the hot stove the pot so big and tall I had to stand on a stupid stepladder to keep it going under the watchful eye of Miss Mary Thurgood. She was running this kitchen with military precision and *no one* dared to question her authority. Heck, even *I* was scared of her and I couldn't begin to tell you why! She was an iron lady born of the bayou and, I guess, knew how to feed a small army of people good food, quick and thus she was in charge of getting the cooking done for today's hungry horde of riders.

Hex was staring at me, and I blinked at him before finally catching up to the fact that he'd just asked me if I was alright.

"Oh! Yeah, just a little frazzled," I said.

"Well, you best unfuck yourself, baby, 'cause these fellers ain't gon' wait on you forever," a woman near me said, and she held her hand out for the giant long-handled wooden spoon I'd been turning in the giant pot. I stepped down and held my hands out in an *after you* motion and she took my place.

Hex took me gently by the elbow and led me out of the kitchen and into the club and asked me again, "Are you okay?"

I grimaced and said, "Honestly, I'm overwhelmed and what's going on with you has me really upset and... I don't know."

He sighed and took me into his arms and held me tight and that? That just seemed to somehow make everything okay. Like... it grounded me like no other thing ever hand.

"Hey, don't you worry about any of that," he said.

"But I *am* worried. It's like they figured out we're a thing and they can't do anything to me directly because of the lawsuit, so they're targeting *you*."

"Fuck 'em," he said with a shrug and I sighed, resting my forehead against his chest while the guilt swirled in my chest.

He'd been pulled into the office the last day before winter break and had been told that he was under review and that it'd come to light he was a member of the Voodoo Bastards and with the club's history of legal complications it was being decided on whether he would be able to remain and I quote here – "*a part of the Lakeside family.*"

When he'd said those words, my mouth flooded with the metallic tang of *I'm going to puke.*

It'd been a shock to the system and didn't seem to matter one wit that we'd put in all of this work and effort to the benefit of the school – a benefit they were contradictorily willing to take with all kinds of surface and very public gratitude, but oh, no, no! Hex wouldn't be able to continue as a custodian there. Not if he remained a member of the club.

"Gods above and below," I muttered. "Just make it make sense."

Hex chuckled and took me by my shoulders and held me at half an arm's length.

"People in power are like this, babe. Do as I say not as I do. What's good for one ain't for the other. This type of corrupt bullshit is a tale as old as fuckin' time. You're going to either kill 'em in court or get yourself a fat settlement and they gotta have their pound of flesh and pint of blood. They're just too fuckin' stupid to realize they're just cuttin' off their own nose despite their face."

I sighed and looked up at him and felt my shoulders slump as I said, "I feel like I'm a walking poison and that I'm ruining your life sometimes."

His face grew more serious than I think I'd ever seen it and he shook his head.

"Don't you ever say something like that again," he said, and his tone was as deadly serious as I'd ever heard it.

I scraped my top lip between my teeth and nodded and said, "Well I hope you're right. I hope I take them to the cleaners and I hope it hurts, and I swear to the God and Goddess, if they *do* fire you; I quit. Because fuck that noise. I am so sick of these people and places standing there like they're some paragon of fucking virtue when they do things so wrong headed and intentionally awful – no, *spiteful* and they expect us to be the responsible ones under all this pressure for these kids when they're acting like- like – like a bunch of mean girls!" I sputtered the last with my increased agitation at the situation and then put on a mock whining voice and said for emphasis, *"You can't sit with us!"*

Hex's shoulders were shaking with silent laughter and finally he just pulled me to him and hugged me tight, saying, "Come ride with me. They got this, let's put our knees in the breeze take the wind therapy, and enjoy the day because—"

"Fuck 'em," I said, voice muffled by his leather sleeve as I burrowed into his arms.

"Exactly! Now you're gettin' it, Fable."

I rested my chin on his chest as the club and kitchen and kids volunteering scurried about to making things ready and said, "You're so smart."

He smacked a kiss to my forehead and winked at me. "Nah, I just figured out when and what I needed to just chuck it in the 'fuck it' bucket and move on. You'll get there."

I grinned like a loon. "Chuck it in the 'fuck it' bucket. I like that – but also, language. I know these kids know it and have heard and said it all but let's try and lead by example."

"Oh, okay, Ms. 'Fuck that noise, fucking paragon of virtue, fuck 'em McGee."

I laughed at that; I mean, he had me there. I'd let myself get worked up enough that I'd maybe let fly just a little too casually but hey, I think I'd earned a few f-bombs with the stress of the last few days.

He hooked an arm over my shoulders and guided me over toward the office, taking out his keys and unlocking it. My coat and riding gear was in here with a bunch of the other things in the club we didn't want or need lying around – like the booze from the bar which was now being set up as a serving line.

I went in and he followed, shutting the door and throwing the lock. I turned and he came to me, putting his hands to my hips and kissing me soundly.

My arms just naturally wound around his neck and shoulders and he naturally just twined his arms around my back, hugging me to his body, his hands on my ass, squeezing, his mouth on mine, kissing me breathless and I couldn't ever help myself when he did this. I *swooned* into his hard chest, body going lax even as my heart throbbed and my muscles went warm and loosened. The whole idiom about your legs being made of jelly suddenly making perfect sense to me when I'd always thought it was just a silly little thing that people said.

He lifted me, and walked me back, sitting me on the edge of the desk, parting my knees and stepping between my legs, one of which nudged one of the boxes of alcohol from the bar, the bottles rattling together with a pleasant ring, the sound snapping me out of it, making me draw back, a hand to his chest as I breathed heavy and said with no little trepidation, "We can't."

"Aww." He pouted and kissed the tip of my nose, but he acquiesced and straightened.

I looked up at him and asked, "What brought that on?"

He winked at me and said, "Woman, if you ain't figured out yet that I want you every time I look at you, I don't know what to tell you."

I blushed and shook my head and slipped back to my booted feet on the polished cement floor.

"And you call *me* insatiable!"

"If I ain't the pot callin' the kettle, I know, I know." He picked up my chaps off the couch that was pushed against the wall to one side and said, "C'mere."

I had figured the leatherwear out by now and could totally put them on myself but that was one of the things he liked to do. He liked to dress me for the ride himself. I think it had something to do with his protective nature. It was like he wasn't satisfied unless he did it himself, and truthfully, it'd become one of our little rituals. One that I cherished. He helped me into my jacket after the chaps were on me securely and handed me my scarf. I looped it around my neck twice and turned around automatically so he could zip my coat for me.

It had been a little strange at first, him dressing me like that but now it was just something that had become uniquely *us*.

His eyes rose and connected with mine and I said softly with a wink, "I have to pee."

He burst out in rich laughter and for now, the melodrama thanks to the school administration was thrust aside and the day had been returned to me.

He was right. Fuck 'em. They didn't get to live rent-free in my head on today of all days when all of our hard work and planning over the last few months was about to bear fruit.

He took up our helmets and said, "C'mon, baby. Your chariot awaits and you're the Homecoming Queen of this shindig. Let's ride."

I let him open the door for me and with a courtly nod of my head, I stepped through. He grinned at me and smacked me on the ass with his free hand as I slipped past him. I yipped and jumped and gave him a warning look over my shoulder but it was too late. A couple of the kids from my fourth period class had seen it and were already whispering behind their hands. He stepped out, caught sight of the two girls and the bastard just had the unmitigated gall to look *amused*.

"Guess that cat is out of the bag," I said out of the side of my mouth as we traveled up the hall.

"Did you seriously just forget about our cuddle and make-out session in the kitchen?" I frowned.

"None of the kids were in the kitchen!" I argued and he laughed at me.

"Damn sure was," he said. "You really had yourself wrapped around the axle, didn't you?" he put his arm around my shoulders while my cheeks flamed.

"Shut up." I huffed and he laughed.

"While I do appreciate your concern for me, Miss Legare, you don't have to worry about me. It's not like I've wanted to remain a high school janitor for the rest of my life."

I nodded and said, "Okay, that's fair... still, the whole thing is shitty."

He nodded. "Agree on that, but who knows? Maybe it's a blessing in disguise, yeah?"

I stopped just before we were to step outside and into the fenced-in lot of the club and looked up at him, that sense of guilt back for a completely different reason.

"I have to confess... I don't think I've ever asked you what you want to be when you grow up." I smiled and he laughed at me for the way I phrased it but he looked thoughtful a second and then the truth slipped free with a nostalgic little smile on his face.

"Y'know, I always thought that I'd like to follow in the footsteps of my daddy," he said, and I cocked my head.

"Moonshine?" I asked. He'd told me about his father plenty of times. Telling stories of helping him with his moonshine stills up in the Smoky Mountains of Tennessee. He always spoke of his time with his dad with such fondness and so much respect, I couldn't believe I'd never thought that could be a thing he'd want to do.

"Distilling, yeah." He nodded. "I got all my pops' old recipes. I'd love to try 'em and figure 'em out and get it all perfected, maybe take 'em legit somehow."

"I imagine that would take funds," I murmured as he tugged me out into the cold sunlight... well, cold for New Orleans and the Deep South anyway.

"A hell of a lot more funds than a janitor makes," he said chuckling.

"You know," I ventured. "I might know a bitch who's coming into some big money."

He laughed and shook his head. "Don't even think about it, baby. That's *your* money."

"Fine." I rolled my eyes, but the seed was planted and already starting to grow as we stopped at his bike.

"Just go for a ride with me and stop worrying your pretty little head," he said, and set his helmet down on the seat. He put mine on me before I could retort. While he'd effectively silenced my talk, he couldn't make my thoughts shut up, and I thought about it as speeches were made and engines were fired and we all threw a leg over the spines of our iron horses about to ride out into these streets like some old west posse.

Hex and I were at the front of the pack, riding alongside La Croix and Alina at the president's right hand. I'd learned there was reason and ritual behind just about everything these men did. That club structure had given them a purpose in a world they otherwise felt had abandoned them or left them feeling shiftless or without purpose. The club life had given them a place to go, to fit, when the rest of the world had seemingly turned their back on them.

There was a lot more to it than that, layer upon layer of reasoning steeped for the most part in bitterness and anger. It was interesting to me, both as a way of understanding Hex further and in an almost anthropological sense – history and understanding people's way of life a secondary passion of mine to the written word.

I held on to Hex, grateful that this ride would be low and slow and knowing it was going to be the longest I'd ever been on.

It was an interesting dichotomy, biker life in general.

These men were among the most feared in the city and surrounding area with a reputation of rage and ruin – and yet, they certainly had their soft spots. Especially concerning kids. I'd listened and talked with some of the men of the Voodoo Bastards and I guess it wasn't uncommon for even bigger and badder clubs that the media liked to sensationalize as gangs – clubs such as the Sacred Hearts which was certainly the biggest and most well-known name in the MC world. I mean, the Sacred Hearts supposedly had ties to the cartels in South America! Anyway, it wasn't uncommon at all for them to do big ticket charity things like we were doing now.

Things like toy runs to make donations to charities such as the Marine Corps led Toys for Tots, or even large sum donations to charities that helped homeless veterans.

While we'd had a surprising amount of support from the community for this particular venture, I'd heard one woman say that even Hitler had managed to do some good things but that didn't outweigh, you know, the whole entire holocaust...

It'd given me some pause. I'd *wanted* to go up to her and tell her to get wrecked and leave if that was going to be her attitude but honestly in that moment, I'd felt the hypocrisy radiating off of her like the heat from the pipes of the bikes I rode. I mean, she was judging the absolute hell out of these men who were trying to do a good thing while they were trying to do it and she was here either by paying for her ticket or volunteering – I hadn't checked so yeah... wasn't that cyclical thinking? She was like the mythological ouroboros. The giant serpent of out of Norse mythos that was depicted eating its own tail.

The irony of her being nasty and judging me and the boys as she was helping us, wasn't lost on me...

My thoughts turned to the glittering sea of tinsel and chrome behind us, we took up both sides of the street which had been blocked off for this spectacle to allow our passing. There were Santa and elf hats a plenty, the speeds kept so low and slow that no one seemed to be taking anyone to task over helmet laws and things like that as we made way through the city – a serpent of our own roaring with one voice made of many engines as we wound through the parade route that'd been predetermined by the powers that be for that sort of thing.

Hex had been right; there wasn't anything as magical as riding in a large pack like this. I felt as though we were the head of a dragon snaking its way through New Orleans and I found myself in a meditative state only a short distance into the ride, riding the frequency of our good intentions as much as the bike. Holding on to the man I loved under a high blue sky, the temperature a pleasant low sixties; an almost perfect day for something like this.

I soaked up the joy and the good vibrations, waving to the kids and parents alike that gathered to watch us pass by. Returning the waves of police officers blocking off side streets and finding that I was smiling so hard my cheeks hurt.

It was everything that we'd wished to put out into the city and the world and I hoped it would pay off in rich dividends for some hungry kids and would feed the spirit of the holiday season as much as some empty bellies.

CHAPTER THIRTY-FOUR

*H*ex...

The ride was nice; a little on the long side, but the day was good for it and I had to like that it seemed to put my girl into a better less worrisome mood by the end. When we got back to the club, we parked outside the gates of the old, converted warehouse while the bikes entering into the best decorated contest – about twenty or so – rolled on in through the gate to back in along the fence where me and the boys usually parked it.

The picnic tables were out in the lot, draped in red and white table-cloths, Christmas trees were up around the place, stable in old tires and cemented in place for the younger kids to decorate with lights and construction paper snowflakes.

Corliss handed me her helmet and gave my hand a squeeze as one of her students came up to get her attention. I gave it a couple of squeezes back and let it slip from my hand watching her as she wandered into the fence line away from me.

That's when dude who was vaguely familiar walked up. He held out his hand and I took it, and he shook it heartily.

"Sup?" I asked.

He looked uncomfortable to say the least, a big fat fuckin' shiner on his left side and he said, "I'll be honest with you, man. I'm taking my family and we're leavin', getting the fuck up outta here tonight."

I raised an eyebrow and gave a slight nod, and he held out a doubled-up grocery sack stuffed with something soft. I looked down in it and the leather vest with its worn patches and Bayou Brethren colors.

"What the fuck is this, man?" I demanded, looking up at him scowling.

He shook his head. "They're pissed, not fuckin' letting shit go – and now I don't know what they got planned but the things they were talking about... man, I got a wife and kids. I wouldn't want no one comin' after them. That's coward's shit."

"They planning on trying for family?" I demanded.

He shrugged said, "Man, I don't know what they got planned. They was just talkin' all kinds of crazy and when I said somethin' about it, I got my ass kicked." He shook his head. "That's not how this shit was supposed to go, man. I don't know."

I believed him, what he was sayin'. There was a sincerity and a pain in his expression. A desperation.

"What the cops have on 'em?" I asked. "Give me as much information as you can."

"I can't," he said, walking backward into the street. "It's a good thing y'all did today, but I gotta get my family away from here, out of this mess. I'm not tryin' to go to prison or wind up dead. I got two young'uns and a wife I can't keep lettin' down. This is the best I can do."

I nodded and he fucked off. Collier came up to me and asked me, "What was that about?"

"Defection," I said and I handed him the bag. "Before you take that anywhere inside the club, you have Saint check that shit for bugs or any other kind of electronics, devices, or signal," I said.

Collier looked in the bag and snapped it closed, bundling it between his two fists real tight. He looked up at me and gave me a curt nod and went to find Saint. I went to find La Croix.

I found our president with his girl at his hip. He stared, bored, at a couple of minister types that were talking at him, Alina being all warm and sweet and making polite small talk with them in her bartender's customer service voice. Yeah, I knew better. The minute they fucked off, she'd be talkin' mad shit behind their backs. She had no time or patience for the hypocrisy of the local churches. As southern and snake bit by corruption as they were.

I leaned down next to La Croix's ear and said low and only for him, "We got a problem." I jerked my head toward the club. He perked up and disengaged himself from Alina's side and made to walk away from the bow tied motherfuckers talkin' their hot air.

"Where you goin', brother?" one asked in surprise and La Croix pinned them with a hard look.

"I'm not your brother," he declared. I winked at 'em as we turned to walk away and heard Alina rush out some kind of thing to smooth shit over.

"What's the problem?" he demanded low and slightly irritated and I shook my head and jerked it in the direction of our office. His scowl deepened and I unlocked the door, setting Fable's helmet down on a stack of boxes just inside it.

I shut the door and he turned to me, I took out my phone and turned it off. He raised and eyebrow and did the same and I let out a breath and finally spoke up.

"We just had an unexpected visitor from the—"

The door opened and Saint poked his head in, Collier squeezing in right behind him. They shut the door and I said, "Phones."

They took them out and shut them off completely and then looked up.

"Well?" I asked first.

"Will you cut the cloak and dagger shit and get to the fuckin' point?" La Croix growled. Saint held out the cut that'd been delivered to my hands. La Croix's scowl only served to deepen as he took the other club's colors out of his hands and held them up to look at them, front and back.

"Bucket," he muttered at the name flash on the front. "What the fuck is this shit?"

I told him and Saint and Col what'd just gone down.

"The shit was clean," Saint said. "I think we ought to take the warnin' to heart."

I nodded. "Me too, man. I think he's a smart bastard."

"Hopefully the smartest one of the bunch o' them inbred back-woods freaks," Collier declared.

"Public place, middle of a charity run – weren't no better time for him to come hit us up." La Croix was doing the same calculations I had in his head and he sucked in a breath, his eyebrows going up as he harrumphed, standing up a bit straighter, his shoulders going back.

"Wouldn't tell me anymore 'n what I told you," I said.

He tilted his head and asked, "You don't honestly think they're dumb enough to try and fuck with any of us, do yah?"

I shook my head. "I honestly don't know. They got their asses handed to 'em in that bar."

"They don't strike me as exactly *smart*," Saint declared.

"Clearly, they ain't if they talk this kind of shit then beat the fuck outta the lone dissenting voice. That's how we end up with advance warning," I said.

"Didn't say I wasn't grateful for it, but yeah – that's exactly what I mean," Saint declared.

"Tell the rest of the boys, quiet like," La Croix ordered.

"Phones off, nothing where anything can be overheard, you know the drill," I told 'em as they went for the door. La Croix looked down at the bag in his hands and went around the desk in here, unlocking the filing cabinet drawer on it and rolling it out, stuffing it at the back behind the files.

I nodded.

"Get it in the safe later," he said and shut the drawer, locking it up.

"It's clean, or Saint wouldn't have brought it in here," I said. "I had Collier take it to him to check it for bugs and shit."

La Croix nodded. "That Moonshiner's paranoia yer daddy instilled in ya is gonna pay off some day."

I snorted. "It already has," I declared going for the office door and holding it open for him.

He nodded. "Yeah, it has," he agreed. "I just meant it's gonna pay off *more*."

I nodded. "That's the whole point of the lessons," I said.

He went out and I was sure to lock the office up tight behind us.

We traded looks that said everything without saying a word. La Croix giving me a nod and then departing to go find Alina, I was sure. Give her some of the lowdown. She could be trusted with vagaries at this point. Shit like 'if something should go down, go here' or 'do that' without asking questions.

I didn't know if my Fable was quite there yet, so I had to think things through. I didn't want to scare her, but I did want her to be safe – so to that end I followed La Croix and when we found his little red head, we got her taken aside.

"Somethin' happens, go to the apartment," La Croix said.

"If you could do me a solid? Make sure to take my little Fable with you," I said.

Alina asked, "Why, is something going on?" We both pressed her with a firm and silent look and she nodded.

"Gotcha," she said.

"Thanks," I told her and I heard her tell La Croix as I turned to walk away, "Whoever's disturbing our peace or trying to, make quick work of 'em if you can."

La Croix simply grunted and I thought to myself, *Good choice for you, good buddy. I think she might be as bloodthirsty as you are in her own way.*

You never would have thunk it lookin' at her. I knew the murder of her friend had changed her some but I was starting to think those changes might be a little more profound than I'd realized.

Seems like La Croix's little Alina was all outta fucks to give.

I caught sight of Corliss through the crowd and stopped a moment. She was laughing, and full of light – the way I'd seen her countless times in the halls of Lakeside. I knew now that I'd been a little in love with her since the first moment that I'd saw her. I'd had absolutely no way of knowing that she was somehow so much better than the image of her I'd had built up in my head back then.

Watching her now was a strong and poignant feeling that stopped me in my tracks and made me want to stop and appreciate what I had something awful, and so I did just that. I don't know how long I stood there, still, staring, the crowd shifting around and between us. I think it might have been my stillness in the crowd that caught her attention.

A prey response, her head coming up, graceful like, her attention attuning to my presence as I stood, but instead of breaking and running, a smile the likes of the full force of the sun lit her face and she waved at me to come closer.

I couldn't keep the smile off my lips if I wanted to, as I threaded my way through the crowd to her side and leaned down to kiss her breathless like I liked to do. I didn't give any fucks about the oohing and ahhing, the sharp whistles and general tomfoolery coming out of the kids from the school. I straightened up and she was blushing a furious pink from being the center of attention, which I knew she hated, but in this instance, it was all in good fun.

At least that's what I told myself for the time being. I knew I was being a selfish prick. The look she turned up to me absolved me of any worries that she might be upset.

"What was that for?" she asked, quietly.

"Just love you," I said, and wrapped my hand around one of hers, bringing it up to my lips to kiss the back.

She glowed and blushed some more and looked like she was fixin' to melt into her socks.

"I love you, too," she declared.

I gave her a wink and asked, "You needed out here?"

"Ah, no! I think I can be spared for a moment, what's up?" I gave her hand a little shake and towed her in the direction of the club.

She laughed slightly and asked, "Where are we going?"

I took her to the office and keyed our way in, my cock already starting to get hard.

"Hex?" she asked quietly.

I shut the door behind us and threw both locks on it and turned, kissing her fiercely, pushing her lithe body up against the door and trapping it there with mine.

I growled into her ear, "I just need you so fuckin' bad right now, so you're gonna be my good little girl, take down those jeans and bend over that desk for me, aren't you?"

"Holy shit," she whispered but her voice was husky with raw need.

"Shhhh," I hushed her. "I'm going to get all the way into that tight little pussy of yours and you're not going to make a sound, are you?"

I bit her bottom lip for emphasis and she moaned so quietly, her body sinking back into the door until the knee I had between her thighs, leg pressed between hers, I was sure was the only thing keeping her up.

"Is that a 'yes, baby?'" I asked her.

"Yes, baby," she echoed finely.

I chuckled darkly and said, "Good girl. Now do a little strip tease for me, sugar."

I put my knee down and she slid off her tip toes which I had her on, flat to the floor. She slowly took off her jacket, and I took another step back to put her in my whole field of vision. Drinking the sight of her in as she tossed the jacket to the side. She undid her chaps and I nodded slowly and she picked up what I wanted fast, slowing her movements down to something careful and easy. The chaps joined her jacket and she was at her belt to her jeans.

"Slow," I told her and she slowed herself down to half speed, unfastening her belt. Desire painted her cheeks so sweetly with the faintest pink across her nose and cheeks, her bottom lip clutched provocatively between her teeth as her blue eyes bored into mine silently begging me for cues that I was gladly giving her.

When she got the front of her jeans open, I was greeted by a triangle of simple white cotton panties and *fuck*, why was that so hot? So pure?

"Stop," I ordered when she went to push her jeans down off her hips. I wanted something different. I wanted a show. "Touch yourself," I told her. "I wanna watch you reach your hand in those panties and rub your clit. I wanna watch you come before I bend you over that desk and fuck you. Hell, I might join you if you make it real nice for me."

She gave me a savage little smile and leaned back against the door, my corrupted little angel, as she trailed a hand over her chest, between her breasts and down the buttons of her shirt. She dipped a hand down the front of the waistband of those panties and closed her eyes, putting her head back against the door as she widened her stance just a bit.

With a soft little sigh, her shoulders relaxed and she touched herself, her hand working against her body as I watched, rubbing fine little circles over her clit as she writhed a little and mm, fuck yes. She was so beautiful, so tempting. I freed my cock from the front of my pants and gripped it firmly, stroking over the head, giving the twist in the wrist that I liked when I worked myself up.

She looked at me, lookin' at her, eyes heavy lidded and filled with desire, pupils dilated with it, swallowing some of the blue as she played with her pussy for me and God fucking damn if she didn't turn me on so fucking much.

I grunted and eased up on my dick, I wanted to finish inside her and I wasn't about to go too soon, not today. I was getting better at that but she still had me going off sometimes like some inexperienced backwoods boy that'd never seen a pair of titties before. It was a good thing I was good to go after some recovery and I had no problem eating her pussy like it was my fuckin' job to make up for my, ah, shortcomings.

She rocked her hips into her own hand and moaned slightly on the tail end of each of her long breaths and *fuck* the sights and the sounds – it was a symphony of desire and a siren's call that was almost too hard to ignore.

"Oh, that's it, baby. Just like that. Come for me, baby girl. I wanna watch you," I encouraged, and she whined slightly, pressing her knees together slightly awkwardly as she quickened the play of her fingers over her clit.

"Oh yeah, fuck yeah, just like that, oh that's good," I praised, and with a muffled cry she almost lost her legs out from under her, doubling over and leaning back hard against the door as she fought to keep from making any sounds and just let her breathing do the prover-bial talking.

I went to her and helped her up, letting her lean on me as I walked her to the desk and bent her over it. She lay prone, gasping as I peeled her jeans and sopping panties down to her knees so I could get a look at her glistening pussy lips and mm, did I want a taste.

I kneeled behind her and put my mouth to her pussy and sunshine exploded over my tongue. She cried out, killing the cry halfway by closing her mouth but the sound pressed at the back of her lips and just served to fire me up some more.

I darted my tongue in and out of her delicious little pussy and she shuddered and shook, her hands lightly smacking and dancing over the desk's top as she struggled to hold still for me.

I stood, and said, "I wanna fuck you raw. I wanna come deep inside you and I want to dress you back up and send you back out there. I like the idea of my spunk sittin' in your panties while you talk to the good people out there."

"Oh, God, *yes*," she said, and she begged for it. "Fuck me, please fuck me. I want that. I need you inside me. Oh, please!"

The sound of her begging over the cadence of her uneven breathing nearly had me lose my shit but I wasn't about to, oh no fuckin' way. Not when her hot, wet, snug little pussy was just begging for my cock. I stood up and slicked my head through her wetness, up and down, up and down, as she panted against the desk and tried for a deeper touch by thrusting her hips back to try and get me inside when I passed over her entrance.

"Oh, that's a bad girl," I said with a laugh. "I'd spank your ass, but we don't want any of the kids out there to know I'm fucking their teacher over this desk now do we?"

"Mm, no," she agreed.

"So, you're going to be good and quiet while you take this cock, aren't you?"

"Yes!" she hissed, and I thrust into her hard and full and to the fuckin' hilt.

She pressed her lips together and muffled her scream with a rough "Mmm!"

I slowed my pace from there, taking her nice and easy, loving the way her pussy lips gripped my cock on every stroke, trying to pull it back in on the withdraw.

"Fuck that's good!" I hissed and worked myself in and out of her at an easy pace while she whimpered and tried to stay quiet beneath me.

I grunted, setting a pace that was half slow and easy, followed by some bursts of rough and fast, working hard at not letting our bodies completely meet in that all too dead giveaway clapping sound that'd tip anyone out there off on the fact we were in here fucking.

When I finished, it was everything in me to keep from shouting as I did it and I felt her sail right on over the edge with me, her pussy gripping and milking my cock for everything killin' me with how oversensitive I was.

I pulled out of her carefully and before I tended to myself, I made sure to help her get her panties and jeans up. She struggled to help but I didn't want that, I just wanted her to enjoy the ride she was on.

"Easy baby," I murmured. "Take your time."

She stood up slowly and turned, leaning her shapely butt against the edge of the desk to do herself up in the front as I tucked myself back away into my boxers and jeans.

"That was… that was *wow*," she said with a bit of a reckless grin. "Do you think anyone heard us?"

I shook my head. "If they did, they'll mind their business or else," I told her and she laughed a little.

I loud knock came at the door and she jumped. I finished threading my belt through its buckle as I went to it and found Chainsaw on the other side.

"Hey, man, I need to grab that bottle of Hennessy some of us adults are grabbin' a nip." I looked into the top of a box on my left and took up a bottle that was the right shape and set it down, moved the top box and Chainsaw reached down and said, "Ah-ha! Thanks, bro."

"No problem," I said.

He winked at Cor and said, "You have fun."

I swear she blushed to the roots of her hair but she didn't cave, instead saying, "You missed the show. I had a *great* time."

Chainsaw barked a laugh and went on down the hall and I shut the door.

I turned to my girl and had to grin.

"I fucking love you," I told her as she tucked herself in and fussed with her hair.

"Right back at you, baby," she said, and her voice held that softer sultry tone that I loved. The one she held when it was just her and me and she was in her feelings.

Fuck, I was already getting hard again.

CHAPTER THIRTY-FIVE

*C*orliss...

Christmas Eve had been spent at the club; the clubhouse decorated with the Christmas trees lining the big room out front that the kids had decorated. Christmas *day,* however, had been quiet, just me and just Hex – and we hadn't gotten out of bed all day which was just how I liked our first Christmas together.

New Year's Eve had found us and the club partying hard, like *really* hard and let me tell you – I had *never* been so hung over in my life on New Years' Day and I still don't know where my clothes had gotten to. Just that Hex and I had woken up naked on one of the pool tables and those that weren't blackout drunk complimented us on our form while he'd apparently railed the shit out of me for their entertainment.

You would think I would have felt *embarrassed* or horrified at myself or something for my behavior. I mean I was a *ninth grade language arts teacher* for God's sake – but no. All I felt was a sense of pride, like I'd accomplished something and what I certainly didn't feel was like I'd done anything wrong or whatever.

Still, the holidays were over and it was back to reality and today was the day that Hex and I were going back to work and *that* felt like more of a death march than anything. I mean, he was essentially walking in to see if he even had a job and I was dreading that he wouldn't when we got there.

I hated that. I hated it so much.

I fully admit hanging around the main office as long as I could, forgoing my prep time for my first period class and watching the clock, sweating absolute bullets while the second hand spun around the dial and the minute hand ticked away as I scrambled for things to talk about with the secretaries about the holidays without revealing too much of what I'd done on mine – in some cases, I just outright made some tame and boring shit up.

When the door opened to the main office's conference room where they mostly handled parental and disciplinary meetings with two families of students (the irony not lost on me at all) Hex looked impassive, and shook hands with the principle and some higher muckety-muck from the school district. I felt my heart sink as he walked past the secretary's wrap and I realized he didn't have his staff identification clipped to his pocket like he usually did.

"I'll see you at home, baby," he murmured and bent at the waist to press a kiss to my forehead.

"No," I murmured, hurt. "They didn't."

He gave me a kind look and a wink and said his goodbyes to Arlyna, behind the desk, and Sal further back.

I turned to the unknown admin and Mrs. Donal.

"I'll finish out the school year, but I quit," I said and I left the office, Hex chasing me out into the hallway.

"Don't do that, baby."

"Oh, I'm *absolutely* doing it," I snapped. "And there's not a goddamn thing you are going to do or say to change my mind!"

"Babe," he tried, and I straightened to my full height and gave him an absolutely *withering* look.

He stopped in his tracks and gave me his silent look the way that he did at home when I dug my heels playfully. I thought of it as his *"do what now?"* Dom look – but right now, we weren't having sex, it wasn't about the club, and I would not be backing down.

His expression softened and he pulled me into his arms and only when he did that did I realize my eyes had become glassy with rage. I did that, cried when I was angry as hell – but the softness and the grace that he showed me cut through that layer of anger exposing the hurt and the grief at losing him here on the day to day and exposed my fear.

I didn't know if I could do this without him. He had become my talisman to make it through the school day knowing that he was here and that I had backup if I needed it. I mean, I didn't think lightning was going to strike twice and that another twenty-something year old man was going to attack me in the bathroom, but still – I avoided the second-floor girl's bathroom at all costs now and one of the things getting me through my days here had definitely been that my savior was right around the corner should I need him and they were taking him away from me... and not even for anything *he* did... but because of me.

And right on the heels of us handing them a check so big it not only had wiped out the lunch debt for this school, but the entire district with enough left on the books to put it in the black to offer more free lunches next year to some of the kids that were merely on reduced lunch whose family really needed it.

The bastards.

"We'll talk when I come pick you up," he said as we'd ridden in together without a single damn care this morning.

I nodded and said, "Okay."

To their credit, Mrs. Donal and the district administrator were arguing behind the glass windows of the front office and hadn't followed us out here. Mrs. Donal looked pissed and the school district official simply looked like the cutthroat corporate psychopath that he likely was.

"I love you," I said and he kissed my forehead and said, "I'm a text or phone call away, but you can do this you little badass."

I snorted a laugh and wiped my eyes and said, "I know I can. Still, this is bullshit."

"Citizens," he said with a shrug and I nodded.

"Citizens," I agreed because the club was right. They liked to make things ten times harder than they needed to be and for what?

I sighed and we parted ways and it hurt, but it wasn't the kids' fault and they still needed an education. An education that I aimed to provide them.

~

MY PHONE RANG after the last bell, I heard it vibrating in my briefcase. I went and got it and saw Hex's name and smiling face flash across the screen. I caught it just before it went to voicemail.

"Hey," I murmured.

"Hey, I'm out here in the employee lot but they won't let me come in the building."

"Bastards," I muttered.

"Yeah, well, I knew it was coming, baby, and we both know it's gonna be alright."

"Yeah, it will," I said with a defeated sigh. "But it should be fine right now."

"Hey, they want to cut off their nose to spite their face, that's on them," he said. "I'll see you when you get on down here, but by no means am I rushin' you. You just take your damn time, y'hear?"

"I'm rushing anyway," I said, rolling my eyes. "I want to see you and be home with you already."

He laughed a little on the other end of the line.

"Don't be stubborn, girl," he warned.

"Have you *met* me?" I demanded and he laughed some more. It put a smirk on my face to hear it. That was one of the things I loved about being with Hex. The laughter and the fact that he fostered my growth and didn't try to change me or put me in a box of what he thought I should be.

"Alright, alright. I'll see you in a few," he said and I nodded, realized he couldn't see it, and said, "Okay."

"Bye, now." The line sent the tone that the call had been disconnected and I slid my phone into my back pocket. I shouldered my briefcase, left my classroom, and locked up behind me.

Mrs. Donal tried to stop me in the hall on my way out to the employee lot.

"Miss Legare, can I talk to you a moment?" she asked politely.

I turned and said, "No," before I hit the doors and was out into the bright afternoon sunshine.

She looked taken aback and almost hurt in a way but that was too bad. I was mad, and I wasn't about to let myself be put into a position where I was apt to say something unfortunate.

I was still working on my *official* resignation letter, which I would email tonight – but I was as good as my word; I would be finishing out the school year – but after that? That was it. I would either find another district or something else altogether.

Hex took my briefcase from me and put it behind the seat of his pickup as I climbed up into the cab. I shut the door and he reached over and massaged the back of my neck with one hand as I buckled my seatbelt.

"Get us the fuck out of here," I said bitterly and he sighed.

"Yes ma'am," he said and let off the brake, turning the wheel to spin us around and out the gate and through the main lot to the street.

"Don't be upset, baby," he said and I looked at him. "Everything happens for a reason and it's probably for the best."

"Oh, you have no idea what they've done," I declared. "I'm so mad I could spit."

He chuckled and said, "What you thinkin'?"

"I'm thinking I am going to go home, finish tendering my official letter of resignation. I'm going to finish out the school year as promised, and then I'm going to absolutely destroy them in court."

He smiled a little sadly but the slow spreading of lips turned that sad little smile into a savage grin pretty quickly.

"That's my girl," he said, and he took his hand from the back of my neck and put it back on the wheel to pilot us in the direction of home.

I stared out the window moodily and said, "You should have brought the bike."

He barked a laugh and said, "I'll remember that for next time."

"You better," I said, then muttered, "I'm sure *that'll* piss them off – but I guess they should have thought of that."

"Hey," He took up my hand and threaded his fingers through the spaces between mine. I looked to him and he smiled kindly. "I ain't worried about them or even myself. I'm gonna be just fine."

"I know," I said. "Some of the kids? Not so much, they're really upset."

"Aw, shit," he muttered.

"I'm not the only one who loves you," I said, and he raised my hand to his lips and kissed the back of it while watching the road.

At home, he let us into the house and I went straight to the bedroom to change into more comfortable clothes. When I came out, my laptop bag and briefcase slung over my shoulder he was in the kitchen.

"I'll be up in my book nook," I said and he nodded.

"Okay, baby. I'll come get you when dinner is ready."

"Okay," I said and I quietly climbed the ladder with my bags into my loft.

It was a bit cool in the house, and so I wrapped my shoulders in a chenille throw and sat on my cushion at my low corner desk in the back. I kept everything so cozy up here, and low. I didn't want to put a full-size desk up here even though I could. I didn't want anything up here except my books and my cozy reading seat and my tea and my comfort.

My little workspace was as little as I could make it and still have one and I liked it like that.

I turned on my little fairy lights which illuminated up here after dark perfectly for reading but the lighting remained low enough to not be glaring or obtrusive, a warm white light that kept everything wonderfully comfortable. A splendid little space that was all *me*.

I looked around at my neat rows of books along the built-in shelves with my little knick knacks and photographs among them. I had to sigh.

I'd never had a space like this before. One that was truly *mine*... something that was wholly for me and about me.

Hex had given me that.

I sighed and set up my laptop, plugging it in and connecting to the house's Wi-Fi automatically, all while staring off into space and contemplating what I wanted to say.

In the end, I realized nothing I would say would matter. Nothing I would say would make any difference, or change, or sway them in any way. All it would serve would be to make me feel better... and honestly, it wouldn't be anything but wasted energy or effort.

So, I simply typed out a generic resignation, giving my notice to the end of the year, and I emailed it off to the powers that be and that was that, I guess.

I sighed heavily, then emailed my lawyer with everything that happened and I told them I didn't think it would make a difference or matter in any way, but reminded them they did tell me to keep them appraised of anything that may or may not be construed as retaliation. I didn't know if this would count seeing as it didn't happen to me – but it certainly hurt and felt incredibly much like a slight against me and that was enough to make me send it.

"Hey." I turned and found Hex on the ladder, half leaning into the loft space with me.

"Hey," I murmured back.

He cocked his head and he asked me, "Can I come up the rest of the way?"

"Yeah, please. Please do," I said.

I scooted over to the plush overstuffed pillows and lounge spot as he crested the ladder and came across to me, settling in beside me and taking me into his arms. I hugged myself to his side and settled in, half draped over him, living for the feel of his arms around me. The comfort he gave me was immense and I soaked up his love and care.

"Talk to me, baby," he murmured and I sighed.

"None of this is fair to you," I said and I sniffed.

"See, I don't see it that way," he said. "I see it as none of this is fair to *you*."

I looked up at him and his expression was as serious as I'd ever seen it.

"You're seriously *unbothered* by what they've done?"

"I wouldn't say *that* per se. I can't say I'm unbothered. I mean sure, it pisses me off but I guess what it really boils down to is that I'm un*surprised*. Shit like this is par for the course for me. Did I like my job? Yeah. Made me feel closer to my dad – you know he was a custodian for a school, right?"

"You'd told me," I said with a faint smile. "But that almost makes me feel *worse*."

"Don't, baby." He kissed my forehead.

"Tell me," I begged. "What do *you* want? I mean, what is one of your biggest desires and childhood dreams?"

"Hm." He smiled, rocking me with the single syllable chuckle he made at whatever thought had occurred to him.

"I wanted to be just like my dad," he said, and I pushed myself up and slung a leg over his hips, straddling him and crossing my forearms on his chest. I rested my chin on my layered hands I fixed his gaze with mine and at first it was amused but the more I thought about what it was that was scratching and tearing and digging its way into my mind the more he lost his easy smile and he asked me, "What?"

"You said you had your dad's recipes, right?" I asked softly. "For his moonshine and all of that?"

He looked at me, his hand buried in my hair rubbing my head soothingly like he did. Like I was a cat, or more realistically because he luxuriated in the feel of my hair in his hands. I mean, it was like he couldn't keep his hands out of it.

"Yeah, I got all that," he said.

"I need you to get out there in the woods and figure them out. Perfect them, put a spin on them. I don't care but I need you to focus on that and on you – can you do that for me?" I asked.

His brow furrowed as he looked me over, and he asked, "Now why you want me to go an' do a thing like that, Fable?"

"Because it's your dream," I said. "It's always *been* your dream, and I want to make your dream into something real like you did for me."

"I did?" he asked, cocking his head curiously.

"Look around us," I murmured. "All I've ever wanted was to be loved and to have a space that was my own. Something small, but mine, and look at you... look at what you've done for me. I want nothing more to give that back. To be your partner and not just a – a – a project."

"Hey!" His voice was whispered, his tone still the harshest he'd ever taken with me. "Don't you *dare* talk about yourself like that. You are *not* a project. Never have been. You're my joy, baby. You make me the happiest I've ever fuckin' been. No more talk like that. D'you hear me?"

I nodded, but I persisted, "And I want to do the same if not more than you've done for me because *same*!"

"Shit, honey. Illegal moon shining ain't easy nor is it safe. Why, you want me to—"

"I *know*," I said. "I know, and I don't know if you can sell it or whatever and I'm not even *asking* you to. I'm just asking you to get out there and get the distilling right."

"*Why*, though?"

"You can't get mad at me and you can't say no," I said, sticking my finger in his face. He bit it gently between his teeth and sucked it into his mouth and I felt my pussy clench and closed my eyes.

"Stop trying to distract me with sex." I pouted and he grinned around my finger in his mouth and teased it with his tongue.

"Hex! I'm serious!" I cried but I couldn't help but giggle.

He relinquished his hold on my finger and said, "Start makin' sense, then."

"I want you to perfect your dad's recipes so that when I get my money from this settlement, we can secure our future – legally, which will be a pain in the ass. I want you to take what you need and start a distillery. The way you talk about your dad's hooch and this being a city virtually pickled in alcohol I think it could be a thing and I want to explore that with you."

"You're serious," he said after a moment or two of stunned silence.

"I'm dead fucking serious!" I declared. "I don't want to try and be dependent on a teacher's salary forever but I also know you… you and the club want to move into more legitimate ventures," I said and he stared up at me.

"You're not supposed to know shit about that, baby," he said and his tone held a warning.

"You wouldn't be with me if you thought I was stupid," I said tiredly. "So don't insult my intelligence now." He nearly choked on his laugh and I gave him a wry smile. "Alina and I know a lot more than you think and we're alright with it, but we also want to help you all realize your goals and call me crazy – but this has a real chance at working for not only you, but all of you and all for the low low price of keeping me and making me a silent partner or whatever the hell you call it. I fund you guys do all the heavy lifting and yeah… You told me once it's not me against the world anymore it's *us,* well dammit, it's not *you* against the world anymore either. It's *us.* So let it be *us.*"

He stared at me hard and I saw it when hardness left his brown eyes and his posture which was stiff beneath me eased some. He stopped fighting me and switched into his thinking mode, and took in a deep breath and let it out swift in a rough sigh.

"This all depends on a lot of things," he said.

"I know, how much my settlement or judgment is or whatever and yes, I also know that isn't going to happen any time soon. It could be months; it could be years – but that's time that I don't think should be wasted. Which is why I'm asking you to magic make your damn spirits so when the money arrives, we are already ahead."

"You been thinking about this a while, haven't you?" he asked.

"How could you tell?" I asked sardonically.

"Fuck, that's hot," he growled and dragged my mouth down to his.

I kissed him back and let my tongue slip between his lips and teeth to stroke against his. I moaned slightly into his mouth, and he smoothed his hands down my body in a way that made my temperature *instantly* spike.

"Was dinner ready?" I asked suddenly, aware that was supposed to be a thing in the near future.

"It'll keep," he growled. "I want my dessert first."

Fuck.

"Get your cock out," I ordered boldly. "I want to ride it."

"Yes, ma'am," he said with an easy smile, delving his hands between us to work his belt and his jeans open at the front and to shove them out of our way.

I wasn't wearing any panties, and my pajamas really had wound up being whatever one of his shirts I pulled on. He liked it, he swore, and they were so soft and comfortable and smelled like him even fresh out of the wash that I just continued doing it.

"Here, baby." He pressed a condom into my hand, and I smiled and tore it open, stroking his cock with my hand and backing off of him enough to roll it on adeptly. He moaned and gasped slightly and panted with effort not to come too quickly and I know it should be annoying that he sometimes couldn't last and sometimes it *was* but for the most part? I secretly loved the fact that I affected him just so much.

Still, I wanted him in me. I needed to feel his hard, thick length filling me out and pressing against my walls.

I knelt up and pressed his cock to my opening, carefully dropping myself over the top of him to take him in.

I loved that we were like this together, here in my space under the warm glow of the little fairy lights, witnessed by the spines of my books standing sentinel and watching. Watching as I pressed hands to his chest, as his cock disappeared inside of me, as he filled me up and filled me out and I forgot to breathe for how exquisite the feeling.

"Oh, shit!" he whispered, and I struck a rhythm of grinding, his cock swishing inside me, touching that place that felt so close to the surface and yet so very deep at the same time. The pleasure radiating, throbbing almost, and certainly building between us.

"Fuck, baby, you feel so good," he growled, and I tightened around his cock, squeezing down on purpose as much to heighten his feel good as mine. I loved it when he talked like that. Loved it when he told me how good I was, how good I felt and how much I pleased him. I thrived on that type of dirty talk and wanted more and so I worked at pleasing him more right along with myself.

"Shit, yeah," he breathed, and I begged him for that last little nudge that I knew would have me coming apart only to remake me whole.

"Touch my clit," I pleaded. "Please, touch my clit and help me come."

"Mmm," he savored the request, licking the pad of his thumb and delving it between us; he touched my clit and it was as though electricity crackled through me, sending shockwaves through my entire system and kicking me into a frenzied movement that was going to send me over the very edge of existence and into the warm black abyss of carelessness that I so desperately wanted right now.

The thing that was different about making love to, or fucking Hex, is that I felt with every fiber of my being that he wholeheartedly took that journey *with* me.

I bit my bottom lip and looked down at him, the way he looked up at me damn near leaving me almost completely undone with just that glitter of desire and madness in his eyes. The one that screamed out wordlessly just how completely crazy in love with me that he was and honestly, *same…* so crazy, madly, deeply, truly in love with him was I that were anything to happen to him I swear I would never recover and so this ploy of mine was honestly two-fold.

Would it make good on his dream? Yes. Would it also bring him part way out of the dark and keep him safe? Also yes, and that was my ultimate goal. Far was I from a fucking goody two-shoes, but I desperately loved him and wanted a long and natural life with him and I was desperate to make that happen. To kiss him, to hold him, to ride him like this as often as possible.

Hell, I wanted to be so old and break a hip fucking him like this in our nineties – and I would do anything, anything at all to make that our reality. Manifest it and make it our destiny absolute.

"God, I love you," he ground out, and I couldn't help it. Couldn't hold out if I wanted to. I came, so hard, so completely, and so absolutely that I didn't need a piece of paper, a band of metal, or anything else to tell me so. I knew completely, that we were wed. Our souls two halves of the same whole and welded together so tight it was a thing that even time couldn't erode and take.

"I love you, too," I panted when we came back to ourselves and each other after the light bursts and fireworks had cleared from our eyes and our sex-frazzled nerves.

He had his arms around me, holding me tight, and sealed it all with a kiss to my forehead and made my dreams a reality once more.

CHAPTER THIRTY-SIX

*H*ex...

"Can you do it?" I asked and stared hard across the table at Bennie who I could already see was running the calculations in his head. He was good with numbers. Was sort of low-key obsessed with them, which was only one of the reasons he ran our books.

"I can do it," he said. "I'd fuckin' fellate it if it'd get me out of working the fuckin' dead-end corporate hellscape I'm stuck in right now."

"So let me get this straight, because I honestly don't know if I heard you right – I mean, this shit seems like it's too good to be fucking true. You want us to help you run an illegal still out there in the swamp somewhere to get your daddy's recipes and shit right so that when your ol' lady lands millions from her settlement or whatever—"

"Which she will," I said, looking Chainsaw in the eye dead to rights.

"Oh, yeah she will – ain't none of that in doubt – but you mean to tell me you give dick so good she wants to hand you a shit ton of that money to start an honest-to-God legit fuckin' distillery?"

The guys around the table were trying to suppress their laughter about my giving Cor good dick – but in fairness, it was probably funnier than it was to 'em since we'd all been smokin' weed together – plus, there was absolutely no denying that I tried my absolute damnedest to give it to her so good she couldn't think about anyone else without comparing me to them and having me come out on top.

La Croix smirked and leaned forward. "Why are any of y'all lookin' this gift horse in the mouth?" he asked. "We all wanted to go legit, and somehow this whiskey-loving bastard has landed us the golden ticket."

"Doesn't mean it might not be without complications," Saint said and heaved a big breath.

Mardi Gras was almost upon us, and he had a fuckin' point. The Bayou Brethren hadn't done shit but I didn't think that wasn't because they weren't interested in fuckin' with us. I think they were biding their time until the festivities started and the cops were too fuckin' tied up with crowd control to look at what the man was doin' behind the curtain.

Everyone was still on edge and uneasy, but that was neither here nor there – we couldn't do shit until something went down unless we wanted to skip right over the whole trying to be more chill.

"I mean, we can definitely do small operation shit and operate well within the front line of our lane financially," Bennie said.

"The question is," La Croix started, "how fuckin' serious were you all with wantin' to establish a new world order within this club and are you fuckers in or out? I'm in." He raised his hand and the hands went up around the table like mushrooms after a rain. Everyone raised theirs, the motion carried unanimously.

"It'll be hard fuckin' work," I declared and Cypress made a noise like what I'd said was stupid and I had to smirk. "Fair, for some of y'all it'll be easier – the main thing is it'll be a long fuckin' road to get there. There's no tellin' when this'll end when it comes to the courts let alone to when she'll get the money or how much or any of that."

"We fuckin' betting now?" Axe asked with his crazy grin.

"I'm betting six mil." Saint threw a twenty on the table.

"Shit, I'd say two," I said. "Fuckin' district is stingy and I know she ain't wanna drag things out through a trial but I also know she will.

She's stubborn as fuck. So, I'm going to see your six and say eight." I tossed in a twenty of my own.

"Twelve," Chainsaw declared and tossed down two tens.

"Nah, I say four." Axe threw in his twenty.

The bets went around, the pot was made, and Bennie collected it to put it in the safe, wrapping the paper the bets were written on around the stack of bills.

"Alright, alright," La Croix spoke over the chatter. "Hex, what we do next?" La Croix asked.

"Next, we need to find a spot out in the woods where no game warden or dumb fuck yokel is gonna stumble on it. Then We gotta fabricate and build our still out there and then I get to work makin' shit work. Then and only then can I start training you fuckers how to do it so we can keep an eye on shit and make some magic out there."

La Croix nodded. "Too right, work's cut out for us," he said.

"When do we start?" Cypress asked.

"Right fuckin' now," I said.

"We wanna use the smokehouse as a launch point?" Axe asked. "Pretty secluded out there."

I thought about that and I said, "I hate puttin' all our eggs in one basket." I sucked my teeth. "Any other ideas, boys?"

I knew something would come to me eventually, but damn if it wasn't exhausting sometimes being the entire fuckin' brains of the outfit. Sometimes it was nice to be able to pass the baton and take a rest.

"I got some places," Cypress volunteered. "Out by my ol' nucky's place there's some flat land ain't prone to flooding in certain spots. It's way out there, though. Like prob'ly an hour's ride then another hour by boat. How often you need to get out there?"

I thought about it, and finally said, "Well, I ain't got a job so I reckon this *is* my job up until things move along a little further in the process. That should work just fine. When can y' take me out there?"

"Any time y' want, brother."

"Tomorrow?" I asked.

He nodded and said, "I'll see what I can get and drive on out to your place. Take some shit with us. If it works, awesome, we've got a start on haulin' some shit in and if it don't? Well, then, I at least got some shit out that way for the next place."

Cypress nodded and said, "Good time to do it, it bein' the off season now."

"Yeah, well, how apt is it to be discovered in the 'on' season is the trouble." I raised an eyebrow.

He looked thoughtful a minute and finally said, "Shit, never mind, this spot might not work after all."

I nodded and said, "Well keep thinkin'."

He nodded and some of the other guys were thinkin' hard, too.

"Let me run these numbers before we get too far ahead of ourselves. I mean, I don't even know what all some of this might cost with the grain and shit until I can get to the internet which ain't happening in here," Bennie declared and I nodded.

"Fair enough," I said.

"For now, we got anything else for tonight?" La Croix asked.

"I think that's it," Bennie said, looking over his notes on the meeting. He only kept the innocuous stuff wrote down. Made us look positively boring, but that was by design if the cops ever came knockin'.

"Alright then, let's call this and get out to our women if we got 'em," La Croix said.

"Rub it in, why don't you," Collier teased.

I huffed a laugh.

"All in good time, all in good time," I told him.

"Easy to say when you got a beauty like Cor sittin' waitin' on you to come home," Axe said with a wink.

"Ain't you hittin' that fine ass down near the Garden District?" Saint asked him.

Axe shrugged. "Yeah, she's older and married, though. Just a way to pass the time if you know what I mean."

We all laughed a little and La Croix rumbled, "Just don't get your ass caught or shot or somethin' stupid."

Axe laughed, "Her husband's a milquetoast motherfucker. Why you think she's riding my dick?"

"Motherfucker, you're one of the quiet ones!" Chainsaw grinned. "You oughta know best to look out for your kind."

"I somehow doubt the accountant is a serial killer," Axe said, and Bennie piped up with a, "Watch it!"

Laughter went around the table and we naturally just sort of broke up from there.

When I got out into the main part of the club, it was to find my woman on one of the couches, a tote bag at her hip with a strand of yarn coming from it as she crocheted her way through something or other, a video up on her phone. She was trying to find something other than reading to occupy her and she'd been into crochet as a kid or something. Something about a foster mom teaching her some things or what not.

"How's it going?" I asked her and she looked up and smiled holding up the triangle of whatever for me to see.

I squinted. "Are those faces?" I asked. She nodded.

"It's called the 'lost souls' shawl and it's got skulls."

"I'll be damned! It does!" I realized when I really looked at it. The moment she said it, my brain making sense of the pattern in it. "Looks real nice, Fable."

"Thank you," she said. "I'm trying to get it down, but after a certain point they're just like 'now repeat this for rows ten through sixteen' and I'm like having this brain block or whatever and can't seem to get it right on keeping this a triangle. Like I know I have to add but…" she blew a breath up and her fresh new bangs out of her eyes.

I hated the bangs, but I didn't get a vote. It was her hair. Thankfully, I think she hated them too and was already trying to grow them back out.

I smiled at her and asked, "You hungry?"

"Starved, actually," she said.

"Home and dinner or are you gonna let me take my girl out to eat."

She tucked her things away. "Depends. Where'd you have in mind?" she asked.

"Favorite place, nothin' fancy."

She nodded. "I could definitely go for that."

"Alright now." I held down a hand and she took it, hauling herself to her feet. She bent over to tuck her work back into her bag and I admired the view.

"You don't smack that, I think we're all going to be disappointed in you," Saint called out from the bar and Corliss straightened up like I'd lit that ass on fire before I could do anything.

"Don't you dare!" she cried and she blushed a subtle pink.

I laughed along with the rest of the guys.

"No worries here, baby. I'll get to that well and good when we get home."

She smiled at me and said, "Well then hurry up and feed me so you can get to fuckin' me."

There were some rowdy cheers from around the room but I only had eyes for her.

"God, I fuckin' love you," I declared and she winked at me.

"Right back at you, baby," she said, and I pulled her into my arms and kissed her soundly to a track of wild cheers, whistling and applause.

"Man, you need to fuckin hurry up and marry her," La Croix declared in his deadpan way, but there was a sparkle of something in his fucked-up eyes. I winked in his direction and he took a pull off his beer.

"Pretty sure he'll get around to it eventually," my Fable said breezily. "Won't if he doesn't get me any dinner, though."

"On that note, boys, I'll see you later."

We left the club and she sighed once we were outside.

"So?" she asked nervously.

"So, I'm going to be out most of the day tomorrow finding a place to set up. Bennie's running the numbers as we speak. It's a go."

She squeaked and threw her arms around my neck, nearly bowling me over kissing me soundly with her excitement and enthusiasm.

"God, I fuckin' love you," I breathed against her mouth.

"On second thought, let's skip dinner. Take me home, please. We can always make a sandwich when we're done fucking."

I barked a laugh and said, "It's like you were made for me."

She grinned. "Right back at you," she declared.

I shook my head.

"Food first," I declared. "I'm fuckin' starving."

She pouted a little and said, "Fine!"

"Hey you two!" Alina called down from her open apartment window. Cor and I looked up. "Well?" she demanded.

Cor put up two thumbs up and Alina squealed with excitement.

"This is going to be so cool!" she declared and then waved down at us and shut her window.

"What's going to be so cool?" I asked. My Fable grinned.

"I said she should do some watercolors, maybe paint some, so we had some ideas for the labels for the bottles."

"You are getting *way* ahead of yourself," I declared laughing.

"Hey, we gotta get our touch on things in somewhere. This is going to be a family business after all."

I cocked my head, "How do you figure?" I asked.

She turned to look over her shoulder as she set her tote on the seat of my bike and took up her helmet to put it on.

"Isn't that what you said?" she asked. "That the club wanted to be more like a family, like you saw with that other club, The Kraken?"

"Yeah…" I trailed off thoughtfully.

"Then it's a family business," she declared. I grinned at her. I couldn't help myself.

"You're just out here fixin' to make every single one of my dreams come true, ain't 'cha?"

"You're goddamn right I am," she declared. "That's what being a ride or die means, isn't it?"

She put on her helmet and gave me a fixed look with those blue eyes of hers through the crisp and crystal-clear visor of her face mask.

"Well, I'll be goddamned," I muttered. "I really hit the jackpot with you."

I put my own helmet on my head and strapped my chinstrap nice and snug while she slung her bag over her shoulder and waited for me to get on so she could get on behind me.

She threw a leg over and got snug up to my back as I fired the engine.

I fucking loved this. Could totally get used to it in every sense. Would cherish and protect my peace with her at all costs. I'd kill for her again a million times over if I needed to and damn sure nothing bad would ever happen to her again.

She was everything my dreams were made of; I just hadn't known until she'd walked into my life.

I turned us out of the lot and up the road in the direction of our favorite restaurant and had ever plan to love her into exhaustion as soon as we got home – and every other opportunity I could get from then on.

How did I get so fuckin' lucky, I would never know – but somehow, some way, I was pretty sure my pops was lookin' down at his boy and was smiling about it.

I put my hand over hers where they rested around my middle and gave 'em a squeeze. The time wasn't right yet, but as soon as it was? I was definitely putting a ring on that finger of hers.

ALSO BY A.J. DOWNEY

The Sacred Hearts MC

1. Shattered & Scarred

2. Broken & Burned

3. Cracked & Crushed

3.5 Masked & Miserable (a novella)

4. Tattered & Torn

5. Fractured & Formidable

6. Damaged & Dangerous

The Virtues

1. Cutter's Hope

2. Marlin's Faith

3. Charity for Nothing

4. Stoker's Serenity

5. Justice for Radar

The Sacred Brotherhood

1. Brother to Brother

2. Her Brother's Keeper

3. Brother In Arms

4. Between Brothers

5. A Brother's Secret

6. A Brother At My Back

7. A Brother's Salvation

Sacred Hearts MC Novella

Christmas with the Brotherhood

Indigo Knights

1. Her Thin Blue Lifeline

2. His Cold Blue Command

3. A Low Blue Flame

4. His Wild Blue Rose

5. Her Pained Blue Silence

6. A Cold Blue Call

7. Her Reluctant Blue Cavalier

8. Forged Under Fire

9. Under A Blue Moon

10. Sound of Blue Thunder

Sacred Hearts MC Pacific Northwest

1. Over the High Side

2. Wind Therapy

3. Apex of the Curve

4. Low Sided

5. Eating Asphalt

6. Hammer Down

7. Only Fool Riding

The Voodoo Bastards MC

1. Bourbon & Blood

Paranormal Romance (with Ryan Kells)

1. I Am The Alpha

2. Omega's Run

3. Hunter's End

Indigo City Darker (with Jared KingPacal Lain)

1. Triple Threat

2. Double Shot

Standalones

Synchronicity

ABOUT A.J. DOWNEY

A.J. Downey is a Pacific Northwest girl living in an East Tennessee world who finds inspiration from her surroundings, through the people she meets, and likely as a byproduct of way too much caffeine. She specializes in real and relatable romance stories featuring that real-life kind of love that everyone craves.

Stalker Information:

Website
www.ajdowney.com

Sign up for her newsletter at
http://eepurl.com/dkQiIH

Facebook Group - AJ's Sacred Circle
https://www.facebook.com/groups/authorajdowney/

facebook.com/authorajdowney

twitter.com/authorajdowney

instagram.com/ajdowney

bookbub.com/authors/a-j-downey

www.ingramcontent.com/pod-product-compliance
Lightning Source LLC
Chambersburg PA
CBHW051941220626
47052CB00004B/745